NIGHTSPARK

A GHOSTCLOUD NOVEL

MICHAEL MANN

HODDER

First published in Great Britain in 2022 by Hodder & Stoughton

13 5 7 9 10 8 6 4 2

Text copyright © Michael Mann, 2023
Illustrations copyright © Chaaya Prabhat, 2023

A CIP catalogue record for this book
is available from the British Library.

ISBN 978 1 444 95978 9

Typeset in Vendetta by Avon DataSet Ltd,, Alcester, Warwickshire

Printed and bound in Great Britain by Clays Ltd, Elcograf S.p.A

The paper and board used in this book
are made from wood from responsible sources.

Hodder Children's Books
An imprint of
Hachette Children's Group
Part of Hodder & Stoughton
Carmelite House
50 Victoria Embankment
London EC4Y oDZ

An Hachette UK Company
www.hachette.co.uk

www.hachettechildrens.co.uk

To Sarah, Chris, Meg & Leia.

I'll never thank you enough.

HAMPSTEAD
HEATH

NORTH LONDON

GREAT ORMOND
STREET HOSPITAL

HOUSES OF
PARLIAMENT

PIMLICO

N
W   E
S

TEDDINGTON LOCK

LONDON

OLYMPIC STADIUM

ST PAUL'S

NEW THAMES BARRIER

AEROPLANE GRAVEYARD

DEAD ZONE

DOCKLANDS

BATTERSEA POWER STATION

SLUMS

GYPSY HILL

CHAPTER 1
HIDE AND SEEK

Click. Swish. Tap. Click.

She was coming his way. There had to be somewhere to hide in this place. He looked down the corridor. There were tall arched windows and whitewashed walls, cold stone floors and thick oak doors. Surely one of them would be unlocked.

Click. Swish. Tap. Click.

The sounds grew closer. She'd see him soon. Reaching the first of the doors, he pressed his ear to the keyhole: nothing. It was as good a door as any. He grasped the iron-ring handle and paused. What if she heard him?

On the breeze came a floral, sharp-sweet smell, and through the shutters, he glimpsed fields of red.

Click. Swish. Tap. Click.

The breeze swelled, a shutter slammed, and he took his chance. He opened the door and dived in, hoping the wind would mask the noise. But the room was not a room at all — it was a cupboard, piled high with moth-eaten blankets. In the corner, crouched down, was someone familiar.

'Ravi?' Luke asked, his heart beating faster.

Ravi put his finger to his lips, then pointed at the door.

Tap. Tap. Tap. Tap.

She was outside already? Somehow, she'd known which door he'd gone through. He heard the ring-handle squeak and slid the bolt shut just in time. The door rattled but didn't open. An amber eye flickered at the keyhole. Luke caught the scent of tobacco.

She'd be angry now. He could hear her breathing. Luke searched the closet frantically for an exit or something and that was when he saw them. Peering out from the blankets were children: he recognised some from Battersea. Wide-eyed, breath held, they faced the door. What were they all doing here?

Tap. Tap. Tap. Tap.

The door rattled again. Then came a strange squeaking noise. Something moved in the keyhole . . . but it wasn't a key. It was a black-painted fingernail. It poked right through, towards Luke's chest, and he leapt back, landing on the floor beside Ravi. The nail paused, as though thinking, then it did something strange: it grew, at an angle, up the side of the door, snaking, searching, till it reached the bolt. It curled tight around it.

Tap. Tap. Tap. Tap.

Luke grabbed Ravi's hand. The blankets tumbled and covered them in darkness. Through the stifling fabric, he heard the bolt slide open.

'Luke?' said a voice. But the voice was not Tabatha's. It was kind, muffled and warmly familiar. 'I've been knocking for ages. Are you under the blanket?'

The blanket was ripped from above and suddenly everything was far too bright.

His sister stood over him, frowning. 'Here.' She thrust a steaming cup into his hand. 'You look like you need it.'

CHAPTER 2
HOME

Luke sat up in bed and took the cup from his sister. He sipped and the malty aroma washed over him. He felt a little more human.

'Nightmares again?' she asked.

Not nightmares, but nightmare. He'd had the same one several nights running. Tabatha chasing, then Ravi, then both of them trapped. Every time, he woke up shaking.

It was surprising he'd dreamt at all, come to think of it. He'd been out all night with Alma – scouting for ghouls in a pre-Hallowmas 'clean-up', trailing spidery shapes through the Walthamstow Marshes. There were so many these days, he'd barely caught an hour of sleep. It seemed that this had still been enough for a nightmare.

He shrugged; he wouldn't dwell on it. That would let Tabatha win. And a dream was just a dream, no matter how often you dreamt it. Or, at least, he hoped so.

He took another sip. It was a liquid hug, washing the taste of sleep from his mouth. 'Why is this never as good when I make it?'

'Nana's some kind of kitchen witch. Everything she makes tastes better.' Lizzy sat down on his bed and looked round. 'This room needs a refresh.'

She had a point. A whole summer had passed since he'd escaped from Battersea, yet he'd changed nothing: the piles of board games in tatty boxes, the moth-eared football and old fishing rod, the shelves upon shelves of detective comics. It was practically a museum to his ten-year-old self. But then, he'd liked being ten. Things were simpler back then.

'You know, I don't mind it. It brings back good memories.'

She leant down and picked up a pair of old trainers. 'Even these?' She threw them expertly into the bin in the corner. 'They don't even fit. Come on, Luke. A photo, a hobby, a book, or something – you must have picked up some new interests down there?'

'Shovelling?' he said. 'That's one I'd rather forget.'

There was another interest, of course, that he had to keep secret – the world of ghostclouds and all that came with it . . . flying through the night sky, changing his shape, making it rain and hopefully, soon, lightning too. As a 'half-ghost', he had the gift of

5

crossing over, of slipping out of his body and into the realm of the ghosts. Alma said it was because his heart had stopped at birth, and because of what he'd been through at Battersea but, whatever the reason, he was glad for it now.

Well, mostly. He'd happily lose the nightmares.

'Lizzy, do you think dreams mean anything?' He saw her expression. 'You know, like fate, signs, that kind of thing.'

She gave her lopsided smile. 'I'd forgotten how serious you could be.' She studied his face. 'If I'm honest, I don't. We're just tiny specks on a planet, beside an average star. But that's just me.' She stood and walked to the door. 'Anyway, drink up, it's banana fritters, they're best when they're hot.'

The door closed. Luke savoured his Horlicks in the quiet of his room. After two years of gruel, it was the little things that mattered.

Scratching sounded from the window. He stood up and slid it open; Stealth stuck his head through. Luke rubbed his cat's fur between the ears. 'I wish I looked as sleek as you in the morning.'

Stealth blinked, then leapt down to lick up some Horlicks that had spilt on the floor. Luke washed his face, put on the shirt he'd ironed, and tucked Ravi's old watch under his left cuff. He hated dressing up. The collar felt even scratchier than his old sackcloth in Battersea. But today was important. He had to make an effort.

He straightened his sleeves and opened the kitchen door. The breakfast table groaned under his grandma's efforts: orange juice and sliced mangos, banana fritters and fried eggs, cereal, toast, eggs and cold beans. Nana Chatterjee was determined to feed him up after his stint underground. She plonked another hot drink on the counter before him.

'I've just had one, Nana.'

She gave him 'the look'. 'You'll drink it, young man. There's still nothing on you.'

He took it and sat next to Lizzy, who picked at a fritter while reading bits from the paper.

'You seen the Mayor's Hallowmas calendar? It's to raise money for the Battersea kids. There's a prize for the best Terence outfit on All Hallows' Eve and they're burning a Tabatha doll on Bonfire Night instead of Guy Fawkes.'

'Hmm,' said their dad, barrelling in. 'That's a little morbid. But I suppose if it's for charity . . .' He adjusted his tie. 'That Mayor's a good man. On the side of the people.'

Luke stirred his tea uneasily. It had been months since the

ghosts had torn the roof off of Battersea Power Station, freeing Luke and a thousand other shovellers. But the person behind it all – Tabatha Margate, the station owner – had disappeared entirely. Her right-hand man, Terence, had vanished too, along with dozens of the children, including Luke's best friend, Ravi.

Tabatha was now public enemy number one. The Mayor had 'wanted' posters hung from every street corner. He'd made public announcements and offered rewards. He'd even appointed a dozen detectives, including Luke's dad. And now this ridiculous bonfire. But Luke knew the truth: the Mayor had been working with her all along. Something told him it was better to keep this quiet.

'Dad, any luck with the Tabatha case?'

His dad turned and squeezed Luke's shoulders. 'Sorry, son, these things take time. We'll get her, though. London wasn't built in a day, you kn—' A burst of coughing cut him short.

Luke reached for a napkin, Lizzy for the water. The coughing came less often than when he'd left prison, but often enough. At the last visit, the doctor's face had been hard to read, unlike his bills.

Luke couldn't help but feel it was partly his fault. If his

dad hadn't fought so hard for him, Tabatha wouldn't have thrown him in prison and he'd never have got sick in the first place.

His dad caught his breath and chose his words carefully. 'You're young, and you've got your whole life ahead of you. Focus on the future, not the past.'

Luke knew his dad was right, but he couldn't forget. He *wouldn't* forget – at least, not until Ravi was safely home.

His dad smiled. 'Anyway, I bet you thought I'd forgotten. Here's your gift.'

Luke's mind went blank. 'Gift?'

'You earnt it,' said his sister. 'Two years off school and you still somehow passed the Detectives Guild exam.'

He'd only scraped a pass, but he'd wanted to be a detective for as long as he could remember, to be just like his dad. For his fifth birthday, he'd even asked for a detective hat. But he'd never expected a gift today. It had been enough just to sit the exam in the first place, unlike Ravi and the other kids, who'd never get the chance.

He felt a rush of anger, a strange urge to smash the gift on the floor. It was all so unfair. He wouldn't even be here if Ravi hadn't protected him, listened to him, taken him under his wing – if he hadn't shown him the ropes when he'd first got to

Battersea. Ravi, who'd had dreams of his own – of running a shop, of seeing his sister, of his parents' boat in the north bank water market. Ravi had wanted Luke to be his business partner, to meet his family, but when he'd needed him most, Luke had failed to protect him.

And now Ravi was gone. Sold to Europe through the Old Channel Tunnel. All because he'd worked hard and earnt his golden ticket, which was supposed to have won them their freedom. Golden handcuffs, more like.

The ghosts and the detectives all said they were searching, but until they had a location, they held little hope. Europe, as everyone kept reminding him, was enemy territory and a very big place.

'You OK, Luke?' his sister asked. They were staring at the wrapped gift squished in his tense-knuckled hands.

'Sorry,' he said. 'It's nothing.' He reached to tear at the wrapping.

'Hold on,' said his nana. 'You have to guess; you're a detective now.'

'Only an apprentice, Nana. But OK, I'll try.'

He observed the present. The wrapping was cheap, but folded precisely, stuck with smudgeless Sellotape that had been cut with scissors. There was only one person that neat in his family.

'Lizzy wrapped it.' She grinned and nodded, but Luke was already hunting for more clues. He weighed the item in his hands, shook it and squeezed. It was firm but gave slightly. Leather, it had to be. A book, perhaps. A detective notepad? No, a box.

But a box this small . . . It wasn't, they hadn't . . .

He didn't wait to guess, he just tore off the paper.

It was a leather box – he'd been right – and inside it lay a gleaming, silver-rimmed watch. It had a dark brown strap, textured and soft. A pattern of moons ran round its edge. It looked used, but well-loved. In good condition. He heard its little cogged heart ticking boldly away.

But Luke's own heart sank. He had a watch already: Ravi's watch.

'To be a detective, you have to the look the part,' said his dad, smiling.

'This was your mum's.' His nana's eyes softened. 'She loved the sky, just like you.'

His mum's? He didn't know what to think. They'd never said she loved the sky. He felt a surge of something – sad but sweet. He missed her more these days now he was out of the station. He turned it in his hands and saw words on the back, engraved like a motto: *Make a difference. Every second counts.*

Luke sighed. He loved it, and he hated it, and they'd never understand.

He forced a smile. 'Thanks, guys. Best present ever.' He took Ravi's watch off, pocketed it and put the new one on. Then he squeezed each of them in oversized hugs.

His dad patted his shoulder. 'Now, go change the world. Make every second count.'

There was a knock at the door. Jess's head peeked through. The paddle in her hand dripped water on the floorboards.

'Power cuts again. There are river jams all the way to Mile End. We'd better go now or we'll both be late.'

Luke nodded, grabbed a fritter and ran out on deck before scaling the ladder to Jess's dinghy. As his hand ran over the last rung, he stopped. There were scratch marks. He placed his fingers in the grooves. They fit. *A human hand.* And the cuts were deep . . .

His neck prickled. Someone was watching. He spun around.

It was only his dad from the boat. Luke took his fingers from the marks and shook off his doubts. He was imagining it, that's all.

'Remember,' his dad called, 'be patient, be thorough, but most of all, be polite. Guildmasters can be tricky, but they're the ones who decide if you pass.'

But Luke wasn't worried. The one good thing about having been a Battersea shoveller was that his new boss couldn't be any worse than his last.

CHAPTER 3
THE GUILD

'So you're finally going to be a detective!'

They'd moored the dinghy in Limehouse docks and caught an open-topped chugger along the Thames. Jess sat, somewhat precariously, on the boat's back railings. The view was better there, not that Jess ever looked. She was too busy talking.

'An *apprentice*, Jess.' Luke fiddled with his new watch. It was uncomfortably tight. 'But yeah, I'm excited.'

'You don't look it.' She grabbed his wrist. 'It looks good, don't worry, and Ravi would agree.' She paused. 'Actually, first, he'd *say* he didn't like it, to see if you'd sell it, but in the end, he'd agree.'

Luke laughed. That was exactly what Ravi would do.

They gazed out over the mud-grey river. To the right, cargo-ships steamed past the arched loading bays of Wapping docks, filled with tar, grain and scented tobacco. A grid of canals ran into the distance packed with pie sellers, tea hawkers and greedy-eyed boat cleaners. It was the last section of the river city, before they reached the flood barriers that kept the old city dry.

'Honestly, Jess, do you think he's OK?'

'Of course!' Jess said. 'He's probably dug a tunnel halfway back already.' It was typical Jess – even in the darkness of Battersea, she'd buzzed with positivity. She stopped to admire the New Thames Barrier. Sprigs of Hallowmas rosemary hung from its pillars and pulleys. 'And if he hasn't, Lukey, then between the ghosts and the detectives, it's only a matter of time. And don't you forget, you're on the Tabatha case too.'

It was true. He'd almost fallen off the houseboat when he heard.

He glanced to the south bank – a sprawling expanse of slums, rubbish and rubble-strewn lands – where a slum boy picked litter from the silty water. Luke was lucky, really, compared to so many others. He had the apprenticeship of his dreams and a chance to fix things.

'OK. You win. No moping, promise.' Jess always made him feel better. 'Here's to the seizing the day.'

He fist-bumped Jess and laughed. Seizing the day was everything to them. After all that time lost in Battersea, they couldn't afford to wait around.

'That's the spirit!' Jess pointed at a riverboat stop in the distance. 'And that's Temple – your stop. Now chin up, Lukey. Today is your day.'

The boat pulled in, cutting through a carpet of floating litter. Luke stepped out on to Temple, a pocket of green at the edge of the river. Luke's nana said it'd once been full of lawyers, that people had given them great piles of money to stop bad things happening – but it seemed unlikely. Surely the bad things just happened anyway? Either way, Luke didn't mind, because the buildings were gorgeous: white-plastered, timber-beamed, ship-like things, floating in a sea of manicured gardens.

He walked up a path, past statues, suited men and crests of arms. Temple was home to the High and Middle Guilds. Over a hundred of them held offices there, from the glittering Industrialists to the bookish Accountants. The Detectives Guild was at the cheaper end, but still, it was Temple.

He felt the excitement bubble up inside him. It was going to be good. Maybe even great. There was so much ahead of him: meeting his master, learning the tricks of the trade, and, who knew, just maybe cracking a case or two.

Moments later he stood poised, brass knocker raised,

before the central branch of the Detectives Guild. It was a pillared, sooty edifice.

Rap. Rap. Rap.

A window creaked overhead. Footsteps skittered, then the door swung open. A thin, grey man, with a thin, grey moustache, ushered him into thin excuse for a lobby. It was essentially a corridor with chairs.

Luke gave his best smile. 'Good morning, I'm—'

The man waved his hand. 'I know who you are. I am a detective, remember. You are Luke Smith-Sharma and you're four minutes early.'

Luke hadn't even checked his watch but he nodded anyway. It was one of Alma's rules: if in doubt, nod. It gave the impression that you knew stuff.

He reached out his hand. 'Pleased to meet you, Inspector.'

The man didn't offer his hand back. Instead, his mouth formed a dainty 'O', as though he was sucking an invisible straw. It was an odd expression. Was he cross, or surprised, or possibly both?

At last, the man spoke. 'Inspector Oberdink,' he said, then blew out through his 'O'. 'And I'm not shaking hands currently. I've a cold. Follow me.'

Luke followed him down a fusty corridor, to the third door along. It was a simple room with a metal desk, three chairs and a lingering odour of spiced coffee. The man sat down and nodded at the wall, where certificates gleamed in cheap frames under spotless glass.

'You will have surmised by now, I hope, that I am your master.' With a grey umbrella, he jabbed each frame in turn. 'Treasurer for the Committee of Detective Hygiene. Inspector for the Office of Officiality. And Chief Examiner for the apprentice entry exam. Which, I may add, you only passed by a hair.'

'I'm sorry, sir, I missed a lot of school, you see—'

'There is no need to explain,' Oberdink interrupted. 'I know all that.' He leant back in his chair. 'Yet I mentioned your results anyway. Can you deduce why?'

Luke could think of a few reasons. Maybe Oberdink had forgotten. Maybe he liked to make people feel small. Or perhaps he just liked the sound of his own voice. But he had a feeling none of those was the answer he wanted.

'Maybe, Mr Oberdink, because you don't want excuses. Because I'll need to work harder if I'm to pass my apprenticeship.'

Oberdink's mouth formed an 'O', once again, but this time the edges of it smiled a little. As though he'd given it permission for a millimetre of joy. Luke felt sure he'd said the right thing.

Oberdink pushed a pile of papers towards him. 'I want these in envelopes. In alphabetical order. I can't possibly lick them on account of my cold.'

Luke hadn't seen evidence of his cold yet, but he nodded all the same.

Oberdink carried on. 'If you want, there are disposable gloves in the corner. Ensure each letter is firmly sealed. There's a "D" in detective and it stands for *detail*.'

Oberdink pointed to a poster on the wall.

The Detective is . . .

D – Detailed

E – Evidenced

T – Thorough

E – Evidenced

C – Consistent

T – Thorough

I – Impartial

V – Valiant

E – Evidenced

Luke wondered if the 'D' should stand for detailed or dull? Though he supposed having evidence three times was 'consistent'. Then he remembered his promise to Jess: no moping. He had to be patient. *These things take time*, his dad had said.

He turned to the pile of envelopes and letters and tried to summon some gusto.

Fold, insert, close, lick.

Fold, insert, close, lick.

Luke hummed the words in his head to pass the time. They were inventories mostly from Tabatha's factories – lists of each weapon manufactured and shovel bought – along with an occasional witness statement of remarkable dullness on import taxes or the price of coal.

Nothing on the base. Nothing on her.

His watch ticked loudly. It whispered to him, *'Make a difference. Every second counts'*, but with this kind of work, he didn't see how it could – not for Ravi, Tabatha, or anyone at all. Was this what real detectives did? Paperwork? Or maybe it was a test. Maybe any minute now, the real work would start.

But an hour passed, then another. Oberdink scribbled at his desk, barely looking up, while paper cuts spread across Luke's fingers and his tongue grew parched from licking. He was contemplating whether envelope poisoning could be a cause of death, when he picked up a letter that stopped him in his tracks.

Another witness statement, but this was one different. Longer, for a start – at least two pages – and it talked of nail marks in doors. Tall, clicking shadows. The scent of tobacco and whispers in the dark.

Luke remembered the houseboat ladder. His fist tightened round the sheet in his hand.

'Sir, have you seen this?'

Oberdink looked up, eyes narrowed. 'Of course. But if it's from the slums, I ignore it. Especially if it's the ravings of some crazy old tramp. Said he'd seen Tabatha's "shadow" in the station ruins. Heard her talking to a man about "tearing down the sky".' Oberdink laughed. 'He was incoherent and an utter waste of time.'

Luke didn't laugh. 'Did he say anything else?'

Oberdink put down his pen. 'And why would an *apprentice* like you even care?' His lip curled. 'Detective work isn't about intuition, it's about evidence. Hard work. Doing your time.'

Luke shrank. He hadn't meant to be rude, but he had clearly said the wrong thing. Yet if he'd learnt one thing at Battersea, it was that you had to speak up. Nobody else was going to speak for you.

'You're right, sir,' he said, treading carefully. 'Evidence is everything. So maybe I could interview him? It might be good practice.'

'It might' – Oberdink's moustache twitched – 'if the man were alive. But he died that night. Heart stopped, apparently.' Oberdink checked his nails for dirt. 'Tragedy, I'm sure.'

Died? Just like that? Luke wanted to ask more, but the door burst open.

'Emergency case,' spluttered the clerk. 'Just had a call from Town Hall.'

'Can't you try someone else? We're busy.'

'I would, but all the other inspectors are out on actual cases.'

'That's probably why they're all behind on their paperwork,' snapped Oberdink.

Luke's dad hid his paperwork under the dinner table. He thought best not to mention that now.

The clerk shuffled. 'But, sir, it's the from the Mayor's office, to do with Battersea. And it's fingerprinting – your speciality!'

'The Mayor?' Oberdink's eyes widened. 'Well, why didn't you say? Be there right away!'

Oberdink signed a letter, folded it twice, stamped it and quickly organised his pencils in height order. Then he rushed to the door.

Luke leapt to his feet.

'Oh, not you,' Oberdink said with a sneer. 'I'd hate to waste your *intuition* on basic fingerprinting. All that evidence is beneath an expert like you.' He allowed himself a thin-lipped smile. 'You stick with the envelopes.'

Luke almost choked. This was a *lead*. A chance to make a difference. He knew Battersea. He'd lived and breathed it for over two years. Couldn't Oberdink see that?

Then he remembered his dad's words: *be patient and polite*. It was only his first day. He had to pass this apprenticeship. Saving Ravi would take time. And he could hardly force Oberdink to take him along.

'Yes, of course, sir.' He nodded, though it went against his instincts.

Oberdink frowned from the doorway. 'And those calluses on your hands, file them down. I can't have people knowing you're a Battersea kid.'

Luke looked at his palms. It had been months since he'd

shovelled, but the calluses hadn't faded. He had a strange feeling they never would.

'I'll do my best, sir.'

But when he looked up, Oberdink had already left.

Luke listened to his steps grow fainter and found his eyes drawn to the tramp's witness statement once more. Quickly, he tucked it into his pocket. If the statement was rubbish, then Oberdink wouldn't miss it.

CHAPTER 4
SOULRISE

He was a thousand feet up. London glistened below. Wedges of grey drifted by in the night all around him, slow and heavy in the wet autumn wind. The air smelt good, of moss and rocks – the opposite of the musty guild that morning. He smiled, watching raindrops fall through his hands then disappear into the cloud underfoot.

'I just can't get used to it. Rain should fall on you, not *through* you.'

'Only if you're alive,' Alma said. 'I prefer it like this. It's like a shower on the inside. A deep clean without scrubbing.'

Scrubbing, Luke thought. He'd scrubbed his hands for an hour after Oberdink's taunt, but instead of softening, they'd become raw and sore. His spirits sank a little; his cloud darkened. Did people really care about calluses? He trudged to the edge of his kite-cloud and peered over. Rain drizzled down on the rooftops of the city.

'Alma, could you zap my calluses off?'

'Don't know,' she said. 'But if you don't stop talking about them, I might zap your mouth closed.' She stared intently at the streets below. 'I'm the Council Deputy now, my time is precious. And if you'd focused more, you could probably have zapped them yourself by now.'

It was a bone of contention. Luke's lightning skills were almost non-existent; he could barely muster a spark. Alma saw it as a slight on her teaching. She worried about her reputation with the Ghost Council, a group of otherworldly beings elected to guard the boundary between the living and the dead. They protected ghosts from ghouls and had lots of rules. Luke felt a lecture coming on.

'I bet your "detectiving" is the problem.' She adjusted her waistcoat and smoothed down her dress. 'Electricity is life. It makes your heart beat. It flows through every nerve and fibre of your being. But if you're as exhausted as you are – juggling two jobs – then nothing's flowing. You need to rest and recharge. Pick one thing and do it properly.'

Luke rolled his eyes. He and Alma bickered affectionately like this all the time. She was too bossy for her own good. If she really cared about his rest, she wouldn't insist on him flying each night. Not that he complained. He *loved* flying. It was when he felt most free.

Alma checked her watch. 'Anyway, look carefully, it's almost time.'

Luke strained to see through the crackling rain. They'd waited above Bloomsbury for two hours now and the novelty of the view had long worn off: the ridged copper pyramids of the British Museum, the over-dainty houses of New Russell Square, the broken minaret of Coram's Fields – they were all splendid, but he'd seen them before.

Nor did he hold much faith in Alma's watch. It was made out of mist, and she was always late. He looked down. 'OK. But what exactly are we looking for?'

'Souls. They tend to rise at midnight this time of year. It's the darkest hour – roughly halfway between dusk and dawn. They kind of look like . . . There! Like that!'

He followed her gaze to Great Ormond Street Hospital, a curving, modest red-bricked building, tucked between residential streets. It wasn't flashy, like other hospitals – as though it didn't want to outshine its well-to-do neighbours.

But it was shining now, with green, blue and red-gold

lights. They flickered in the windows, then drifted right through the glass.

'Aren't they gorgeous?' said Alma. 'They're called soulglows. Nightsparks. And they move quick, so don't let them out of your sight.'

Luke couldn't have, even if he'd wanted to. Alma was right – they were beautiful things, pure and light. They drifted and circled like butterflies in summer.

'Shepherding souls is my new initiative. It's gone down a treat.' She glowed bright as she spoke. Since being elected the Ghost Council Deputy, Alma had been coaxing them into action after years of reluctance to 'interfere with the living'. Ghosts were now allowed to watch over their loved ones with appropriate supervision. Or to rain on gardens or farms, when the plants looked parched. Little things, really, to brighten someone's day. They wouldn't change history, but they might make the present more comfortable.

'Anyway,' she continued, 'tonight's a practice run. There'll be a big one after All Hallows' Eve, when the moon is full. That's when the wall between this realm and the next is thin.'

A wind caught and scattered the glows through the rain.

That's when Luke saw the others. All around the city, many-coloured lights rose in the sky in clusters, and waiting to meet them were ghostclouds of every shape and size. If this was all Alma's doing, it was quite the turnout.

The nearest ghost stood less than a breeze away – a waist-coated man, on a poodle-like cloud. He caught Luke's eye and smiled, before turning back to the lights.

'Shouldn't we spread out a bit? We'll never catch them all this way.'

'Most of them find their way in the end.' She gestured towards Great Ormond Street Hospital below. 'But the little ones, and the frail ones, don't know their ups from downs. So we focus on hospitals, nursing homes, that kind of place. A little nudge here and there can go a long way.'

Luke watched a light by the river market – a hazy red thing – get swept on a breeze east along the Thames. *Seaward*, he thought. 'What about the ones who don't find their way?'

'You can't save everyone, Luke. That's just life. We do our bit and hope for the best.' Alma followed Luke's eyes to the red soul on the river. 'Don't worry about him. A lot of souls visit places first, places that mattered. He was probably a sailor.'

Luke was about to reply when he saw something flicker through the rain. 'Alma, over there – I think there's one coming!'

They ran to the opposite corner of the cloud and, sure enough, a green glowing light was butterflying closer. It pulsed bright and quick like a heartbeat.

'Hold out your hands, palms up,' Alma said. 'You're welcoming it. Soothing it. Shepherding it on.'

'But what if it wants to stay?'

'Then let it.' She peered down. 'But somehow I don't think this one will. The young ones rarely do.'

'What do you mean, young?

The green-glowing soul danced higher, then stopped, dead level with them. It hovered silently, then sank into their cloud, right at Luke's feet.

'It's chosen you,' Alma said. 'That's good luck.'

It doesn't feel like it, Luke thought, because there at his feet, with its eyes still closed, was the tiniest baby he had ever seen. It must have only just passed over, the moment it was born. He'd never held a baby before.

The thing started wailing and wriggling at his feet. Before he knew what he was doing, he'd bent down and picked it up and cradled it in his arms. It stopped crying and began searching with its mouth.

'It's a reflex. It wants milk.' Alma passed him a bottle made of mist, which she'd conjured up. 'Try this.'

He couldn't see how it would help, but he offered it anyway, and the baby began suckling quietly.

'It's so sad,' Luke said.

'I guess,' she said. 'But we all have a time. At least we're able to give it what it needs.'

'But it won't make a difference. It'll still end up in the End Place.'

'So will we all – and nothing you do will change that.' Alma watched the child. 'It's the journey that counts. And we just made this one's journey a little bit better.'

Luke wanted to disagree but he couldn't. He'd been a baby like this once. He'd almost died too. But they'd saved him in time. And now he was a half-ghost. Was it really too late to save this one?

'You know,' Alma said, 'there's one more thing it needs.'

Then softly, in a voice gentler than Luke thought her capable, Alma began singing. It was a lullaby of sorts. He didn't know the tune, and he couldn't quite catch the words, but he was moved all the same.

And the baby was too, because a moment later, it faded and was gone.

Luke breathed. It had weighed nothing, but he felt lighter.

Alma slapped him hard on the back. 'Told you it was worth losing sleep over.'

Luke smiled and nodded, though he wondered if he'd feel the same in the morning.

'How are the nightmares?' Alma asked. 'Any better?'

'No, not really. They're so real sometimes. This morning, when I woke, it was like I could feel her. And there was this scratch on the ladder . . .' He trailed off – it sounded so silly – so instead he stared at the quiet streets below. The last few smatterings of souls were spilling out from windows on to the street. Some rose straight up, others danced like plastic bags in the wind.

'There are ghosts who read dreams,' Alma said. 'We could get it checked out.'

Luke nodded, but his mind was elsewhere. One of the souls wasn't like the rest. It was fainter, darker, and instead of rising, it was drifting steadily down the street like a shadow. And when it passed the houses, he could have sworn he saw their window lights flicker . . .

'Alma, down there, in the street. Do you see—'

But Luke never finished, because at that moment, the sky flashed blue, and the flickering light in the street disappeared. Thunder rumbled and he glanced behind. The sky lit up with two bolts of bright green.

Alma's cloud darkened. 'Blue, green, green,' she muttered. 'That's the code for Battersea.'

Dread rose in Luke's chest, along with something else too: a ripple of excitement – or was it relief? 'Battersea? But they destroyed it. How's that possible?'

Alma leapt off Luke's kite-cloud towards the rooftops of Bloomsbury, unfurling her swan-cloud beneath her as she fell.

'I don't know,' she said, 'but I've a feeling we're about to find out.'

CHAPTER 5
THE GHOST COUNCIL

Luke plunged his arms into the moist grey cloud fluff and breathed, letting more of himself flow into its droplets. He rode the cloud, but it was part of him too – darkening and brightening with his mood, rising to meet him if he fell. It was a shape-changing, rain-making magical carpet, and he never grew tired of it.

'The south wind's strongest,' he said. 'Let's take it to the river.'

'Roger that.' Alma darted down.

He dived after her, tilting his cloud just in time for the breeze. It shoved him towards the river, over a forest of spires, pointed-rooftops and squat, hot chimneys. He whooped and glanced up, to where other ghostclouds moved slow and safe: a ram with curled horns, a whale with legs, and other swirling creatures, inkblots and brushstrokes on rain-soaked paper.

Battersea. The very word unnerved him. He hadn't been back since they'd escaped. And then there was the Ghost Council. Many of them disliked him just for being a half-ghost. They said he didn't belong, that he should become a 'full ghost' or not come at all. Alma told them to bog off, but it still put him on edge.

He breathed in the city to calm his nerves, from the sticky-sweet coal-smoke to the rain-scented tiles, from the grave-quiet alleys to the whispering windows. The city at night was strangely soothing – sleepy, subdued, but never still. He soaked it all in. 'We should reach the river wind, any second,' he said.

'I know, I know,' Alma said. 'No need to state the obvious.'

It hit them wet and fast and they swerved to the west over churning brown waters. Within minutes, the cracked chimneys of Battersea Power Station loomed ahead. Luke shuddered. It was worse than he remembered – roof caved, windows shattered, cracking walls. It was a reminder of what the Ghost Council could do if they put their mind to it.

Instead of approaching it, Alma tilted her cloud up, towards a bulging black storm-cloud overhead.

'Aren't we meant to steer clear of storms?'

'Real storms, yes.' She winked. 'But this is just a meeting.'

He knew Alma too well to ask what she meant – there were few things she liked more than a good surprise – so he swallowed his fear and followed, watching the storm swell as they got closer. It pulsed and crackled with thunderous blue light.

He braced himself as a wall of black cloud engulfed him.

Everything seemed to slow down. Black droplets spun in the air around his body. The thunder became muted. Then through the black, he spied flickers of blue.

They burst through the cloud-wall and his feet landed on grass. It was storm-grey in colour and dewy underfoot. Above, a dome of dark rumbling cloud lit up with occasional crackles of lightning.

A field within a cloud? It didn't make sense.

'They hollow out the cloud out to stop people noticing.' Alma pulled him towards the field's centre, where a circle of blue ghostly eyes awaited. 'Of course, the grass isn't real. Methuselah just adds it to make it feel like the Heath.'

Luke glanced around. 'He made all this?'

The Ghost Council's powers never ceased to amaze him: thunder, lighting, snow, mist and rain. You name it, they could do it. And yet, for the most part, they didn't. They refused to 'interfere' because they feared that if they did, it might upset the balance between the living and the dead, between this realm and the next.

'Welcome, all,' the sing-song voice of Methuselah greeted them. The Head of the Council wore a top hat and tails the colour of dusk, and stood in the centre of the circle of hazy figures. Beside him were Luke's three least favourite ghosts: the white-collared Reverend, the beak-masked Plague Doctor and the wizened Crone with her bonnet and cane, who gave a smile even frostier than the blizzards she cooked up. Luke could just about see through them, their edges shifting with the breeze.

Methuselah clapped his hands and the circle fell quiet. 'This evening, news has reached us of a break-in at Battersea. And the culprit got away.'

The councillors broke out in shouts of dismay.

'How did this happen?'

'Wasn't it guarded?'

Methuselah raised a thin-fingered hand, silencing the gathering. 'We don't have time for posturing. See for yourself. I read these memories from a guard.'

Reading memories was a skill all ghostclouds possessed, but Methuselah was a reader of the highest order. The principle was simple enough: ghostclouds and humans were both mostly water, and when their waters connected – through rain or mist – their thoughts did too. But Sal went further. He painted a picture more vivid than any televisor could.

He touched the cloudgrass and a spray of mist rose from it. It hovered lazily, then shimmered with colour. With a click of his fingers, it snapped into focus.

They were standing in Battersea, chimneys towering above, while apprentice builders waded chest-deep in mud, hammering the foundations of the plant's outer wall, alongside yellow-clawed diggers. Suddenly, a crack tore through the wall.

'Yesterday, they uncovered a new section of the lab. Then, this happened.'

At first, Luke noticed nothing – except that every fibre in his being had tensed. Officials passed in and out of the opening. Soggy apprentices cleared a path. Policemen arrived next, a detective too, but it was a builder who caught his eye. Stooped and lanky, he carried a large metal box. Something about his walk was unpleasantly familiar. He entered the crack, re-emerged, then boarded the digger. A second later, it accelerated away.

People ran in pursuit, but the digger was too fast. It shot across the boggy earth, churning mud in its wake, swinging its claw at anyone in its path. A guard fired a gun, but it didn't make a scratch.

'We had no choice,' said Methuselah. 'If the goods were worth stealing, then they were worth stopping.'

Metres from the riverbank, a bolt of blue lightning exploded from the sky, hitting the digger squarely above the driver's seat, blindingly bright. Luke stepped back. He knew the man was a thief, but did he deserve that?

Then the impossible happened. The digger emerged from the light – steaming, paint peeling, but otherwise unscathed – then leapt over the bank and into the air. It plunged under the water, resurfaced, then was swept with the current under Battersea Bridge.

'When the digger emerged,' Methuselah continued, 'the driver's seat was empty. The box was gone.'

The muttering began at once.

'The bolt must have missed them.'

'But what did he steal?'

'Who even cares. He's clearly dead.'

Luke frowned. The man had headed straight for the water. And with a lightning-proof digger? It didn't add up. And there was something else too . . .

He had to speak up. 'Methuselah, can you zoom in on the driver?'

The eyes of the councillors turned to him, hostile. Alma nudged him hard, but fortunately for him, her elbow slipped right through.

'Quiet, half-ghost,' the Reverend hissed. 'This isn't a televisor. We can't just zoom in.'

'Actually, I can,' Methuselah said. 'And the half-ghost knows Battersea. My interest is piqued.'

The scene played again, closer, slower, and this time they saw it. Just before the digger hit the water, the driver did something strange. He glanced right up at the clouds – and smirked. It was a smirk Luke knew only too well.

'It's Terence,' he said. 'Tabatha's right-hand man, I'm sure of it. And wherever he is, Tabatha's not far behind.' He looked around. 'Whatever he's taken from Battersea, it can't be good.'

'Luke's right.' Alma nodded. 'This is serious. We have to catch him, and fast. We should spread the word in in the sky – ask everyone to look out. Cancel all other duties and fog up the ports.'

The Crone shook her white shawl and jabbed the ground with her cane. 'I disagree. Why cause panic amongst the ghosts? Tabatha is in Europe, beyond our jurisdiction. For all we know, this Terence is just some desperate man. We should wait for more evidence.'

The Plague Doctor gave a gurgling rasp; others mumbled in agreement.

Luke looked around, uneasy. They wanted to wait? Were they blind? He had to convince them. 'But there's already more evidence. I saw nail-marks this morning. There's the rise in ghouls. And there was this tramp at Battersea, who says he saw her shadow . . .'

Luke trailed off. The ghosts were looking at him funny. He supposed it did sound far-fetched.

'Her shadow?' The Crone laughed. 'Our resident half-ghost is clutching at straws and do you know why? Because he's the real reason that the ghouls are on the rise. If he would become a full ghost, like we asked, we'd all be safe.'

Alma cut in, 'That's gossip, not fact.'

'But they are the on up,' said the Reverend. 'Just yesterday a groundghoul grabbed two ghosts by the river!'

Alma's eyes flashed. 'Who cares about some silly groundghoul! Last time, Tabatha almost destroyed us – she's still a danger to us all.'

The sky rumbled with thunder, silencing the argument.

'Enough,' said Methuselah, his suit now the colour of night. 'Since you're so confident, Alma, let's put it to the test. You and Luke may drop your duties and hunt for Terence and this case, but only if you hunt down this "silly ghoul" too. You've until All Hallows' Eve.'

'What?' said Alma. 'But that's in three days!'

And yet the council nodded. Methuselah, diplomatic as always, had found a solution that displeased both sides equally.

Luke still had one thing to ask. 'And if the case he's stolen has a lead on Tabatha's base, will the council stop her?'

'Of course, but let's not get carried away. You need to find it first.' Methuselah smiled, but not with his eyes. 'And in the meantime, if I were you, I'd watch my back. The last time we saw Terence, he was lowering you into a furnace. He might try to finish the job.'

Luke nodded. He had a feeling he wasn't going to sleep much that night.

CHAPTER 6
THE NORTH BANK WATER MARKETS

The nightmares had come thick and fast that night. The usual nightmare – *with Tabatha and Ravi* – was followed by a bonus one of Terence. He was standing in Luke's bedroom, reaching towards him, as Luke lay unable to move on his pillow. He'd woken up sweating.

The trouble was that it was all too possible. Terence hated Luke, and he was petty and vindictive. It'd be just like him to seek Luke out. But the one day Luke might have felt safer staying inside the office, what had Oberdink done? The opposite, of course. He'd taken Luke to the water markets – the busiest place in the city.

Every stall-keeper and street-sweeper looked horribly suspicious. Terence could be anywhere.

'Every third Tuesday, Smith-Sharma,' Oberdink said, 'I fingerprint new and fascinating items. Items that others deem impossible to fingerprint. Today, it's pineapples.'

'Pineapples, sir?'

'Oh, I forgot, you've been underground.' He prodded a sorry-looking pineapple through plastic gloves. 'It's an exotic fruit. No doubt smuggled in by a foreigner or criminal.'

Luke bit his tongue. Of course he knew what a pineapple was. What he didn't know was why he should care. His dad had left for Battersea at dawn to investigate the break-in, like a real detective, but Oberdink would rather inspect fruit with a magnifying glass.

His boss whipped out a splodge of blue putty, pressed it into the pineapple, then peeled it off.

'Aha! I knew it.' A swirling fingerprint etched across the putty. 'Highly suspicious. European, I'd wager. They sneak across the Channel in boats at night.'

'But are pineapples used in many crimes these days?'

'Who knows? Until now, we've never had the means to find out.'

Oberdink turned to pay for the incriminating fruit and Luke felt a growing frustration mixed with nerves. They finally had a lead – a chance of finding Ravi – and he was wasting time here. And then there was the council. Only giving them three days off duties to find Terence. They weren't taking it seriously.

Hang on in there, Ravi, he thought. *I'm trying, I promise.*

'Inspector,' Luke said, 'you know your job in Battersea, yesterday . . . did you notice anything odd?'

'If I had, Luke, I wouldn't tell you. It's confidential.' Oberdink wedged the pineapple into his briefcase. 'Incidentally, I've decided you'll just be "Smithy" from now on. It's neater. Shorter. Smith-Sharma's such a mouthful.'

His name? Seriously? Luke felt like giving Oberdink a mouthful. He watched his boss straining to close his briefcase over the pineapple. He didn't offer to help.

And it was just as well that he didn't, because a second later, both Oberdink and the pineapple went flying, knocked to the ground by a sprinting guard, followed in turn by a galloping robot-horse carriage.

SCREEECH!

The robot-horse skidded to a halt an inch from Oberdink's face, splattering him with pineapple from beneath its hooves. A crowd gathered. The horse whinnied and tossed its chainmail mane.

Oberdink stood. 'I don't care who you are,' he spluttered, waving a fruit-covered fist. 'I'm fining you for speeding, in the name of the Lord High Mayor!'

The carriage door opened and the crowd fell silent, for behind it stood none other than the Mayor himself.

Broad-shouldered, strong armed, with a mane of lion-gold hair, he gazed down at the crowd. He had to be well over six feet tall, Luke thought.

'Citizens,' he said, in a resonant voice. 'I apologise. My guards and I are chasing a criminal.'

The people nodded, almost gratefully, then the Mayor strode to where Luke and Oberdink stood. His boots crunched pebbles. His leather gauntlets creaked. His velvet black cloak stirred the earth as he moved. All of his movements were heavy and quiet.

'My apologies, good sirs, but this must be fate. A detective is exactly what I need right now.'

This man had worked with Tabatha. By all rights, Luke should hate him. But somehow, he found himself nodding like the rest.

'Last night,' said the Mayor, 'a man stole something from Battersea. We traced him near here. We think he wanted a boat.' He ran his hand through his hair. A few locks fell across his forehead. 'We just caught him, but then he slipped right through our fingers. And I mean that literally. His hands were so greasy, the cuffs slipped right off.'

Luke shivered. It had to be Terence.

A gleam appeared in Oberdink's eyes. 'Well, Mr Mayor, I may be the man to help you. I have at least ten certificates in finding criminals. And I have just discovered how to fingerprint pineapples.'

The Mayor frowned. His talkometer beeped. 'Ah, a development.' He nodded to the pair of them. 'Walk with me, do.'

It had the tone of a request, but the power of a command, and Luke and Oberdink found themselves scrambling to keep up with his strides. They left the market and reached the Strand – a huge boulevard of once-white pillared buildings – and soon reached a pub on the corner. The Mayor nodded towards a narrow set of steps beside it. 'My men say they chased him down here, to Vaudeville Square – deliberately, of course: it's a dead end.'

'And have they questioned him yet?'

They reached the bottom of the steps. It was a shady, paved courtyard that smelt vaguely of drain water, with a lonely pear tree slouched in the centre. At each side of the square, tall, red-doored houses stooped inwards; their shabby net-curtains twitched in the windows.

'That's the problem,' the Mayor said. 'He wasn't here. He disappeared. And now I'd like you to find him.'

'Curiouser and curiouser,' muttered Oberdink, pacing in stiff strides around the square. He scoured the rooftops with his eyes. 'Nothing. Not even an ounce of a clue.'

'Sir,' Luke said, 'what about that mark on the stairs?'

Oberdink looked round, peeved, then his eyes widened. 'The boy's right. It's a skid mark, from a hobnail boot. Recent, too. The culprit must have headed across the square to one of those two doors.' Oberdink gave a tight-lipped smile. 'Of course, I saw it first – I was just testing the lad.' He withdrew his fingerprinting brush like a sword. 'Leave this to me. This won't take long.'

Luke felt a rush of excitement. A real case, with fingerprints, and he had helped, kind of. Even the Mayor looked impressed. Luke rushed to Oberdink's side.

'Not you, Smithy. Unless you've learnt to fingerprint?' Oberdink smiled. 'No, I thought not. Now sit down and put those hands away.'

Oberdink glanced at Luke's calluses, and Luke's excitement withered. How could he learn if Oberdink wouldn't let him try? He slumped on to the bench under the tree, with his hands in his pockets. He felt Ravi's watch, still there – wasted, unused – and he knew how it felt. In Battersea they'd asked him to do many horrible things, but not once had he ever been asked to do nothing. It was almost worse.

Luke looked to the sky, but the tree blocked it out, taunting him with fruit that was out of his reach. His stomach rumbled.

'Hungry?' said a voice from behind. He hadn't even heard the Mayor approach. 'I bet they still pay apprentices a pittance.' The Mayor plucked a golden pear from a branch. 'Here, take this. Nobody ever solved a case on an empty stomach. I'll have one, too.'

Luke hesitated. Important people rarely spoke to apprentices. Especially friends of Tabatha's. It made him uneasy. But if he refused, it wouldn't look good.

He reached for the pear and the Mayor's eyes locked on his callused hand. Luke pulled it back, but too late.

'Those marks,' the Mayor said. 'You're a Battersea kid.'

'No – it's just . . . just . . .' But the fight had left him. What was the point? He'd never been that good at lying. 'Yeah, I suppose I am.' He looked over to his master, diligently dusting for prints. 'But I'm not meant to say.'

'Don't worry, your secret's safe with me.' The Mayor placed the pear in Luke's hand. 'What people don't know can't hurt them. That's what I always say.'

Luke nodded, but avoided his gaze. He bit into his pear. It'd been a strange twenty-four hours, between holding babies in the sky and munching pears with the Mayor.

He finished his fruit and realised the Mayor was still watching, his own pear uneaten.

'Now, son, answer me this.' The Mayor nodded towards Oberdink. 'Could a boy who beat Battersea really be beaten by man like that?'

Luke swallowed. He felt sure the pear had stuck in his throat. But the words came out, strong and clear. 'No. Never. Not in a million years.'

'Good,' said the Mayor. 'Because we need people like you to find that stolen case. My sources say it's linked to a weapon. One that might threaten everyone in this city.'

Luke's hands felt clammy. It made sense, he supposed. Tabatha had been making new weapons to use against Europe, but now she was banished, would she use them for revenge? He wouldn't put it past her.

He thought of his family. They'd been through enough.

'I'll try my best, sir.'

The Mayor smiled. He dropped his pear and it rolled to the foot of the tree. What Luke saw then made him jump.

'Lord Mayor, I think I know how he escaped. Look!'

Tucked away by the tree roots was a rather large drain. And shimmering on it, in the sunlight, were fingerprints. Fresh, greasy, Terence-shaped prints.

There was a cough from behind. Mr Oberdink stood there, eyes narrowed. 'Luke, I told you not to talk to your superiors.'

The Mayor laughed. 'Well, I'm glad he did, because he's cracked the case. Our man escaped down the drain.'

Oberdink's mouth smiled; his eyes did anything but.

The Mayor passed them his card. 'I'll ask the Plumbers Guild to seal the sewers, then you and my guards can check them properly.'

'Sewers?' asked Oberdink. 'I can't check the sewers. It's unhygienic.'

'But you must,' said the Mayor. 'I'll expect a report first thing tomorrow.' He walked off as his men filed into the drain. Oberdink watched, pale-faced. Luke couldn't help but feel bad for him.

'If it helps, Inspector,' he said, 'I think I know the culprit from Battersea.'

'OH WELL DON'T YOU KNOW EVERYTHING!' shouted Oberdink, right in Luke's face. 'In fact . . .' His moustache began twitching, then an unwelcome smile crept across his face. 'Since you're the expert, *you* can go down into the sewers. Yes, I like that idea very, very much. In the sewer, with the rats. And the rubbish. And the germs.' Oberdink grinned. 'While I drink tea in the office and write this report. How does that sound?'

Luke didn't even bother to reply. He walked up to the manhole and peered in. Terence was probably down there with the case, which could be Luke's only clue to finding Ravi. It looked dark, creepy and probably dangerous. Basically, it looked a lot like Battersea. And he'd beaten that once, so he'd beat it again.

There are worse things, anyway, he thought. He'd take rats over reports any day of the week.

CHAPTER 7
THE SEWERS

Water hissed, tunnels coiled, and bricks glistened like scales. It was almost as if he'd been swallowed by a python. An enormous, drain-drinking, slow-moving python, which lived under the city gobbling rats and rain.

All around him guards shouted, rushing back and forth on a ledge. Beside them trickled a stream of grey water, brightened by torch beams.

'Footsteps northwest.'

'Might be a decoy.'

'Roger that. Let's splinter.'

The guards barked military phrases that meant little to Luke and dabbed the walls with glow-paint arrows.

'What about me?' Luke said. 'What should I do?'

'Not our problem, kid.'

They dispersed through the tunnels, leaving Luke alone. The

red light flickered on Luke's walkie-talkie. Oberdink's voice crackled out, tinnier than usual. 'So, Smithy, found any clues?'

'There were footsteps, but the guards just trampled all over them.'

'Oh dear. Has our expert lost the trail already?' Oberdink chuckled. 'I'll make sure I put that in the Mayor's report.'

'No, it's fine. I'll follow their tracks.'

But the walkie-talkie breathed static: Oberdink had already hung up. And though he was somewhat relieved, Luke suddenly felt very alone.

He shook his head and swallowed his fear. It was better, really. This way, he could focus.

He followed the tracks east and his ears adjusted to the sewer. The chitter of rats. The drip of water. A rumbling undertram somewhere nearby. The sounds mixed together in chorus, like some underground song. The crisp sounds of the surface – birds, wind, the rustle of trees – didn't belong here. Everything was muffled by slosh and squelch, as though the sounds themselves had been soaked and buried.

He followed the arrows on the wall. The tunnel curved, straightened, curved again. His legs grew tired and his boots soaked up water. His spirits dampened too. What if they didn't find Terence? And even if they did, would he tell them what they needed to know?

The tunnel grew darker, so he wound his torch handle twice to brighten the beam, and in the yellow-white light, he made out a fork ahead. A secondary tunnel, smaller than the one he was in, veered off to the left. It looked old. The brickwork had crumbled in places and had the darkened sheen of years of sewage. The guards had put an 'X' above it – a dead end, he supposed. But for some reason, he paused.

There was a rat, sniffing the wall, below what looked like a grease mark. At about the level of Terence's hand. The rat disappeared down the tunnel. Luke stepped after.

Inside, the ledge curved then widened out and the bricks became older, crumblier and haphazard. The ceiling rose, forming an arched chamber, with a drain near the top at least twenty feet up. Strange white marks ran up the wall towards it, glowing less like glow-paint, more the light of the moon. But it was what was below that made him almost drop his torch. Set into the wall were shelves filled with bones. Brown, oozing, peeling bones.

He could smell them – rancid and dusty and dank. And he

could tell from the size that they weren't from rats.

Fear caught in his throat. What was this place? What had happened down here? Before he knew it, he was backing away. What had he been thinking? Old tunnels were dangerous, he knew that much from Jess. They could be structurally unsound, could contain noxious gases. And one with bones – well, that couldn't be good.

As he reached the entrance, he stopped. The chamber was horrible, but that was the point. He bet the guards had backed out just like he had. And he bet that was exactly what Terence would have expected. But a place this horrible wouldn't have worried Terence at all – he'd have loved it.

Luke stopped, breathed, and forced himself back inside. He shone the torchlight across the walls. Engraved in the brick was 'St Paul's'.

He must be near the cathedral. Perhaps it was the catacombs, or a plague pit of sorts. He breathed a sigh of relief; that was all it was. Nothing sinister, just people long dead. He saw enough of those each night with Alma.

He walked to the bone-shelves and cast his torch beam over them. Skulls with empty sockets looked back at him, some cracked, some deformed, but all uniformly creepy. But then, on one shelf, he saw something different: metal, glinting, right at the back.

Resting his torch on the brick, he cleared a path through the bones with his hands. Set in the shelf was a case just like one used in the break-in, and a trumpet-like contraption. Luke shuddered. He recognised it. It was from Tabatha's lab – a version of the ghost-gun she'd used to trap Alma.

This was it. He'd found it. Terence must have hidden them here!

He dragged both items out. The case weighed a ton and was sealed shut with a combination lock. He pressed his walkie-talkie to call for help, but the light began blinking. *Strange*, he thought, he was sure he'd charged it that morning.

Then, in the distance, he heard footsteps. Not the military clip of the Mayor's guards, but heavier, uneven. Was it Terence?

Or her?

Click. Drip. Click. Drip.

Steps in the sewer, nearer now. It could be anyone, and yet he held his breath. Should he call out or stay quiet?

Click. Drip. Click. Drip.

The steps grew quicker. Had they heard him? Suddenly,

inexplicably, his torch began to flicker, plunging the room in and out of darkness. He'd changed those batteries . . . it didn't make sense.

Click. Drip. Click. Drip.

In the flickering light, he made out a figure – stooping, scurrying down the tunnel towards him. Unnaturally fast. Distorted, like a shadow. With strange, curved arms. Luke looked behind: there was no way out. He grabbed a shard of bone from the shelf. It wasn't a weapon, but it'd have to do.

Click. Drip. Click. Drip.

He crouched, ready, then took a step back – right on to a bone, and went tumbling to the floor.

Everything seemed to spin and slow at once. A tobacco tang spread, bitter in the air. Bone dust choked him. He tried to scream but no sound came.

She was going to get him. Just like in his dreams.

A shadowed arm stretched out towards him. The darkness swirled and poured down his throat.

BANG!

Bright orange light exploded through the tunnel. The shadows disappeared and air flooded Luke's lungs.

He lay on the floor, gasping, as a very different silhouette appeared over him.

'Lukey, is that you? Why are you covered in bones?'

Even half-blinded, he knew that voice a mile off.

'Jess!' Luke leapt to his feet and hugged her. Then he remembered himself, and checked the tunnel. No shadow, just her.

'Did you see that *thing*? What was it?'

'Thing?' Jess frowned. She was wearing her plumber overalls and gas mask round her neck. 'There's nothing here, Luke, except for some rather toxic sewer gas. It can make you hallucinate all sorts of weird stuff. Didn't you see the 'X' on the door?' She nodded to the floor, where an orange flare fizzed brightly. 'That should have fixed it, but here, take a gas mask, just in case.'

Luke took it, still reeling. Toxic gas . . . had that been it? Had he imagined it all? He supposed the footsteps *could* have been Jess. 'I don't get it, how did you find me here?'

'The Plumbers Guild's all frantic – sealing sewers for the Mayor. When I heard Oberdink's name, I volunteered to help.' She picked a piece of skull off his shoulder. 'You smell rank, by the way. Like a grave. And that's coming from someone who works in a sewer.'

'Sorry,' Luke said, still unsure of himself. It *had* only started when he'd entered this tunnel. And the smell, the shadow – there was no trace of them now.

He looked around and saw the ghost-gun and the case. At least they were real.

Jess followed his gaze. 'Oh my gosh, you found the case!' She started skipping about, and a bone shattered under her foot. 'Oops. Will that annoy some ghost?'

'No, that's not really how it works.'

'Phew.' She sat down on a crumbling ledge and sighed. 'I miss our adventures. Your life's so much more exciting than mine now. You solve crimes. Hunt ghouls. While I spend the whole time fixing toilets.' She paused in thought. 'I wouldn't mind, you know, but they treat me like sewage. I do everything well, but they turn up their noses. And the boy apprentices get to do everything cool: ventilation, zeppelins, boats, you name it. But my master, I dunno, I guess he's just . . . *thorough*.'

Luke sat next to her. 'Mine too. If by "thorough", you mean dull, mean and jealous.' He shook his head. 'It's funny – at least in Battersea I knew who the bad guys were. It was black and white. These days, it's all grey. I know I'm in the guild and all that, but how much difference is fingerprinting a pineapple going to make?'

'A pineapple?'

'Don't ask.' He picked up his torch. Odd. It was working fine again now. His walkie-talkie too. He thought back to the flickering in the street at soulrise.

Jess watched him. 'What is it, Luke? You know something, don't you?'

'Not *know*, exactly . . .' He ran his mind back. 'The last few days, I've noticed strange things: nail-marks in the houseboat ladder, a figure in the street, and I read a witness statement from a tramp who said he saw Tabatha's shadow at Battersea. Oberdink laughed, and I know it sounds silly . . .' He sighed.

'Not silly,' said Jess. 'Sinister, more like. And *exactly* like Tabatha. But how?'

'I don't know, but I keep thinking back to the lab, when she had me and Alma cornered. She wanted to know how I travelled between realms.' He paused. 'What if . . . Well, what if she's found a way?'

'Like a half-ghost? Like you?'

'Yeah, or something worse.' Luke remembered the shadow in

the tunnel earlier. 'She's up to something, I know it. I tried to tell the Ghost Council, but they wouldn't listen.'

'Adults never listen. You know, sometimes I wish we could have a guild of our own. Me and you, Alma too if she wanted. The Ghostplumber Detectives, or something like that. We'd search for Ravi, or shadow-monsters, or whatever we liked. And if that didn't work, at least we'd get to hang out.'

Luke looked at the ghost-gun. The Mayor's words echoed in his mind: *What they don't know can't hurt them.*

'You know what, Jess? That might not be such a crazy idea.' He lifted the trumpet-like contraption and passed it to her. 'Meet me tonight at Paternoster Square. Let's put our Ghostplumbers Guild to the test.'

CHAPTER 8
THE GLIMPSE

The night was darker than most. It was black-on-navy, with a scuttling wind. Even the moon cast a damp shade of gloom. Luke waited in the sky. A mile or so down, the canals of east London squiggled back and forth, like black spaghetti, looping round islets and under rickety bridges. It wasn't as neat as the streets of the north, but for Luke, it was home.

His cloud, however, felt anything but. He rode a slithering slug-cloud, complete with a slime-trail and a pair of feelers.

'Alma, are you sure we can't fly something a little more cheery?'

'New rules, I told you. Apparently we need to be "less conspicuous".' She shrugged in the shadow of her slug's twin antennae. 'Not that anyone looks up. Most people in London don't even look at one another.'

Luke glanced down at the city as they drifted south: the Olympic stadium wrapped in white-flowering bindweed, the Stratford swamp reeds with their sweet-rot scent, the red-brick water mill with the witch-hat roof. They all looked so empty. Not a soul in sight. And yet part of him wondered. Was something down there, in the shadows, slipping between realms?

He pushed the thought from his mind. He didn't have proof yet. And he should focus on the positives. It had been quite the day – his find in the sewer had made the evening news. Obviously, Oberdink had taken the credit, but his dad knew the truth. He had hugged him tightly and said he had the makings of a great detective, and Luke's heart had swelled with pride. His nana had cooked dosa, his sister had brought chocolates, and that night, they'd cracked open a brand new board game.

Only two things niggled him. Firstly, Terence. He still hadn't been found, though the guards had traced his grease-marks to the port. And then there was the Ghost Council.

'I still don't get it. Were they really that mad?' Luke said. 'I found the stolen case, just like Methuselah asked!'

'And then you gave it to the Mayor! He's bad, remember?' Alma shook her head. 'The Crone and her cronies had a field day.'

'Look, I'd have been fired if I hadn't given it to him. And it was locked – we needed someone to unpick it.'

'That's basically what I said, but with more charm and panache.'
She shrugged. 'And I won them over – for now. Let's just keep them sweet by catching this groundghoul before All Hallows' Eve.'

'Fine. But they'd better bloomin' save Ravi when we've done it.'

'Of course they will! Now: groundghouls are sneaky, hard to find. They slip through the wall between realms in places where it's thin, like cemeteries and so on. But it just so happens that I've a friend in the know . . .'

Alma waxed on about her friends with connections as they crossed over the river to the southern slums. If the east was all water, the south was all craters, scars left over from the war with Europe. It was like a switch had been flicked and you'd flown to the moon – a black-earth moon, filled with thin, ragged people huddling round bonfires. The crater slopes teemed with slums, teetering storeys high, and in the centres pooled lagoons, where dogs drank and splashed.

Though it sounded rather hellish, it was Alma's haunt, and as she showed him round, it sparked into life. She pointed out landmarks, from overgrown parks to sunken cemeteries, from artillery barracks to abandoned lidos. There was even, to Luke's amusement, a place called 'Broccoli'. At least, that's what he thought she had said.

'But if they've got no electricity, what do they do in winter when it's cold?'

'This is England, Luke, it's cold in summer. That's why they've got all the fires.' She frowned. 'But it's bad in winter. I wouldn't show you round then.'

Luke looked at the run-down streets. The people looked happy enough, but it didn't seem fair. The city had written them off. 'Maybe Tabatha had a point. She always said she wanted to bring power to the slums.'

Alma's cloud darkened. 'If she wanted power, it was only ever for herself.' She nodded ahead. 'Anyway, we're here: Gypsy Hill. Look smart, Ma Boxhill's waiting.'

Luke followed Alma's gaze to an archipelago of tiny silver cloud-islands, scattered through the sky above a rubble-strewn hill. On each stood a dark cloud-tent of sorts, and as they rose to meet the nearest, Luke spied a figure out front. It was a cross-legged old ghost lady with prominent cheekbones, a wide smile, tattered trainers and turbaned hair. A beaded shawl hung from her shoulders and shimmered transparent with the passing breeze.

'Alma, my sweet, it's been too long. If only Hallowmas came more often.' Laughter lines wrinkled her eyes. 'And this dapper young man must be Luke. I do love a bow-tie.'

A bow-tie? Luke looked down. She was right, he seemed to be sporting one. Not only that, but a three-piece suit that shone like satin. He wasn't sure how it had got there, but it didn't look half bad.

'Indeed it is,' Alma said. 'He's normally quite feral, but I dressed him up just for you.'

The clouds touched, and Old Ma Boxhill beckoned them on to her cloud. It was an intimate thing, boarding someone's cloud – something you did with friends, not people you'd just met, but Luke got the sense Ma Boxhill wasn't one for formalities. His feet moved across misty scrub and sand before settling on the rug opposite her.

'So, tell me,' said Alma. 'Any news from the south?'

The lady cracked her knuckles and lifted a teapot from the floor. Carefully, she added some herbs and vapour. 'No sign of Tabatha, but they found a new warehouse on the southern coast.'

Alma leant in, nodding. Ma Boxhill stirred the pot and filled three rough-hewn cups to the brim with steam.

'What else? Let me think. Storms are down, refugee boats are up, and they say the Crone is plotting again. Wants your half-ghost to be a "full ghost" – and wants your job as deputy, of course.'

'Nothing new there, and nothing I can't handle.' Alma laughed.

It didn't sound funny to Luke.

Ma Boxhill went on. 'Oh, there are tales in the slums of a new type of ghoul. When it flies past houses, the lights blink.'

Luke's chest tightened. The flickering again, just like at soulrise and the sewer. A type of ghoul? Or something travelling between . . .

'Pah!' cut in Alma, before he could speak. 'Ghouls have better things to do than go around causing power cuts.' She turned to Ma Boxhill and stirred her tea. 'But the other stuff is perfect. Now, about the business I mentioned, do you think you can help?'

'If the waters will it. I've collected drops from the Thames this evening. They carry whispers of this groundghoul. But this Terence of yours is not so clear.' She turned to Luke. 'Your thumb, dear. I just need a drop.'

'A drop? Of what?'

'Of your soul,' said Alma, matter-of-factly. 'It's for your memories so that she can find a match on Terence.'

'Err . . . but don't I need my soul? And my memories, for that matter?'

'It's not like that,' Alma said. 'Your soul's like blood. You need it, yes, but losing a drop or two never hurt anyone. What matters more is that it's flowing.' She frowned in thought. 'And I guess the memories are like DNA. They're etched in each drop. Every choice, every action, it all leaves a mark.' She nodded to the old woman. 'Ma Boxhill reads them – she's kind of an expert.'

It sounded strange, Luke thought, but if it helped find Terence, then it could help find Ravi. He held out his hand. 'If you're sure it's safe.'

Old Ma Boxhill took his thumb and pricked it lightly. A drop of light fell into her palm. She smiled. 'What a vibrant soul. A good place to begin.'

At once, all around, the sky disappeared, replaced by a dome of gauzy, grey mist. Colours flickered on its surface. A pretty cobbled street, dripping and dark. A broken cart lay to one side. Luke knew it at once.

'That's Carter Lane! It's right by St Paul's.'

'Go there, tonight. The ghoul lies there. But be vigilant. It hides well.'

Excitement leapt in his chest. Was this actually working? He had never bought into fortune telling, but this felt different. 'What about Terence? Any sign of him?'

Ma Boxhill's brow furrowed. At first nothing happened . . . but then he heard footsteps. Louder each step. It was Terence, he knew, from his loping gait. But the image stayed the same.

'Strange,' she said. 'He's heading that way. There's something he seeks.'

'His case, maybe?'

'Perhaps. And there's something else . . . something odd . . .' The street lights in the image began to flicker, convulse, then the scene melted into black.

A door appeared in the darkness. Thick, oak and bolted at the top.

'This isn't mine,' whispered Ma Boxhill. 'I don't understand.'

But Luke did. He knew that door. And more importantly, he knew what was coming next. The eye at the keyhole. The *tap tap tap*. The fingernail snaking up the side of the door.

It was the door from his dreams, but for once, he couldn't wake up.

He grabbed Alma's hand . . .

. . . but instead of an eye at the keyhole, the door creaked open.

Luke held his breath. Was this where he found out the end of his dream?

Behind the door lay darkness, and out of the darkness stepped a figure: raven-haired, amber-eyed, her hand on her cheek right where he'd burnt her. Luke shivered. It was Tabatha and she was staring straight at him, as if she were right there with them.

Then from the shadows behind her, a second figure emerged: dark hair cut short, glasses chipped. He looked taller, Luke thought, older, tired.

'Ravi! I'm here!' Luke couldn't help but call out.

Ravi didn't respond. But it was what happened next that stayed with him. Behind the pair, a full moon rose, over a field of red, and the air grew suddenly thick and hot. Luke smelt burning, from the sky itself. Then the moon and the figures melted like wax.

The grey dome vanished. They were back in London. Ma Boxhill sat, pale, her cup knocked to the ground.

'What on earth was that?' Luke said. 'The door, that's from my dream . . . but the bit after – I've never seen that.'

'Not *yet*.' Ma Boxhill shook her head. 'Dreams are in-between things, and time, like water, can flow both ways. If I'm not mistaken, that was a *glimpse*.'

'A glimpse?'

'A nothing,' said Alma, though her eyes said otherwise. 'They're unreliable. Unsafe. The council doesn't approve.'

'Which is why many of us don't approve of the council.' Ma Boxhill stood. 'But perhaps I should go, before I say something I regret. Good night, both, and maybe good luck. I know that's a place I'd rather not go.'

'Wait,' Luke said. 'Ravi was there. I need to know what it means.'

Ma Boxhill paused. 'As you wish.' She weighed her words carefully. 'It means that to save your friend, you must face her first. And you must be ready to sacrifice everything, perhaps even more. She will try to take it all. Every last drop.'

Luke swallowed. It sure sounded like Tabatha. 'And the moon? What about that?'

'That's how long you have. Till the next full moon.'

Luke looked at the sky. The moon was cut in half, a perfect semi-circle. He knew one came each month, but if they were already halfway . . .

'Two weeks to save Ravi? That's all we've got?'

Alma shook her head. 'Less, Luke. It's seven days at best.'

He turned to Ma Boxhill. 'But that's impossible. What if we don't make it?'

'Let's just say that for his sake, and all of ours, I hope you do.'

CHAPTER 9
GHOUL-HUNTING

'I'm not saying she made it up. I'm just saying it's *unlikely*.'

Since they'd left Ma Boxhill with a polite goodbye, Alma's irritation had grown with the wind. She now crouched on her slug-cloud as it slithered beside his, ranting to Luke and the dark night sky.

'The intel is fine, but the rest is mumbo-jumbo.' She threw her hands in the air. 'That stuff about Tabatha, the moon, and the flickering too – I mean, lights flicker all the time these days!' She tutted. 'It's those herbs in her tea. She had one too many cups.'

Luke dug his fists into his slug-cloud and shot away on the wind. She was getting on his nerves. Since when had 'unlikely' ever mattered? Tabatha's experiments on ghosts had seemed 'unlikely', but if they'd looked into them earlier, then a lot of trouble could have been avoided. And then there was the 'glimpse' – it had felt so *real*. There were details she couldn't have taken from his memory.

Ravi had looked older. Tabatha's burn had healed. And the silvery moon – it had looked just like the ones on his mum's watch.

The detective inside him knew that the guild – and Oberdink – wouldn't see any of this as proof, but whatever they said, he couldn't ignore it. It meant something, he knew it, and he knew Alma did too. But only seven days, really?

He sank into the cool, moist fluff of his cloud and gazed up at the moon. Perhaps his mum was right. He'd have to make every second count.

'Luke, wait up.' Alma pulled alongside him. 'I'm sorry. I got annoyed. It's just, I thought she'd solve our worries, but she gave us new ones. You've enough nightmares as it is.'

'Well, that's true.'

Alma sighed. 'Let's go one step at a time. We'll try St Paul's and if the ghoul's there, we zap it, then worry about the rest.'

'Fine,' Luke said. 'Whatever it takes to find Ravi in time.'

So they flew on quietly, looking down over the city. To the north, by Barbican, glass-domed roof-gardens glowed gold and alive, steamed up from the heat of bubbling coal stoves. To the west, by Covent Garden, people spilt out from bars and on to the curbs, umbrellas popping up like little dark starfish. But as they neared St Paul's, the quiet was thick. Nobody was out. Did they sense something out there – the ghoul perhaps? Luke guessed they'd find out.

They finally stopped at Paternoster Square and peered down. It was eerily still.

'Wait, did you hear that?' Alma's eyes narrowed.

Screech. Screech. Scrape. Clunk.

In the flickering red light of the undertram sign, a manhole cover unscrewed and clunked on to the pavement. From the darkness leapt Stealth, his fur bright in the lamplight. A second later came a head of messy blonde hair. Jess grinned right up at them, the ghost-gun slung over her shoulder . . . then promptly jabbed Stealth with her thumb. The cat yowled.

Alma frowned. 'What in the skies is she doing?'

'I think,' Luke said, 'she was trying to give a thumbs up.' He allowed himself a smile. Jess always managed to make him feel better.

'A thumbs up. Of course.' Alma shook her head. 'For the record, I still think bringing her is a terrible idea, but you know me, I'll try anything once.' She grabbed the slug antenna nearest to her. 'Now, let's head down and save that poor cat.'

Luke grabbed the other feeler – it felt slimy, somehow – then with a sharp tug, the slug-cloud split into a pair of sluglets. He sunk his fists into spongy, wet grey, tilted down and right, and caught the edge of a cold, fading gust. It gave him just enough momentum to glide down, past pockmarked chimneys and bomb-proof steel shutters before landing in a puff of fog next to Jess.

'Hunting with ghosts, well, isn't this fun?' Jess chirped, stifling a yawn. 'If a little past my bedtime.' She squinted at the pair of them. 'You're rather hazy at the edges, but you almost look normal.'

Most people could only see a ghost if the ghost made an effort, but after all those days hanging out in the summer, Jess had grown quite attuned. She was a better ghost-spotter than most clairvoyants.

Stealth leapt from her arms and licked his little tongue right through Luke's misty foot. It tickled and Luke laughed. It relaxed him somehow.

He filled Jess in as they crossed the square, making their way towards Carter Lane. 'Here's what we know. This ghoul's grabbed a ghost each night this week. But nobody sees it coming.' They entered an alley. Soot-stained walls rose steeply either side of them. 'Jess, you got that torch?'

She rummaged in her bag. 'Yes! A UV torch, like you asked.' She pulled out a squat brass torch, flicked a switch and shone a purple beam on the walls. The bricks glistened darkly from the recent rain, but there was something else: glowing streaks of what looked like white paint.

'Abstract art?' Jess frowned. 'Or pigeon poo?'

'No. They're ghoul marks,' said Luke. 'And they start at ground level, which is how we know it's a groundghoul. That's why they don't see it coming: it comes from beneath.'

'Yuck,' said Jess. 'But I thought ghouls came from the End Place? Isn't that up there?'

'It's mostly up there,' said Alma. 'But it's all around us, too. You can feel it, sometimes – in cemeteries, churches – that shivery feeling of something beyond. It seeps through the wall between realms where it's thinnest.'

'So if it seeps' – Jess frowned, thinking – 'it's kind of like water. Does that make the ghouls a bit like leaks?'

Luke grinned. She was plumber through and through. 'Yeah, I guess. Normally, the ghoul-leaks come from above, through the "roof" as it were. But sometimes, there's a problem with bricks lower down.'

Alma looked ready to pull out her hair. 'Fine, whatever. Ghouls are leaks in the wall . . . leaks that try to kill you. And what matters is that we plug this one, sharpish. For Ravi, and also your reputation with the council. They can't call you a part-timer if you pull this one off.'

'But I *am* a part-timer.'

'I know.' She waved her hand dismissively. 'But it's appearances that count.'

Luke sighed. He wished they didn't.

At their feet, Stealth began to hiss. His black ears pricked up and he stared ahead.

'Listen!' Luke said. 'Do you hear that?'

They all held their breath. A quiet moaning could be heard on the breeze. Luke looked towards the sound. The sign on the corner read *Carter Lane*, just like he had seen in his 'glimpse' with Old Ma Boxhill. They'd got what they'd asked for, though part of him wondered if they might live to regret it.

The bells rang midnight. The moaning faded.

'Well,' Luke said, 'here goes nothing.'

CHAPTER 10
DEAD END

Luke realised he'd been to Carter Lane before, in the day, when it thronged with tradesmen heading to market. The drivers normally sang, but there was no song now. Only the drip of water on cobbles and the rustle of rats.

The moaning had stopped, but he knew its source lay further down. They just had to spot it before it spotted them. Or smell it, perhaps. Ghouls had no eyes, so they preferred to sniff out their prey. Groundghouls, Alma said, were small, so one zap of lightning might do it, but they were also quick, so they'd have to keep their eyes peeled. Unlike Jess, who was currently crouched with Stealth, eyes inches from the floor like she was counting ants.

Luke sighed. 'Jess, what are you doing?'

'It's the manholes. They're off-centre.' She looked up hopefully. 'Might that be a clue?'

'No,' Alma said. 'It's entirely irrelevant.'

'What about that rat?' Jess said, as one skittered past them. 'Could that be something? In the sewer, they're never that shade of grey.'

'Jess,' Luke said. 'Maybe leave us to the clues and have the ghost-gun ready?'

Jess's face fell.

'No, Jess is right,' Alma said, with sudden enthusiasm. 'The rat does look odd. Quick, Jess, follow it! It's getting away!'

Jess nodded and sprinted after it down an alley, Stealth scampering behind, leaving Luke and Alma alone on the lane.

'Did you say that just to get rid of her?'

'Maybe. Anyway, at least it's quiet now.'

They walked along the cobbles, but Luke found his annoyance from earlier creeping back. She always had to have it her way. She didn't care what he thought.

'Alma, that's not OK. I invited her for a reason. Her master is horrible. She's having a hard time at work—'

'Well, I don't know if you've noticed, but I'm having a hard time too,' Alma snapped. 'I've had to pause all my special projects. The Crone and the Reverend are on my back. And now you don't only want to save Ravi, but Jess as well?'

'I'm not trying to save her, I'm trying to be nice!' Luke realised he was shouting, and stopped himself. He took a deep breath. 'We thought it could be like a guild. The Ghostplumber Detectives, or something like that . . .'

'Ghostplumbers?' Despite herself, Alma broke into a grin. 'That, Luke, is a bonkers name.'

He couldn't help but grin too. 'I know, and yet—'

A sharp, cold breeze cut down the alley. In the square ahead, a lantern flickered.

The pair of them froze. Had they imagined it? There was nothing now. Only dark walls and rooftops, warped and huddled against the rain and the night.

There it was again! At the edge of the square, the windows on the side street blackened one by one, like dominoes. It was just like Old Ma had said.

'It's getting away, quick!' Alma shouted.

Luke was already running, his misty feet zipping over silver-black cobbles. He reached the centre of the square, then turned down the side street, and for a fleeting moment, he saw a figure – a shadowy figure.

Bang!

Bright amber light burst from the streetlights. The power went out, blanketing the way in darkness.

Alma caught up.

'I saw something,' he said. 'A shadow. Do you think it might be . . . her?'

Alma frowned. 'I don't know. It doesn't seem like a groundghoul. They hide, not run. Come on, stay close.'

They stepped down the street, treading slowly past pub signs, bricked windows, and painted pillared doorways. The pavement twisted left, to reveal a dead end.

The air tasted cold. A rustle from the corner.

Squinting, Luke made out a shadow in a doorway, about twenty feet away. It moved a little and he could see a figure. A hunched, ragged woman, squatting under an arch, shoulders rising and falling, with grunts of sleep.

She wasn't like the figure he'd seen at all. She looked like a beggar. Except for one thing: her head was in her hands. This was possible for anyone, of course, but it seemed a little convenient, given the eyes – or lack of them – was the giveaway of a ghoul. It was all so confusing.

'Is it the groundghoul? Should we zap her?'

'We have to be sure. I can't just zap a little old lady.'

A crash from behind. Luke and Alma whirled round.

A bin lid spun on the floor. A rat peeked out behind it.

'Ugh. Just rats.'

'Wait,' said Luke. 'They look *different*. Do you think—'

A chittering started, then a pitter-pattering. First quiet, then louder, from the other side of the street.

He turned back round. The woman was gone.

'Where is she?' shouted Alma.

But it wasn't the woman Luke was worried about. 'The floor, look!'

A seething mass of rats was running towards them, the colour of mist, baring their teeth in an eyeless stare. These weren't rats at all. They were part of the ghoul. But though Alma's fist crackled blue, the rats were too quick – they were already upon them, scurrying up their legs and over their bodies. Their tiny claws and teeth dug into his skin.

Luke tried to shake them off, but he couldn't move at all. To his right, he saw Alma's fist fizzle then fade. The rats stopped moving and the chittering stopped. A terrible silence fell on the alley.

'Alma, can't you zap them? Why can't I move?'

'I'm trying, but I can't. It's the groundghoul, all right, and it's got us. Its water's mixed with ours. It's taking control.'

Frozen, they watched as the rats on the floor began to pile on top of one another, like a strange circus trick – a tower of rats. Then the tower bulged and blurred into the haggard old lady. She gave an eyeless grin and a guttural chuckle.

Luke tried to move, run, but his body wouldn't co-operate. A cold numbness crept up from his toes. 'Alma, come on! What do we do now?'

'We get swallowed, basically, then taken to the End Place.' Her voice trembled. 'Apparently, it's nice once you get there . . .'

The old lady sniffed and stepped closer. She loosened her jaw. It slid slack and wide like a hungry snake's. Luke saw right inside, into the sparkling black of what lay beyond.

'Hey, guys, guess what?' Jess burst round the corner with Stealth. 'That rat didn't have eyes! Then it just disappeared.' She froze on seeing them. 'Erm . . . who's that lady?'

The hag gave a hideous squealing sound, fell on all fours and began scuttling towards Jess. But Jess was too quick. She had the ghost-gun at her shoulder, her hand on the trigger, and a slurping, air-ripping sound filled the air.

The rats and hag disappeared into the gun. Jess flicked off the switch and patted it in wonder. 'Well, that was neat. Were you saving her for me?'

Alma exhaled. 'Something like that.'

Luke flexed his fingers and bent his knees. He looked at the ghost-gun – he'd never felt so grateful for one of Tabatha's inventions. 'Jess, you saved the day.'

'Technically,' said Alma. 'It's night, not day . . . but he's right. I'm sorry for doubting you.'

'It's OK.' Jess shrugged. 'I doubt myself all the time, so we've something in common.'

The lights flickered back on around the alley. If that had been the groundghoul, what about the lights and the shadow they'd seen just before? It hadn't looked a bit like the rat lady. Were the two separate or linked?

Luke noticed something in the doorway and walked over and picked it up. It was a piece of amber. In the centre lay an ant, frozen in time.

He shivered. 'Tabatha had a paperweight just like this.' Luke turned it in his hands. It glowed orange-yellow in the street light. 'What does it mean?'

'I don't know,' said Alma. 'Something bad, no doubt.'

'It can't be a coincidence. We have to tell the council.'

'But it doesn't prove anything.' Alma shook her head. 'It just raises more questions. We need to do this right. Let's tell them about the groundghoul, to get in their good books, but keep the amber and flickering lights quiet until we've got answers.' She unfurled her swan-cloud. 'Pick your battles, and all that.'

'Pick your battles?' Luke asked. 'Or just pick the ones you can win?'

'Both, of course. Why would you want to lose? It's Ravi's life we're talking about.' She stepped on to the swan's wing. 'If Ma Boxhill was right about the ghoul, then she's probably right about the full moon too, which means we don't just need the council's help, we need it pronto. In the next seven days, to be precise.' She chewed her lip. 'This All Hallows' Eve meeting is our last chance to convince them. I say we hit them with everything we've got – not speculation, but facts. Proof of Tabatha. Evidence of what she's up to. And, most important, the location of the base. Then there's a chance they might act there and then.'

More waiting? Luke couldn't bear it. Ravi needed them now. The council should be helping them look for clues! But then he remembered the last meeting, how they'd mocked his suggestions, and he knew Alma was right. He just hoped they could gather enough proof in time. There were only two days to go.

'OK, I'm in. We keep looking, then hit them with it all at the meeting.'

Jess grinned. 'It's like we planned. Our own secret guild!'

'I guess it is,' Alma said, her swan rising to the rooftops. 'But can we change the name? I wouldn't be seen dead as a ghostplumber.'

With a salute, she was gone and Luke began walking Jess back, while she prattled on about possible names and secret handshakes. Before they knew it, they were back at Paternoster Square and saying their goodbyes.

'It's weird,' said Jess, glancing up. 'The fresh air's so nice. After all that time underground in Battersea, the sewers aren't quite the same. Tonight was fun.'

'It was, wasn't it?' said Luke. 'Though next time, let's skip the almost dying part.'

'Deal,' she said, with a fist bump that went right through his fist.

'Now I, for one, am ready for bed.' But as he reached down to stroke Stealth, the cat's ears pricked up. His little brown eyes fixed further down the street.

Screech. Screech. Scrape. Thud.

The pair of them froze. The manhole ahead twisted, then abruptly stopped.

'I knew they were askew!' Jess said. 'But it can't be a plumber or they'd have the key.'

Luke swallowed. 'It's Terence, it has to be. He's come to get his stuff from the crypt.'

'Then I'll bet he's going to be mad.' Jess swung the ghost-gun on her shoulder.

Screech. Screech. Scrape. Thud.

This time, the noise came from further down the street. Another manhole twisted.

'He's trying to get out,' Jess said. 'But they're locked for miles.'

'Good.' Luke walked towards the noise. 'That'll give us time to plan how to catch him.'

CHAPTER 11
MANHOLES

Screech. Screech. Scrape. Thud.

They'd been following the manholes for several blocks now, and Terence, assuming that's who it was, was clearly getting desperate. The manhole twists were now followed by shouts of frustration, and though the precise words were muffled, Luke felt sure his nana wouldn't approve of what was being said.

But if it *was* Terence, he sure had stamina. He tried a new manhole every couple of minutes. It would have been impossible to keep up if they'd been normal detectives, but the Secret Guild weren't normal at all. With Stealth's good hearing and Jess's knowledge of the sewers, they had no trouble tracking him.

'There's a junction here,' Jess whispered. 'But I bet he'll turn right. The other paths really stink.'

A minute later, as expected, metal screeched to the right,

followed by a particularly foul-sounding curse, which wafted out from a drain.

Forming a plan, however, was not as easy. Luke had hoped for some ropes or a net by Threadneedle Street, but no such luck. Or a weapon of sorts, at Artillery Row, but again, nothing.

'You sure we can't bash him with a manhole cover?'

'I'd love to,' said Luke. 'But Terence is strong – it might not work. And if we hit him too hard . . . well, we don't want to kill him.'

He considered flying off for some ghosts to help, but he didn't fancy leaving Jess alone. Fierce as Stealth was, he was still only a cat. And part of him wanted to catch Terence on his own. After all the misery he'd inflicted on Luke in Battersea, surely it was his right?

A waft of spices hit him, like his grandma's cooking. The glow of lights rose over the hill.

'It's Indytown, look!'

It was an electric jungle. Tropical neon signs perched on shopfronts like parrots. Bulb-studded doors flashed white like waterfalls. A canopy of waxed lanterns arched overhead, while tangled cables hung down like creepers.

'Jess, does the sewer lead down there?'

'Yeah? Why? Shall we get a takeaway?'

'No, but I've an idea. Come on, quick!'

It was simply a matter of choosing the right knots. Just like fishing, except instead of thread, they'd use cables. And instead of fish, it'd be Terence. Who, come to think of it, was at least as slippery as an eel. He'd have to make the knots tight.

They ran up the street. Past curry houses, samosa stalls and a giant plastic mango wearing retro sunglasses. The light from the signs spilt wet and gaudy on the puddles of street water, which pooled ineffectively around litter-clogged drains.

But he didn't care about drains. He needed a manhole. But not that one. Nor that one. It had to have . . .

Yes, that was it! At the roadside under a flashing pink sign, which spelt in curled letters *Radhika's Rice* and swung jauntily in the breeze – no doubt against regulation. Cables hung off it like braids of hair.

It would do nicely. The cable pooled by the manhole: thick, safe, and with plenty of slack.

'Are you sure this will work?'

'Kind of,' Luke said. 'So long as he doesn't wriggle. Now quick, unlock it.'

Screech. Screech. Scrape. Thud.

It was the next manhole along. Whoever it was would be with them any minute. Luke arranged the wires in a loop round the opening.

'When I give you the signal, pull hard.'

Jess nodded and they retreated into the shadows.

Nothing happened. The sign above rattled with a lurid pink glow. The mango in sunglasses seemed to wink in the distance. And they waited.

Had he heard them? Had he changed his mind? Luke turned to Jess, but before he could speak the noise came again.

Screech. Screech. Scrape. Clunk.

The manhole cover slid off and landed with a *thunk*. There was a whoop of triumph from the sewers. Warily, a head peeked out.

Rat-black ponytail. Grease-stained forehead. Yellow-toothed, dull-eyed, stooped and vicious.

It was definitely Terence: he hadn't changed a bit. A greasy waft caught in Luke's throat, and memories assailed him. Terence lowering him towards the furnace. Tossing Ravi into the van. Sneering. Smirking. Hateful. Petty. Then the one from his nightmare: Terence leaning over his bed, his vice-like grip clasped around Luke's throat.

This man was dangerous. Not to be underestimated. He hoped the knots he'd tied would be up to the job.

Terence's eyes scoured the streets and he sniffed twice. Then slowly, like an insect unfolding, he pulled himself from the manhole and up to standing.

It was now or never. Luke signalled to Jess and they both pulled at once.

Terence didn't know what had hit him. The thick rubber cables tightened round his ankles, and he shot up into the air, dangling upside-down like butcher's meat.

'Put me down!' he hissed, venomously. 'Or I'll rip you in half!'

Luke stepped into the light so Terence could see him. Jess and Stealth followed behind.

Terence's eyes widened. 'You!' he growled, then looked to the ghost-gun. 'And you stole my stuff!'

A light flickered on from the building behind them. Terence looked round, nervous. 'Look, I don't want the police and I'm sure you don't either. I'll make it worth your while. I've plenty of money.'

'No. I'm calling them.' Luke turned to shout, then stopped. He didn't need money, but there *was* something – something he wanted more than anything else. And if the police arrived, he might lose the chance. 'Wait. What about Ravi? Where's he being held?'

A smile slithered across the dangling man's face. 'Ravi, let me think . . . grumpy, with glasses. Smart, too. Though not smart enough to escape, I suppose.' Terence chuckled.

A crash from behind. They all looked round. A scowling face peered through the window.

'What the heck are you doing with my sign?'

The voice sounded familiar, but when the window opened, Luke's heart almost stopped. There, glaring in the window, was Ravi.

No, he thought, as his eyes adjusted. It was a girl just like Ravi, with a white streak of hair. Luke's brain put the pieces together – Radhika's Rice was the name of the stall, so it was Ravi's sister, Radhika. He seen her in the water market once, with Alma.

She didn't recognise him, of course, but Luke was sure of it – her mouth was scowling just like Ravi's had done. In fact, it was scowling right behind him at Terence.

'Sorry,' he said. 'We've just tied him up temporarily.'

'Then what's he doing with that knife?'

Knife? Luke spun round, but it was already too late. Terence had slipped a blade out from somewhere and with a flick of his wrist, he cut right through the wires, and fell to the floor in a shower of sparks.

'My sign!' said Radhika, running inside. 'I'm calling the police!'

But Terence didn't run. He rose slowly to his feet as the cables sprayed sparks in the air behind him. 'The police take time. This will only take a minute.' He wiped the knife on his leg and stepped closer. 'Now, who's first? The girl, the ghost-boy, or maybe' – he snatched Stealth from the floor – 'the cat. I hate cats.'

Stealth clawed and writhed, but all in vain.

'Stop it!' Luke shouted. 'He's an innocent animal!'

'But it's so much fun seeing you squirm.' Terence locked his greedy eyes on Luke. 'And don't worry, it'll be your turn soon. Once I've got that ghost-gun.'

Stealth yowled as Terence tightened his grip.

Luke felt sick. He tried to think, but it was all too much. How had things changed so quickly? One minute, it'd been fun, tracking him in the streets, but now he could see that he'd put his friends in danger.

He'd been stupid thinking he could help. Thinking a boy like him had a chance of changing things. He should have left it to the experts. But then, where *were* the experts? They were probably off somewhere having a meeting.

Anger pulsed inside him. There had to be something he could do.

Terence raised the knife.

'No! Don't!'

But as Luke shouted, something odd happened. The sparks from the cable seemed to slow.

Thump. Thump. Thump. Thump.

Luke's heart beat loudly. He felt funny. The sparks had just frozen, mid-air. Nobody else seemed to have noticed.

Then suddenly, with a fizz, they whizzed to Terence's hand.

'Ow!' Terence dropped the cat to the floor. 'Stupid wires!'

He reached again for the cat, but the cable wasn't finished. It fired another burst of sparks at his knife this time, which he dropped, then another two bursts at each of his legs, sending him hopping in a desperate jig.

Thump. Thump. Thump. Thump.

Luke's heart drummed even harder. It was almost as if he could feel it – the sparks, the static, building around him. Each burst at Terence, he'd felt that too.

The illuminated signs all down the street began to stutter.

'Luke,' Jess whispered, 'look at your hands!'

It was only then that he noticed. His hands were crackling like Alma's, but instead of lightning blue, they pulsed hot orange like sunset.

Thump. Thump. Thump. Creeeak.

The heartbeat was joined by another sound. A strange creaking, like ice on the Thames. The air almost seemed to ripple.

Terence had stopped, his eyes fixed on Luke's glowing hands. 'Well, Smith-Sharma, it seems you've been busy.' He smiled, nervously. 'But I've given you the cat, as per the deal, so shall we leave it at that?' He edged closer to the manhole.

The air crackled. Luke felt something swill inside him. Sparks hung in the air like fireflies.

Thump. Thump. Thump. Creeeak.

Terence dived for the sewer, as fast as an eel . . . but the light moved faster. The bolt from Luke's hand hit Terence square on the bottom, blasting him back into the stall.

The signs stopped flickering. The air stopped rippling. Terence lay still, steam rising from his trousers.

Luke felt sick. What had he done?

Jess took a breath then walked over to where Terence lay. She crouched down. 'It's OK,' she said. 'He's breathing. Just about. But he's not going anywhere soon.'

Police sirens sounded nearby. Luke looked at his hands: the glow was fading. How was he going to explain it? To the police or the Ghost Council? He couldn't think straight.

There was a cough behind them.

'If I were you, I'd go before they get here,' Radhika said from the window. She looked around. 'As far as I'm concerned, this never happened.'

Luke and Jess nodded. Stealth miaowed. They slipped back into the manhole and locked it tight.

CHAPTER 12
THE MAYOR

It was breakfast. Luke was tired. And the toaster filled him with dread.

'Just toast them,' said his sister. 'It's not a big deal.'

Luke had never been good at decisions in the morning – jam or honey, water or juice – but toasting crumpets had never been an issue. Everyone toasted crumpets. It was just what you did.

And yet he stood there, uncertain, because this morning, every electronic thing he'd touched had exploded.

First had been the bulb of his bedside lamp. He'd reached over to it, and a spark from his hand had shattered the glass. Then when he'd fumbled around for the torch, the same thing had happened. *Fizz. Spark. Bang. Dark.*

Then finally, worst of all, was his poor sister. When she'd brought his Horlicks, she'd got the shock of her life, leaping back two feet and dropping the mug to the floor. Thank goodness it hadn't been his grandma, or it might have finished her off. Electricity might make hearts beat, like Alma kept saying, but it could stop them dead too.

Thump. Thump. Thump. Thump.

That feeling again. His heart drumming in his chest. Each time, this morning, before a spark, it'd happened, just like the night before with Terence. It was like he could hear – no, feel – the pulse in the wires. True, it was exciting; he was finally finding his lightning. But he wished he wasn't finding it quite so frequently.

In fact, he could feel the static building right now . . .

He stepped back. He couldn't handle this at the moment. 'Actually, I'll try them untoasted for a change.'

He sister looked at him funny, but he was saved by his dad bursting in through the door.

'They caught that Terence!' He clutched a newspaper in his hand. 'He electrocuted himself on some wires in Indytown!'

'Wow,' said Luke, attempting surprise. 'He's alive though, right?'

'Unfortunately,' said his nana, reading over his dad's shoulder. 'The Mayor has him in for questioning.'

Luke felt relieved. He didn't like Terence, but he was glad not to have killed him. Though his sister was looking at him funny again.

A knock at the door. A tired-looking Jess popped in her head.

'Jess, my dear, you look like death.' Luke's nana thrust a crumpet into her grateful hands. 'But great news about Terence, eh?'

Jess paused mid-bite and looked at Luke in alarm. 'You told them?'

'Told us what?' said his sister.

'That . . . Errr . . .' Luke couldn't cope. It was all too much. 'Err . . . that . . . we have an early start today! Gotta go, bye!'

Grabbing Jess by the hand, he practically dived off the boat and into her dinghy.

A few minutes later, he had filled her in, while they paddled the green-water canals of Hackney Wick. He felt better already. The paddling and the air soothed him somehow. He bit into his crumpet: dry. He threw it into the water and made a few ducks happy.

'But that's great, Luke! It's like you're learning your superpower.'

'A stupid power, more like,' he said. 'What kind of hero blows up toasters?'

'But you didn't blow it up.'

'You know what I mean.'

They passed another boat and fell quiet. Luke focused on paddling. The rhythm of it reminded him of shovelling, but softer.

The water trickled off the oars, cool down his sleeves. Was Ravi doing something like this right now?

Ravi had been the best shoveller of the three of them. He'd taught Luke how to hold the spade, how to avoid the blisters, how to keep his arms straight and protect his back. Luke hoped someone was looking out for his friend now.

The static in the air lifted. He felt normal again.

'You know, I wonder . . .' He reached out to touch one of the lights in Jess's dinghy, and to his relief, nothing happened. 'I wonder if it's linked to stress somehow. Before I felt on edge, jumpy, but now I'm calm, it's like it's switched itself off.'

'I suppose that makes sense. Jumpy, like a livewire.' Jess shrugged. 'I guess we'll find out soon enough. But for now, let's cross our fingers for an uneventful day in the office.'

And though wishes rarely came true, that morning they did. The day with Oberdink proved spectacularly boring. Oberdink informed him that they'd been taken off the case, and Luke was back to licking envelopes. He was disappointed, but he tried not to show it, not least because Oberdink was in the foulest mood, up to his nose in piles of papers. If Luke so much as breathed, he was threatened with dismissal.

His thoughts drifted. If today was the 30th October, and All Hallows' Eve tomorrow, when would the full moon land? He quietly twiddled the date dial forward on his watch. But as he did, something odd happened. The pattern of moons on the watch moved too.

An idea began to form in his mind. He counted the moons: exactly twenty-nine, growing from new moon, to crescent, then half-moon and full – and suddenly, he felt stupid for missing it before. It wasn't a pattern, but a lunar calendar, tied to the date.

He wound it forward and his excitement gave way to unease. The next full moon fell on 5th November – Bonfire Night. Was the fire in Ma Boxhill's vision linked to that? It didn't feel like the best of omens.

The talkometer buzzed. Luke picked it up – carefully, in case it sparked in his hand – and recognised the resonant voice of the Mayor.

'Luke,' he said. 'What a pleasure. I'd like to invite you both here, for a visit.'

Luke felt a wave of unease. The Mayor's voice was warm, friendly again, and yet he'd worked with Tabatha. What was he up to? Either way, it wasn't an offer he could refuse.

'Sure, Mr Mayor, when were you thinking?'

'Now, ideally. Unless you've other plans?'

They didn't.

Moments later, Luke found himself straining under the weight of his boss's overstuffed suitcase, trying to keep up.

'Hurry up, Smithy. I won't have your dithering make me late for the Mayor.'

'Yes, sir. Sorry, sir.'

Oberdink strode ahead, his legs grey and stiff like tiny lamp-posts.

'Stop dawdling, boy!' Oberdink called back, as they passed the swirling stone snakes of Apothecary Square. 'We're almost there.'

Though the Mayor hadn't said anything, Luke felt sure it had to do with the stolen case or Terence. Maybe Luke could help in some way. Or maybe they'd noticed the missing ghost-gun . . .

'Slow down!' hissed Oberdink, now Luke had finally caught up. 'We're there. Important people walk slowly, not fast.' He snatched the briefcase from Luke. 'And remember, not a word, if you want to keep your job.'

Luke nodded grimly. Apprentices were meant to be seen but not heard.

They emerged from an alley before Mansion House: a

dusty-pink, many-pillared building, ribbed with reinforced steel – it was a cross between a cake and a bear-fighting cage. Oberdink marched up the steps and into a glittering foyer. Overhead, men polished a tinkling chandelier.

A jowly, coiffured lady, with pearls on her ears and neck, greeted them on reception. 'The Mayor is expecting you both upstairs.' She sashayed towards an elevator with interlocking iron doors. 'The Mayor's personal elevator, powered by pollution-free energy.' She ushered them in and turned to a group of well-muscled men. 'Floor three, please.'

The men nodded then heaved a series of ropes on pulleys. The lift rose in spurts with each heave.

'Well, isn't this delightful,' said Oberdink as the foyer and chandeliers opened up before them. 'Perhaps green energy is the future after all.'

Luke glanced at the straining men. He wasn't so sure.

Finally, the doors opened and they stepped into a light-flooded room, floor to ceiling in gold-veined marble. In the centre sat a mirror-table piled with books and papers. White curtains fluttered against the opposite wall. The Mayor stood before a tall gilded window, his hand resting on his chin in some deep and dashing thought. He wore a black velvet suit. His curls and cloak billowed in the wind and light.

'Perfect timing, gentlemen.' He clasped his gloved hands together. 'Just in time to see my new installation.'

The Mayor gestured towards the corner, and to Luke's shock, there lay Terence: arms shackled, lying down, apparently asleep, locked inside a particularly thick-barred cage. He couldn't help but recoil. Even Oberdink had stopped.

'Oh, don't worry about him.' The Mayor laughed, as though keeping prisoners in one's office was entirely normal. 'He's very secure, but hasn't spoken since we caught him. The shock perhaps. But he mutters in his sleep, so I like to keep a close ear.' He winked and poured two glasses of water from a crystal carafe. 'Sit down, do. I owe you my thanks for finding that case.'

They both sat. Luke tried to sip politely and ignore the prisoner.

'When we unlocked the case that was taken from Battersea Station, we found three things inside: blood samples, amber and several documents.'

Blood? Luke thought. *And amber, again?* But it was the documents that intrigued him – if there were clues to Ravi's whereabouts, they'd be in there.

'My lab have the first two,' the Mayor continued, 'but the documents are here. What did you make of the extracts I sent?'

Extracts? What extracts? Then Luke saw Oberdink nodding smugly.

'Well, Mr Mayor, I've been studying them all day.' He laid some sheets on the table just out of Luke's reach. 'Unfortunately, they're records. Coal quotas, mostly. I imagine they were used to cushion the samples.'

The Mayor turned to Luke. 'And Apprentice Smith-Sharma, what did you think?'

Luke was reeling. His brain tried to process what he was hearing.

Oberdink had told him they were off the case. He'd had Luke licking envelopes all morning. But in fact, it seemed the papers Oberdink had been reviewing were the ones from the briefcase. The briefcase that Luke had found.

Oberdink interjected. 'Alas, my apprentice was rather useless.' He ruffled Luke's hair roughly. 'Not the smartest cookie. But how about that prisoner, shall we take a look?'

'Shame.' The Mayor sighed, getting to his feet. 'But of course, Inspector. I would appreciate an *expert* opinion.'

Yet as the Mayor said 'expert', for the briefest moment, he

looked straight at Luke. What did it mean? It was then that Luke noticed a set of papers laid before him on the desk. His heart beat faster. The Mayor must have put them there. What was he playing at? He supposed it didn't matter – he couldn't pass up a chance. He studied them while the two men walked towards the cage.

Yellowed and thick with spidery handwriting, the sheets were divided into eight neat columns. On the far left were names. He recognised them at once: they were shovellers from the plant. Some strong, some weak. Some clever, some slow. Some kind, some not. He wondered what they were all doing now. After Battersea, many of the families had moved, changed their names and started afresh. Jess was the only one who'd stayed in touch.

The other columns had numbers and dates at the top. A record of the coal they'd shovelled each day. But it was more than that. It was a window to his past. He felt a swell of nostalgia for simpler times, when his worth was measured in numbers, and nobody could take credit for what he'd done. Then he saw Ravi's name – and pain stabbed in his chest.

Ravi's name was above his. They'd shovelled the exact same amount that day. It seemed right, somehow.

But it was the row below that stopped him in his tracks.

It couldn't be right. It had to mean something. And then there was the handwriting – he'd seen it before.

Luke looked up, to where Oberdink was prodding Terence, without luck, with a long pointy stick. The Mayor was glancing down at his watch.

Luke had to say something. He might not get another chance.

'With respect, sirs, this isn't a coal quota,' Luke said. 'I think it's code.'

A terrible silence washed over the room.

Oberdink turned, eyes pointier than the stick in his hand. 'Ridiculous!' he spat. 'I'm a trained code-breaker and I've checked it twelve times! You're only an apprentice, what would you know?'

The Mayor, however, nodded him on.

'I know, Inspector, but I was a shoveller.' Luke swallowed. He knew Oberdink hated him mentioning Battersea, but there was no way round it. 'It's the amounts, they're not right. This girl Jess, at the bottom, it says she shovelled twice as much as me. That couldn't have happened in a million years. And there are other kids, too.'

Oberdink turned puce. 'A clerical error! It means nothing.' He turned to the Mayor. 'I'm sorry, but this useless apprentice barely passed his exams. I let him in out of pity. But if he speaks one more word, I'll happily kick him out.'

But Luke couldn't stop. Not if there was a clue to finding Ravi.

'Inspector, please, it's not just the figures – it's the handwriting. It's Tabatha's, I'm sure, and she was too busy to write quotas. The guards did that. It must be important.'

'Right, that's it!' Oberdink shrieked. 'You're fired, immediately. The impudence! The ignorance! The indignity of it all!'

Oberdink forced a tinkly laugh, then he marched up and grabbed Luke firmly by the wrist. And though Luke's body lifted up, his heart sank to the ground.

Fired? The word echoed in his mind.

He'd wanted to be a detective for as long as he remembered. Since he was a child. He'd worked so hard for it, too. Even in Battersea, he'd tried to practise. What would he do now? What would his dad say? Why hadn't he been able to hold his tongue?

But a cloaked shadow stilled his thoughts. The Mayor stood over them. He smiled and let out a deep, velvet laugh.

'Writing this much code – well, it's precisely what Tabatha would do. She came top at Cambridge. If she hadn't been a woman, she would have made professor. Or mayor, perhaps.' He squeezed

Oberdink's shoulders a little too hard. 'But we're in agreement on one thing. *You*, Inspector, are fired, immediately.'

Oberdink paled. He let go of Luke's hand. His moustache twitched. 'Sorry, Mr Mayor, I think you misheard. I'm not firing me, but the boy.'

'Then I'll tell you what I heard.' The Mayor flashed his teeth. 'That you sent a minor into the sewer unprotected. That you took credit for this boy's work. That you hampered the investigation by refusing him these extracts. And that you treat him downright terribly.' The Mayor leant in so closely, Luke could feel his breath. 'Come to think of it, Oberdink, it's almost like child labour. And we know what the penalty for that is, don't we?'

Oberdink wobbled. His mouth formed an 'O', then curved down at the edges. He looked ready to cry.

Luke felt bad for him, really, even after everything he'd done. Though the Mayor had only spoken the truth.

The Mayor took Oberdink's hand and walked him to the door. 'I'm promoting you, Luke, to Inspector Smith-Sharma,' he called. 'Effective immediately. We'll give you his office. But do excuse me a moment, while I show him out.'

They stepped into the lift and juddered out of view. Luke sat back down and caught his breath. It had all happened so quick.

'Just you wait,' a voice hissed from behind.

Luke spun round. Terence stood in his cage, face pressed against the bars. His eyes sharp, with not a hint of sleep.

'He'll turn on you, just like he turned on Tabatha.' Terence smiled. 'And when he does, I hope I'm here to watch.'

CHAPTER 13
THE SECRET GUILD

Luke's leg was shaking a little. It was hidden beneath the table, so the Mayor hadn't noticed, but he wished it would stop.

Nerves, he guessed. Exhaustion, too. He'd stayed up all night decoding the documents in the mayoral library, with the moon watching too through an open window. Normally, he found the moon calming – it made him think of his mum – but ever since Ma Boxhill's words, it was anything but. All night it had seemed to whisper with the tick of his watch: *Six nights left. Six nights left. Six nights left until Ravi is gone.*

In many ways, he had even less time than that. The council's All Hallows' Eve meeting was only nine hours away. If they didn't get enough evidence by then, who knew what they'd do?

'So what about these sheets, what did they say?' The Mayor took a folder from his desk with a gauntleted hand.

Luke felt exhausted but he had to stay focused. 'We decoded

those first,' he said. 'They're the names of Tabatha's partners in London.'

There was a grunt from the corner from Terence but they both ignored it.

'Good. I'll have them all sent to the Tower.'

Luke hesitated. The Tower of London. His dad had been held there when Luke was in Battersea. They did terrible things there to make people talk. Then again, he had a feeling the Mayor was no stranger to such tactics. Terence's face had fresh bruises this morning and several fingers looked bent and bandaged.

It's for Ravi, remember, Luke told himself, trying to push the doubts from his mind.

'And these?' said the Mayor, picking another file up.

Luke's heart beat faster. These were the good ones. 'Those give details on her bases. There are journey times, rivers and roads nearby. The main one is on the coast, near a church of some sort. The children are kept there for a few months before they're moved on. We've no co-ordinates yet, but I'm going to the water market tonight to get maps.'

'Bravo, Smith-Sharma. You've excelled yourself.'

And despite his misgivings, he really had. It had turned out each sheet from the case had a different code, each based on the name of a Battersea shoveller. It would have been nigh impenetrable to anyone who hadn't worked there. Even Alma, with her dislike of 'detectivy' matters, had been thoroughly impressed. She'd visited him that night in the library loos and given him an update. Apparently, the council were amazed they'd stopped the groundghoul. If they could find the base before the meeting that night, she felt sure it'd swing it. His attempt to demonstrate his lightning to her had been an utter failure, though – he'd barely got a spark.

'And this one?' The Mayor held up a thin white folder.

'That one?' Luke said. 'I haven't finished it yet.'

The Mayor observed him, then the talkometer beeped. He looked down and Luke could breathe.

The truth was that the file covered Tabatha's experiments but he felt uneasy about sharing it with the Mayor. It made for creepy reading. She'd been investigating cemeteries, plague pits and places of death. The 'soul-residue' in the soil, apparently, could generate power, and she'd planned to burn it like coal to power the slums. The best source, it seemed, was from the poppies in battlefields, whose roots were soaked in the souls of soldiers long dead. The document mentioned a weapon and amber too, though how that worked wasn't clear to him.

The Mayor closed his talkometer, stood and took Luke's hand in his glove. 'I must go, it seems, but well done, Luke.' He paused. 'Why don't we meet later, to discuss your future? I've got a jetty at the water market, I could give you a lift home?'

Luke nodded, the Mayor smiled and released Luke's hand. There was a silver sovereign in it. 'Jetty 239, don't forget. Now take the afternoon off. Treat yourself to some snacks at the market before looking for those maps.'

A silver sovereign? He could buy a three course meal and still have change to spare. And he knew exactly who to spend it with.

'Would you rather,' Jess said, biting into a steaming crab pasty, 'have just one of these a week, or gruel, for a lifetime?'

Luke looked down on the water markets from 'Bertha & Violet's', a third-tier tea-house in the north bank water market run by two old friends of his and Jess's. Below him stretched a maze of jetties and stalls swaying on stilts, and above, the sun hung sleepy and pink. Crowds heaved. Pans clattered. River water swelled. And the pong of dried fish seasoned the air.

They had climbed up here to get some fresher air and quiet,

but with Jess, perhaps 'quiet' had been a little ambitious.

'Come on, Luke. It's an important question.'

He shrugged. 'So would I get any other food? Aside from the pasty?' He sipped his spiced tea. 'Because if not, I'd die of hunger, or definitely scurvy. So I guess, all in all, I'd rather live and have gruel.' He looked around. 'Now, please, can we talk Secret Guild?'

'Sure, boss, let's get down to business.' Jess reached into her bag. 'I asked my electrician friend about the power cuts like you said, and you're right, they track them.' She unfolded a map of London on the table, covered in lines. 'There's a pattern at midnight. Cuts that move in house by house. This shows where they've been – where *she's* been, I figure.'

He studied the lines. A cluster by St Paul's, where they'd caught the ghoul. Another at Battersea, which he supposed made sense. One by Aldgate. Clerkenwell. Another in Stokey . . . wait. Not Stokey High Street, but the cemetery up there.

An idea began to form in Luke's mind.

'The groundghoul, Jess – it was by St Paul's crypt. And this is by a cemetery. Do you think it's a pattern?'

Jess put down her pasty. 'I think you're right. These clusters, here, they're above plague pits. The sewers veer round them. All of these places stink of death.'

Luke thought back. 'The leaks to the End Place, where the groundghouls get in – Alma said they often happen by cemeteries. Places where the wall between realms gets thin. What if Tabatha is trying to make leaks?'

'Why would anyone *want* leaks?!'

'Because it hurts the ghosts. All the time we were there, Tabatha was trying to collect ghosts to harness their energy, and she must hate them after what they did to Battersea. More leaks means more ghouls. *And ghouls kill ghosts.*'

Luke felt hot, excited. Horrid as it was, they were getting somewhere. With evidence of a threat, the Ghost Council would act. It was another step closer to saving Ravi.

But Jess didn't look pleased. 'Erm, Luke, have you seen this one?'

He followed her gaze. In the map's east quarter lay a cluster of lines.

'My house?' he whispered. 'There's no cemetery there . . .'

A rush of unease. Had she visited his boat? It would explain the nail marks on the ladder. He shivered at the thought. Maybe he should call his dad, but what would he say?

'Gah!' said Jess. 'Look at the time! We'll be late for those maps if we don't get a move on. She's grumpy at the best of times. I'd hate to make her wait.'

They paid up, Jess grabbed a kebab for the road, then they climbed down the rickety ladder and headed east out of the dried fish stalls and towards the metalwork ones. The sky had darkened now and candle-kids scurried overhead lighting strings of lanterns. The moon shone the biggest lantern of them all.

They took a left, then a right, then a right and left, through sandalwood, rose and thick jasmine plumes, then suddenly burst out of the cover on to a rickety jetty. The dark Thames water flowed on all sides.

'A dead end,' Luke said. 'She said the stall was here, I'm sure.'

They stared at the water. It churned and bubbled brown. A shirt drifted by, tangled with a piece of fishing net.

A cough from behind. They turned to see Radhika, just like she'd promised. She stood on a plank that hadn't been there before: it stuck out through a rip in some tarp.

'Do you want these maps or not?' She grabbed Luke by the hand and pulled him up. She sniffed the air and scowled at Jess. 'And you'd better swallow that quick – it stinks. I hate kebabs.'

CHAPTER 14
MAPS

Radhika ushered them along the plank through the rip in the tarp on to the rot-stained deck of a boat in the shadows. She pulled in the plank and the rip closed suddenly, plunging them into darkness. For a moment, there was only river-smell and sloshing. Then Luke made out the shape of Radhika, tiptoeing down the side of the boat. He gestured to Jess, and they followed, coming to a stop before a large, painted sign on the wall: *Rajendra's Emporium*.

This was it: the boat Ravi had talked so much about. But the sign was peeling and faded now. The decking splintered. The windows boarded. It didn't look at all like Luke had imagined.

Radhika stood still, listening a moment. Once satisfied, she pushed a screw in the corner of the sign. There was a *click* and the sign swung silently inwards, on well-oiled hinges.

A secret door! Jess beamed, but mercifully, she didn't breathe a word.

They stepped inside. The smell of mould vanished. The air was warm and dry. A lonely bulb flickered, showing a varnished-wood room, the floor strewn with trinkets and beaded necklaces. In one corner lay a bed, in another, a desk, and in yet another, a table with circuits and gadgets. On the wall hung a photo of Radhika and Ravi. They looked so alike, from their bright, shrewd eyes to their thin brown hands, from their angled eyebrows to their straight white teeth.

Radhika walked to up to the photo and reached out – tenderly almost – then removed it to reveal a box-like space set in the wall.

'Another secret space?' Jess said, unable to help herself. 'Best boat ever!'

Radhika rolled her eyes, but Luke thought he saw a smile too. She pulled out book from inside it. On the front, embossed letters read, *Northern Europe – Naval Map.*

So she'd found it, after all! Ravi's family were traders. Even in Battersea, Ravi had managed to source all kinds of things. It seemed his sister had the same gift. Luke had phoned her from the Mayor's office this morning, on instinct more than anything, and it seemed he'd been right.

'It cost more than expected.' She nodded to his pocket.

'Come on,' Jess said. 'We're doing it for your brother.'

'And I'm doing this for our parents.' Radhika shrugged. 'We need food on the table. And I know a wallet when I see one.' She opened the book, giving them a peek of labelled lands, before folding it shut. 'So you know, this was the *only* copy left. All the others were bought by a certain Ms Margate.'

Luke counted out three coins in his hand – his week's wages. But it was worth it. 'It's OK. I've money – a perk of promotion. How much?'

Radhika took all three and gave Luke the book.

'Anyone have a pencil?' Luke placed the tome on the table and flicked through the pages, his fingers clumsy with expectation. 'This is it: the North Europe coast. The files suggest Tabatha's base is in a cove, only three hours by boat. If we plot from Dover – can you pass me that ruler? – it has to be around here.'

He circled a section of the coast a hundred miles long. It didn't help much.

'Didn't it mention a church?' Jess stood by his shoulder. 'What about that? It's the only one there.' She pointed to a cross between two bits of green. 'It has to be here.'

Luke ran his eyes over the spot. A forest encircled it, and

beyond that stretched fields with no town nearby. It would be the perfect place to hide a base filled with kidnapped children. The authorities would never look there. He forced himself to breathe. Had they finally found it? Could Ravi be there right now?

Hope warmed his chest. If they had the base, the Ghost Council would act, that's what Methuselah had said. Jess was grinning too.

There was a cough from behind. 'I hate to break up the party, but let me get this straight,' Radhika said. 'You're just going to sail from Dover, into enemy territory, and invade a forest? That's your plan?'

'No,' Luke said. 'We'll get help from the ghosts. Jess told you about them, right?'

'Of course, the flying ghosts.' Radhika looked less than convinced. 'Either way, you might as well do it properly.' She joined them at the map. 'You're a narrowboater, right? Well, my parents were traders and, let me tell you, the sea isn't a canal. There are currents here and here. And the boats move much faster.' She took his pencil. 'And Tabatha wouldn't use Dover. She'd use a smugglers' port, like here.'

Radhika moved quickly with the pencil and ruler, and the circled area was soon three times larger, including four more churches. That made five possible sites in total, each leagues apart.

Luke frowned. 'Could we just sail along the coast and tick them off?'

'Firstly, that would take weeks. Secondly, they'd spot you,' said Radhika. 'And even if they didn't, there are sea-mines everywhere. This whole stretch of coast was battlefield. Millions died. That's why this map's so valuable, it's got the mines on it too.' She handed the book back. 'I guess you've got more research to do.'

Luke sighed. It was two steps forward, but one step back. Though at least the steps were now in the right direction. Radhika knew her stuff.

'Is this your parents' boat?' he said. 'Ravi talked about it all the time.'

'It wasn't just their boat,' she said. 'It was their everything. They escaped a war in it, made a new home here, and when we were kids, it was the heart of the water market . . . Then Ravi disappeared and it all fell apart.' She looked out the window; the river rippled darkly. 'After Battersea fell, I bought the boat back with the compensation money. Thought it'd cheer them up. But they wouldn't set foot in it. Too many memories.' She sighed. 'They've not been the same since it happened, not really.'

'None of us are. My dad's got this cough from jail that won't go away.' Luke looked around. 'But I bet Ravi would like it here.'

'He wouldn't like it, he'd love it.' Radhika gave a rare smile. 'Those gadgets in the corner, he built those, you know. I can't throw them away. He wanted to set up a shop and sell them. I guess that's another dream down the drain.'

Luke remembered Ravi's shop – he'd wanted Luke to be his partner. It had meant so much to him. It had kept him going.

'It doesn't have to be,' Luke said. 'Help us, Radhika. You know about maps. You could help us find him.'

As quickly as it had come, her smile was gone.

'No,' she said. 'We spent years looking for Ravi. It cost us our home, our business. I'm not putting my parents through that again. He's gone, that's that.'

'But you don't know that.' Jess pointed at the map. 'He might be there, waiting.'

'And if he is?' Radhika glared. 'What can I do against some European army? I'm just a kid.'

Luke could see Radhika was angry. She needed time, but it was time Ravi didn't have. He looked down at his watch and remembered its words: *Make a difference. Every second counts.*

'You're a kid, true, but so were we, at Battersea. Anyone can make a difference. You just have to try.'

Though Luke had said it to inspire Ravi's sister, it had the opposite effect. Radhika's eyes widened in fury. 'Do you think I haven't tried?' she snapped. 'And as for making a difference – a difference for who? The Mayor, maybe? He's doing well out of you, isn't he? Or perhaps for yourself? You're looking flush these days.' He could see the whites of her eyes. She shook her head. 'We used everything looking for Ravi. Every last penny. It made no difference. And now we're stuck selling rice to make ends meet.'

Luke didn't know what to say. Radhika looked even more like her brother when she was angry. The curl of her lip was classic Ravi – a stop-before-I-spit-in-your-face kind of scowl. Come to think of it, she really did look like she might spit.

'I got you what you wanted, now get out, I'm busy.' She lifted a carpet hung on the wall to reveal another door. Luke couldn't help but feel that a third secret door was little excessive. 'Cut a right behind the stalls and you'll reach the docks soon enough.'

Jess stepped through, but Luke held back. 'When will we see you again?'

'You won't, hopefully.' She shoved him out and shut the door in his face.

'Well, I didn't think it possible, but she's ruder than Ravi,' said Jess, pulling him along. 'But it's definitely progress.'

'But is it enough? There are still five locations. The Ghost Council will want one. I need to narrow it down . . .' He trailed off, deflated. It wasn't just the map; it was Radhika too. 'I wish she'd help us. She reminds me so much of Ravi.'

'Do you know who she reminds me of?' Jess lifted some tarp and they stepped on to a fancy boardwalk with gated jetties. 'Of me, in Battersea. At first, I survived by pretending I'd be rescued. She survives by pretending Ravi *can't*. But the truth is he can, it's just very, very hard.' Jess pulled some gum from her pocket and popped it in her mouth. 'Maybe harder than in Battersea, because we've so much to lose.'

Luke remembered Ma Boxhill's words. Maybe that was what she meant about sacrifice. They had to risk so much.

'And then,' Jess added, 'what if the ghosts say no?'

It was the question he'd avoided thinking about, because if he was honest, he didn't have an answer. Though there was one thing he knew. 'We're not giving up, if that's what you're asking.'

'Good,' she said. 'That's what I hoped you'd say.'

They fell silent for a moment, save for the sound of Jess chewing. He caught a whiff of pineapple.

'Jess, are you chewing my fingerprinting putty?'

'Well, I can't meet the Mayor with kebab breath, can I?'

They came to a stop by Jetty 239. It was the biggest of them all. A clump of willows swished on the banks, making it hard to see what lay beyond the gate, but to Luke it looked more like a warehouse, or a hangar, than a mooring for a boat.

'It must be massive,' he said. 'That's the size of three yachts.'

Jess popped the gum behind her ear and tried to tidy her hair. 'Do you think they'll let me check the hydraulics?'

'I'm sure he will,' said a voice from behind the gate. A guard stepped out of the shadows and smiled. 'Now come along. His ship's waiting. Though I doubt it's quite the ship you're both expecting.'

CHAPTER 15
THE AIRSHIP

The zeppelin curved sensuously, like the body of some magnificent, black-silk whale, bobbing sleepily against the roof of the enormous hangar. Grey-glowing bulbs strung round its body like pearls and below it hung a dark glass gondola the size of a bus.

'It's beautiful,' Jess said. 'Like some creature from the deep.'

'Yeah,' Luke said. 'One that gobbles you up.'

A hatch clicked open in the gondola base and a velvet rope uncoiled towards them. It stopped an inch from the floor then swayed – almost swaggered – as the Mayor's boots descended. Save for an ermine trim and his golden mane of hair, he was dressed all in black. His boots, belts and gloves gleamed like polish.

'Luke, Jess, what a pleasure. It's my zeppelin's first outing. Join me, do, we can celebrate your findings.'

Jess practically ran – zeppelin plumbing was a dream of hers – but Luke felt a shiver of unease. It was impressive, sure, but something was off. Why would he keep something this beautiful so private?

They grabbed the cord and it immediately began winching them up. The hangar roof opened and the ship rose, lifting them into the wet-black sky. The world shrank away to dollhouse-like proportions and the water markets became blurs of steam and lights.

The rope juddered, and Luke felt suddenly fragile – at the Mayor's mercy. As a ghost, when you flew, the sky was your friend, but here, one slip or gust was all it'd take . . .

They burst up through the hatch into the warmth of the gondola. The guard lifted them down opposite the Mayor.

'Luke, do sit down. Reggie, why don't you show Jess the engine?'

The guard took Jess through to the next room and Luke looked round the cabin. The inside was decked in leather and plush velvet, refined in a first-class carriage kind of way. In the corner stood a black lacquered table with crystal tumblers on it, and beyond, through the glass, blinked a control room full of monitors, levers and grey-glowing lights.

The lights . . . Instantly, Luke knew the source of his misgivings.

'This airship – it's Tabatha's. It's just like her lab.'

'It *was* hers but now it's mine.' The Mayor ushered Luke to the table then poured golden liquid into each glass. 'I think it's time we talked.'

Luke tried to think but instead he found himself looking down. Through the tinted-glass floor, he saw the ship's whirring turbines, the Temple and the City twinkling like cats' eyes as they made their way east. There was no way out, he thought, so he might as well sit.

'I see you found a map.' The Mayor took it off Luke and opened it on the table. 'These five marks, I presume they're bases?'

'Potentially,' Luke said, weighing his words. 'The friend I mentioned, Ravi, there's a chance he's there. I need another day to be sure.'

'I'm impressed. At times, you remind me of my younger self. When you put your mind to something, there's really no stopping you.'

'My nan sometimes says that.'

'Then she's a wise lady.' The Mayor paused. He reached into his case. 'But it does make me wonder why this particular file is taking so long?'

The white file: the one about Tabatha's experiments and

weapons. The glass floor seemed to lurch and Luke felt queasy. He'd hoped the Mayor wouldn't have noticed, but like Alma said, putting things off never worked.

'Why? Well . . . because I don't think we should.' Luke's voice sounded surer than he felt. 'You saw what happened in Battersea.'

The Mayor knocked back his glass. 'I disagree. From the snippets I've seen, the research is ground-breaking. There's much to learn. Like those battlefield poppies making lightning-proof metal. Or the plague pit studies – the earth from just one pit can power a city for a year. This stuff could save lives.'

'But digging up graves? It has to be wrong. And don't get me started on the weapons.'

'Wrong? Weapons? Then you don't know war. If Tabatha's making them, then we must try too. We've already started.'

He drew back a curtain to reveal something quite odd. A glass pyramid, as tall as the Mayor, stood almost in the centre of the gondola.

A weapon? That?

Triangular glass panels made up its walls, each criss-crossed with wires. Thicker cables trailed from each corner, disappearing through to the gondola glass to who knew where. Inside it – stranger still – stacked from top to bottom, lay chunks of amber, each coiled in more wire.

'What on earth . . .' Luke said.

'The Greek word for amber is "elektron". That's where the word "electricity" comes from. We think Tabatha was working on a lightning gun – an artificial storm that could take down cities.' He smiled. 'Or at least, that was idea.'

A terrible idea, Luke thought, *but it sounds like Tabatha.* 'So, does it work?'

'Not yet.' The Mayor poured another drink. 'But we know she's still at it. We've stopped a dozen amber shipments to Europe this summer. It's only a matter of time before she finishes. And if she has this weapon, then we need it too.'

'You're starting to sound just like her.'

The Mayor laughed. 'You distrust me. Perhaps she mentioned that we had an agreement.' He sighed. 'Well, now we've some privacy, I'd like to change your mind.'

'If you want to change my mind, why not—'

The creak of leather cut him off. The Mayor was untying his black leather gauntlets. For some reason, Luke found himself holding his breath.

The Mayor's hands were pale, broad and strong. There were angry scars in a couple of places and his left ring finger was missing a nail. But none of those things shocked him. What drew his eyes were the calluses: deep, thick, faded with time, in the exact same places as the ones on Luke's hands.

Luke couldn't help himself. He reached out and touched them. They were rough like his.

'Now do you trust me?'

He looked up at the Mayor but no words came.

'I was in Battersea, for over six years.' The Mayor's lips tightened. 'It was under Tabatha's father, before your time. I was released because I had skills. Could be useful. And indeed I was . . . but only because I had to be. Until you blew the roof off the place last summer.'

Luke's head spun. The timings made sense. The calluses were real. It was too much at once to take in. 'But I heard Tabatha talking to you. About weapons, the chimney. You were working together.'

'Like I said, I had to. If I didn't, I'd lose a loved one, a job, that kind of thing.' He cracked his knuckles. 'But now it's Tabatha's turn.' He leant closer. 'So, I'll make you a deal. If you decode these files,

I'll save your friend. I'll send a boat right down there with my very best guards.'

Luke watched him speak, so calm and confident, but he wasn't reassured. How could he have stood by all those years knowing they were trapped underground. What kind of person could live like that?

It was like Radhika had said. Luke had made a difference, but for who? He was no longer sure. And what had the Mayor said in the square? *What they don't know can't hurt them.* He couldn't trust him an inch. Once he had his weapons, what would make him keep his end of the bargain? What if he kept Luke waiting?

He saw the moon out the window and glanced at his watch: only five days now – he didn't have time. 'I won't do it,' he said, 'unless you get Ravi first.'

The Mayor's face changed. He clenched his glass. 'I set the terms. Not you. If you don't want to do it, I'll get someone else.'

'You can try. But it will take time. Time you don't have.'

'Then let's up the stakes. If you don't help, I expel you from the guild. How does that sound?'

Panic rose in Luke's chest. 'Y-You can't do that! They won't allow it.'

'I can do anything I want.'

135

The zeppelin stopped. Through the glass, the black canals of east London squiggled below. The control room door hissed open.

'You won't guess what I did!' Jess cried. 'I steered the zeppelin! With help, of course, but still. And he gave me a manual, and a rope-gun too. Reggie said he'd even put a word in with the guild.'

Luke tried to smile, but his face felt tired.

'Think on it,' said the Mayor. 'You have till tomorrow.'

The hatch opened and the red rope coiled out. He took it without thinking. It was only when he reached the ground that he remembered, and wished that the ground would swallow him up.

'What's wrong?' said Jess. 'What happened up there?'

'He kept the map, Jess. He kept the map to Ravi.'

CHAPTER 16
CHECKMATE

Luke warmed his feet by the fire while his dad took his move. In the kitchen, his nana boiled chai and tidied, while Lizzy read, curled on the sofa. Luke didn't like sofas. He preferred the floor – it felt grounding. And after the events of tonight, he needed that more than ever.

His dad moved a bishop. 'Check again.'

Luke had returned from the zeppelin two hours ago, his head spinning with questions. How would he get back the map? Why would the Mayor want such a weapon? What would his dad say if he were expelled from the guild? He'd thought chess might help, but it was giving him a headache.

'Your move, son,' his dad said gently.

Luke frowned at the board. He'd started strong but things had gone downhill fast, like everything else. He moved his pawn. It was the only way to avoid losing a piece. He should have been bolder –

you didn't win chess without a sacrifice or two – but he didn't want to. Not tonight. Because every piece he threw away reminded him of Ravi.

He'd wanted to be a detective for as long as he remembered and if he helped the Mayor, he could stay one and free Ravi too. At least, that's what the Mayor said. It sounded logical . . . so why couldn't he bring himself to say yes?

'That's checkmate.' His dad put down his knight. 'Not your best game. Something on your mind?'

'Dad, how do you know what's the right thing to do?'

'I take it that you're not talking about chess?'

Luke shook his head.

'I don't think you ever do, not with the big decisions.' His dad began putting the pieces away. 'Like when I took the case on Tabatha, I thought I'd done the right thing, but it got you kidnapped, me in jail, and left Lizzy alone. It was right by me, but was it right by my family?'

'But look, we're together – it was right in the end.'

'It only seems that way because it all worked out. If you hadn't stopped her, we might feel differently.' His dad looked to the photo on the wall. 'Take your mum, for example. The doctors said it'd be risky, but she chose to have you anyway, even though her friends all disagreed.'

Luke's sister put her book down. They were all listening now. His dad rarely talked about their mum.

'But you know what she said? "When you know, you know."'

'"When you know, you know?" What does that even mean?'

'It means there's no right choice, only *your* right choice. The choice depends on who you are.' He took Luke's hand. 'She made the right choice for me too, I know that now. But it was the only choice she could make to stay true to herself.'

His dad's hand clutched his tightly.

'Well,' said Nana Chatterjee, 'I think it's time for some tea.'

Luke didn't have the head for more chess. He walked to the window and breathed. He wondered what happened if you weren't true to yourself. Over time, did you end up as someone else? Was that what had happened to the Mayor? Could you find your way back? He didn't know the answer, but he knew some things for sure: he couldn't trust the Mayor about the weapons, nor his promise to save Ravi. Nor he could he put his job above saving his friend. He'd never be able to live with himself if he did.

But if he couldn't count on the Mayor, that only left the

Ghost Council. It was the meeting tonight and he'd just lost the map.

He gazed at the sky. The clouds had thickened, blocking out the moon. What if the council blocked him? Or questioned his claims? If Ma Boxhill was right, they only had five days.

A pat on his shoulder. He turned. It was his grandma offering him a cup.

'Thanks, Nana,' he said. 'I think I'll head to—'

Luke stopped. For a fleeting moment, the boat lights had flickered.

'Power cut,' said his dad. 'I'll go and check the generator.'

Luke looked out the window. None of the other boats were flickering. It was only theirs . . . which meant, it wasn't a power cut at all.

'Dad, wait!'

The boat plunged into darkness.

Thump. Thump. Thump. Thump.

Over the beat of his heart he heard his grandma shriek. His sister stood; her book thudded to the floor. He felt the static in the air, felt it building inside him. His nerves must be setting his lightning in motion.

'Nana, Lizzy, we have to leave now.'

They both nodded. They must have felt it too. This dark was different. Even the light of the moon felt dimmed. Stumbling, they made their way to the door and burst on to the deck.

Luke's relief was cut short; there was no sign of his father.

'Dad?' he called out.

No response. But there was something. A smell. Sickly and chemical, sharp and seeping. It was the scent of petrol.

He ran back into the boat.

Thump. Thump. Thump. Thump.

His footsteps ran loud on the wooden floor as the dark air grew thick with fumes. His chest filled with guilt. This was his fault. He should have warned them moment he'd seen Jess's maps with the power cuts. He'd sensed something was wrong, even if he hadn't known what.

But then perhaps he had? Part of him felt sure about who had caused this – who was lurking ahead, somewhere in the shadows.

He pushed at the door to sister's room: empty. His nana's room too.

Thump. Thump. Thump. Thump.

His heart beat louder. The static grew inside him. This wasn't good.

He couldn't afford so much as a spark with petrol in the air. He had to get a grip. Keep calm. Soothe it somehow. But the more he tried, the tougher it got.

Thump. Thump. Thump. Thump.

Up ahead, oil seeped out from under the engine room door. But before he reached it, he stopped. By his bedroom door, over the stench of petrol, drifted something else too. Something earthy, peaty, that he knew all too well.

Tobacco. *Her* tobacco.

'Luke, is that you?' said a voice from within. 'Come on in. Your dad doesn't have long.'

He pushed the door open.

A shaft of moonlight slipped through the window. His decoding notes lay on his desk. On the floor was his dad, eyes-closed, breaths laboured. And standing above him, heel resting on his chest, was Tabatha herself.

Or something like her. The black lab coat, the pipe in hand, the amber eyes – they were all there. But in the light of the moon, her features blurred darkly as if the moonlight itself drained away through her. A ghost mixed with shadow.

And when she spoke, her voice sounded faded, like a long-distant call.

'Don't step any closer. For your father's sake.'

Luke couldn't if he'd wanted to. His dad was in danger. Quite how, he wasn't sure, but he knew he'd never forgive himself if he came to any harm.

'Good.' She seemed to smile, but it was hard to tell. 'Now, a word.' She ran her nails over the papers on the desk. 'This research – *my* research – I care for it deeply. Like a mother for her child. A father for his son. And yet it seems you're giving it away . . . and to the Mayor, of all people.'

'I'm not doing it for him. I'm doing it for Ravi.'

'Then you're a fool,' she said. 'The Mayor won't help you. He'll take credit for your work, and then he'll take mine. They always do. And when he's finished, he'll cast you aside.'

'You can't talk. Look what you did to us. What you're doing to Ravi.'

'And look what happens to the slum kids each day.' Tabatha leant in. 'Things are broken, Luke, and I am trying to fix them. If that requires a sacrifice or two, so be it.' Her shadow grew darker. 'But back to the papers. Tell me, what have you learnt?'

'Nothing. Not really.'

'Liar.'

She dug her heel into his father's chest; it slipped right through. At once, his dad began gasping for air.

'Stop it!' Luke begged. 'I'm sorry. I'll tell you.'

She eased her foot. His dad breathed deeper.

Luke felt himself shrinking. He was ten years old again on the furnace room floor, answering her questions, playing her games. He didn't have a choice. He had to answer.

'You've found fuel in plague pits, battlefields, places like that. And you're making holes – leaks – in the wall between realms, that's how the groundghoul got in. And you've found a way to cross over. But not quite like me. You're darker, fainter.' And as he said the words, he knew it was true. She was hazier than a ghost, especially at the edges, where the moonlight was weakest.

He glanced down at his dad. Where was this leading?

'That's all you've learnt? Really?'

She lifted her heel.

Thump. Thump. Thump. Creeeak.

It was his heart, his lightning, it was building again.

No, please, not now.

But it was, he was sure of it. He could feel it drawing from the cables that lined the canal. That strange creaking too, like before, with Terence. But with this much petrol on board, he had to get out, and quick.

'I know more,' he said. 'Please.'

He edged forward, the sparks building inside him. If he could just keep her talking, he might reach his dad unnoticed. 'There's a weapon – a lightning gun – in a pyramid in the zeppelin. It uses amber somehow.' A second step forward. Then another. He was almost there. 'And . . . And . . .'

He'd run out of ideas.

Tabatha's head tilted suddenly and she saw him move. With a piercing hiss, she brought her foot down on his dad's chest.

'No!' Luke shouted.

Thump. Thump. Thump. Creeeak.

A blinding light. The air rippled and cracked. He'd lost control of his lightning. He readied himself for the explosion as it hit the petrol . . .

Nothing happened. Instead, the room fell oddly quiet.

He opened his eyes. His hand glowed sunset orange, but

without a spark in sight. It was as if it knew his purpose: his fear gave it shape. And in the blaze of its light, Tabatha's shadow had become faded, insubstantial. Her outline began to melt, her nails dripping down to the floor.

Her voice crackled like static. She was trying to speak, but the words were unclear.

Luke didn't stop to listen. He just grabbed his dad and dragged.

Thump. Thump. Thump. Creeeak.

He pulled his dad across the floor with every ounce of his strength. First to the threshold of his room, and then out into the kitchen. Past the half-spilt chess set and down the creaking corridor. Past his nana's room, his sister's room, and over streaks of black oil. He felt like his muscles were on fire, and sparks zinged inside him.

Thump. Thump. Thump. Creeeak.

He was nearly at the door. He could hear sirens blaring in the distance, the voices from outside, when from the door to his room stepped a hideous shadow – a half-formed, melting spectre of a woman.

It slipped and slid down the corridor after him. Neck craning. Eyes blazing. All nails and limbs. It moved with a scratching, scuttling sound.

'What about Ravi?' it hissed. 'Don't you want to know?'

Ravi? Luke stopped, despite his fear. His fists glowed brighter. The ghostly Tabatha – or what was left of her – cowered back from the light.

'Is he all right?'

'Why don't you see for yourself?' the voice went on. 'I'll tell you where he is for a little something in return.'

Luke was at the door, the ramp right behind him. His hands still glowed bright. She couldn't hurt him now. 'Fine. Tell me. What is it you want?'

The moonlight swelled through a door. Tabatha's shadow sharpened, clear once more. She rested her nails against the wall.

Her voice, when it came, was smooth like dark glass. *'Everything. My power station. My home. My city. My reputation. Everything you took – I want it back.'*

The sirens grew louder.

'What? That's impossible.'

'I'm not so sure. Give me a week.' She smiled. 'But in the meantime, I think I'll take something from you. So you know how it feels. So you don't forget.'

She ran her nails down the wall and a shower of sparks

fell towards the petrol-stained floor.

Luke didn't think. With his legs in the doorway, he pushed back hard, pulling his dad and himself through it and down towards the canal water as his home above him burst into bright amber flames.

An hour passed before the fire brigades came and tried in vain to put the raging blaze out. Luke and Lizzy watched their houseboat burn from the banks, while his nana took the ambulance with his dad to Great Ormond Street Hospital.

It had been their only home. Where his parents had married. Where his sister had been born. All his books, his kites, all his photos were in it. It'd been what he'd dreamt of, what had sustained him during his time in Battersea: the little yellow boat in the eastern canals.

But it wasn't yellow any more. It was charred and black, like just about everything Tabatha touched.

His sister squeezed his hand. 'Nana phoned. The doctors say he'll be fine. Smoke inhalation, they say, though how he breathed in so much before the fire is anyone's guess.'

Luke knew how. Tabatha had done it. He watched his sister walk off to a neighbour.

They'd all been so nice, brought them food, blankets, made them feel safe. But he couldn't help but wonder how long it would last? What if she came back? They wouldn't be safe until the ghosts stopped her.

As if on cue, the heavens opened. An unimaginable amount of rain fell on the boat, quenching the flames, and from the rising steam stepped the shape of a girl. The shape swirled, then steadied. The girl wore a dress and a waistcoat under long dark curls. She leapt down on to the bank beside him.

'Luke, I'm so sorry,' Alma said. 'I came as soon as I heard.'

'It's OK. We're alive. For now, at least.' He looked at the boat, or what was left of it. 'It was Tabatha. And I know she'll be back.'

'Well, she went too far. When we tell the council at the meeting, they'll be sure to act.' She stopped. 'Wait. Was the map in the boat too?'

And despite everything, Luke smiled. For once, something had turned out better than expected. The map was safe with the Mayor.

'No. But it's a long story. I'll explain on the way.'

CHAPTER 17
ALL HALLOWS' EVE

Luke's grandma said the place had once been a floating airport attached by chains to the sides of the Thames. It had bobbed steadily on a monstrous pontoon – a feat of engineering, a Mayoral brainwave – and it had succeeded swimmingly for a year a or two.

Then the waters rose. The chains snapped. And the planes slid into the hungry river.

Now it was known as the aeroplane graveyard and was quite a sight at low tide. The perfect spot for a ghostly meeting. Rusted tailfins and wings poked through dirty brown water, pointing to the sky at melancholy angles. Paint curled and flaked. Hinges squeaked and flapped. And through the mist, red lights blinked to warn off the boats.

Tonight, however, passing boatmen might have glimpsed something else: eyes in the mist, whispers of words, spectral figures in the shifting spray.

'Stop fidgeting,' hissed Alma. 'It's almost your turn.'

Luke scanned the crowds with unease – the great, good and ghostly had all come along in every haze and hue, shape and size. Alma said it was for Hallowmas, but he couldn't help wondering if recent events had something to do with it. He supposed it didn't matter. He had bigger worries: his dad in hospital, his home burnt, the hideous slippery Tabatha shadow he'd seen. He had to focus. Persuading the council was the only way to protect his family and Ravi.

'Any ghoul sightings, Reverend?' Methuselah asked from his position in the centre, standing on the wing of a rusting spitfire.

'A dozen or so, including the groundghoul.' He smiled thinly at Luke. ' Though Alma and the half-ghost have dealt with that now.'

'His name's Luke,' Alma said with a smile even thinner than the Reverend's. 'How would you like it if I just called you "ghost"? It'd soon get tiresome.'

'Frankly, Alma, you're already quite tiresome.'

'Enough, you two,' snapped Methuselah. 'Council members must show decorum.' He checked his papers. 'Luke, you're next.'

Luke nodded. 'I've good news. We found the case, the culprit and five possible bases. With a day or two more, I'll know which one.' He paused for effect, like Alma had told him to, but all he saw was a sea of sunken eyes. 'But there's bad news too. Plenty of it.' And Luke explained about Tabatha's research and weapons, Terence in his cage, the zeppelin, the map, the Mayor's gloved hands, and finally, worst of all, Tabatha's visit that night.

The silence when he finished was nothing short of deafening. The wind seemed to stop. Then the whispering started.

'She was here, today?'

'And as a . . . a half-ghost?'

Sal raised his hand. 'Luke here suggests we strike first once we've the base location. We'll hear for and against.'

Alma nodded and walked to the centre, like an actor on stage. She turned to speak, then waited, until every last whisper stilled. 'As many of you know, I'm the only ghost to have escaped Tabatha's experiments. I was trapped for a minute, but it felt like a lifetime.' Her voice quavered.

The ghosts were hanging on every word. She loved the drama and she sure pulled it off. 'And now she's at it again, there is only one choice.' She stood taller. 'We must stop her, now. We destroyed Battersea, now we must finish the job. It is the only way to be safe. The only way to guard the boundary between the living and the dead.'

There was a rumble of agreement, a crackle of light in the air. Hope bubbled in Luke's chest.

It was punctured by the rap of ice-hard cane.

'Tabatha's not a threat, she's weak.' The Crone hobbled to join Alma in the centre, her bone-white cane shaking. 'She is desperate. Banished across the sea. Reduced to crossing between realms like a second-rate shaman. She doesn't stand a chance of taking London back. The best she could do is burn some mangy old boat.'

Luke flinched at the words. The Crone smiled. 'But if we cross the sea to her base, the risk is greater. That's what she wants. Who knows what she's built there? Or what perils the sea will bring? We may lose many ghosts.' She rubbed her gloves together, causing a trail of snow to fall to the water. 'I say leave her. Let her rot. She's Europe's problem now.'

Rumblings followed from the crowd after her speech, at least as loud as those after Alma's.

Luke couldn't bear it. 'But she won't rot, she'll take root! Look what happened last time!'

'Last time,' snapped the Crone, 'we destroyed her in a second.'

'But not a second too soon—'

'Enough!' Methuselah glared at Luke. 'You speak out of turn. It is clear we are split. And without a decision, we must delay—'

'Wait.' It was Reverend, who had a new ghost by his side, whispering in his ear. 'We have found new memories, relevant to the case. Methuselah, will you read?'

Luke felt foreboding. It seemed too convenient.

Methuselah nodded and took the ghost's hand. A spray of mist rose up, images dancing across it – images of Luke. Of the Mayor giving him a pear in the square. Of the weapon in the zeppelin and the Mayor's gloves coming off. Of the groundghoul and Tabatha's ghost-gun. Of sunset-orange lightning bursting forth from his hands.

Nausea swelled inside his throat. They'd been watching him all along?

Whispers rolled through the crowd. He felt their stares. Put together like that, it looked horribly suspicious.

'Wait. It wasn't like that—'

'These are memories, Luke. Memories don't lie,' the Reverend said. 'But they do make you wonder if the threat isn't a little closer to home . . . The half-ghost and the Mayor. They are in league. Luke is spreading access to Tabatha's research. Using her weapons. And no doubt he will help the Mayor build them too!'

'No!' shouted Luke. 'I was doing it to find Tabatha. To protect you all.'

'Perhaps. Or perhaps you were putting your friend Ravi first. It doesn't matter, really, because there is more. Methuselah, can you zoom a little closer on the lightning?' The images flickered into life once more: Luke's hand glowing in the alley, the flickering lights. But this time, it was the sounds that drew the gasps.

Thump. Thump. Thump. Creeeak.

The beat of his heart. That strange creaking, like ice on the Thames, followed by ripples in the air around him.

The Reverence leant in. 'You hear that sound? That's the wall between realms.' Luke's thought spun. Unease rolled through him.

'This half-ghost lightning is unnatural,' the Reverend went on. 'It disturbs the boundary. You can hear the wall straining, creaking, see the fabric of our realm rippling. He and the Mayor are the real threat now.' He looked round at the captive crowd. 'My solution is this: we deal with Tabatha later, but now, right now, we must destroy those documents before any more of her research gets out. And as for the half-ghost, he must become a full one.'

Become a full ghost?

Luke's thoughts were drowned out by a thunder of agreement.

He looked for Alma, but he'd lost her in the crowd.

Methuselah clapped and silence fell. 'Well, that was decisive, thank you all. Reverend, see to it that the documents are destroyed. And as for the half-ghost, why don't we take a vote?'

'Absolutely not,' Alma cried from somewhere near the centre. 'You can't vote on someone's life!'

'Then let's give him the choice,' said the Crone. 'Become a full ghost now, or never return.'

Never return? Never fly again? Yet the crowd was already murmuring their approval. They were afraid of him. He could see it in their faces.

It wasn't fair. He'd brought them everything they'd asked. He'd risked his life and his friends' to help them. But he'd never been one of them – not truly – and they'd turned on him just like that.

He looked up to where the Reverend was already flying away, to destroy the documents and the only means of finding Ravi. He couldn't let that happen.

'I'll do whatever you want,' he said. 'If you tell the Reverend to wait. I need more time with the maps. We need to them to save Ravi.'

Methuselah's eyes narrowed. 'May I remind you of *our*

loyalties, half-ghost. Our primary duty is to the ghosts, not to your friends. We do not interfere with the living unless—'

'But you *are* interfering,' Luke interrupted, anger driving his words. 'If you destroy those documents, you condemn Ravi and all those children. You're putting your lives above theirs, and they've barely lived.'

'Watch your tongue,' hissed Methuselah. 'We've voted. It's over.'

Luke stared back at Sal's glassy eyes. The Ghost Council leader's lip curled into an irritated sneer: it was the first time all night that he'd shown real emotion.

Above him he felt the west wind swell downriver, towards the seat of the Mayor. He looked at Methuselah and shook his head.

'It's not over till it's over.' He leapt into the wind and didn't look back.

CHAPTER 18
THE DOCKLAND TOWERS

He heard shouts behind, but kept his eyes fixed ahead. He had to get to the maps before the Reverend. If he didn't, then all his hard work would be lost.

But how? He glanced down to where the moonlight rippled on the river. The wind would be strong there, but it left him exposed.

'Luke, look out!'

It was Alma's voice, and he followed it on instinct, darting left, just as a scythe-shaped cloud swooped past. The Plague Doctor turned his long-beaked mask towards him. His scythe turned into a claw and grasped towards Luke.

Luke steered out of reach, losing him, but spied many more silhouettes joining the chase behind. One was gaining on him already. He tried to summon his lightning.

'It's me, you idiot,' shouted Alma, her swan pulling up beside him.

'Oh, phew, you came!' Luke said. 'I thought you'd be mad.'

'I am mad, but with them!' She shook her head. 'That's no council I want to be part of. They're cowards. They'd rather hunt you than a real threat like Tabatha.'

'What about the wall stuff though?' Luke said, remembering the Reverend's words. 'Is it true?'

'If it is, we'll figure it out. But right now, let's worry about surviving the night.'

Luke glanced back at the gathering ghosts. 'Perhaps you were right. I should have picked my battles.'

'Sometimes, Luke, the battles pick you. Now, please tell me there's a cunning plan?'

Luke tried to think. They couldn't outrun that many – they had to lose them somehow. He scanned the horizon. The one nice thing about the aeroplane graveyard was that it was in the east, close to his home. Surely there was something . . .

Then he saw it, where the river bent left. The flooded streets, mirror walls, and the cracked glass towers: the Docklands skyscrapers. That was it.

'It's less plan, more surprise. You like surprises, right?'

'I did until now, but you're making me nervous.'

'Trust me, OK?' Luke squeezed her hand, then let go as their clouds split apart, veering down towards the towers. He lowered his cloud a little further – the height was important – until he was heading straight towards Canary Wharf, an avenue of towering abandoned skyscrapers. They speared the sky, making a network of narrow, shadow-soaked passages. But there was something else about this strip that Luke felt sure the council couldn't know.

'Alma, when it hits you, whatever you do, don't fight it.'

'Hit me? Who's going to hit me?'

'Three . . . Two . . . One . . . Dive!'

The wind tunnel hit him like a brick wall, flipping his cloud into a sickening spin, propelling him through the air at eye-watering speed. His stomach lurched to his mouth. The wind tore at his skin. His eyes stung as everything blurred around him.

But he didn't fight. He surrendered to the wind.

Out of the corner of his eye, he saw the shadow of two councillors following him. Within seconds, their clouds ripped in two, and they were thrown into the cracked glass of the buildings either side.

They didn't know these wind tunnels like Luke. His friends had called it Death Alley. Each year they'd raced their kites along it; he'd lost dozens of kites in practice runs. And as any champion knew, if you fought the wind, it beat you. You couldn't beat a wind of that strength. You had to wait it out.

He spun further, tumbling lower, passing floor after floor of dusty glass and concrete. When it looked like he was about to hit the ground, the overgrown trees on the street broke the wind, weakening it just enough to allow him to pull his cloud out of its death rattle into a steady glide only feet from the floor.

He stole a glance back. Alma was flying a little behind him, looking quite nauseous.

'I'd like to say that was fun. But it wasn't at all.'

'I know, but it worked.'

Luke looked back. The group were a mile away now and much depleted. More must have tried and failed to follow. They'd try to come over the top next, but it was far too late. They'd never catch them now.

He dipped right, down an alley, staying low to the ground. Finally, the water came into view, open and clear, save for a smattering of cirrus clouds many thousands of feet up.

A glimmer of hope fluttered in his chest. There was a chance they'd make it to the maps and the documents in time.

Luke and Alma flew close to the water, a drift of dark mist on the great churning river. They turned the bend at Limehouse, past sleeping Thames chuggers, then the brown Wapping Docks and the green New Thames Barrier. The rising blue arms of Tower Bridge appeared ahead, followed by the shaking steel of Millennium Bridge. The Garden Bridge came next, cracked and splitting with vicious knotweed, trailing a curtain of ivy into the Thames.

'It's the next one,' he shouted back. 'Then we turn right to the City.'

Through the hanging foliage, the Old London Bridge burst into view, piled high with houses and teetering walls. Peeking over the tops, sheltered in the safety of the old city walls, reached the frothy white towers of Mansion House, where, even at this hour, the lights in the tower library and Mayor's office still glowed.

At least, they did for a moment. Before Luke's very eyes, both windows exploded. Crackling blue flames leapt out like monstrous tongues, licking and singeing the white walls black.

'It's the Reverend,' Alma said. 'It has to be him.'

Through the billowing smoke, a hazy figure took shape. A man made of smoke, with a flicker of blue eyes.

'Keep low,' Luke whispered. 'We can't let him see us. Our best chance now is to salvage what's left.'

He needn't have worried. Confident, as always, the Reverend didn't even look back. He just rose into the sky, triumphant, and drifted north.

Luke and Alma turned off the river and slipped through the streets, amidst a skid and rush of police cars and sirens. Mansion House was in chaos. Flames burst haphazardly from windows. People screamed in the street. Fire engine hoses waterfalled in the air. Luke could taste the smoke, spray and sweat in the mist.

'An electrical fire,' cried a firefighter. 'Some kind of surge in the office.'

'Have you seen the Mayor?'

'Not yet. They said he ran back into the building.'

Luke's heart leapt. The Mayor was inside? The Ghost Council couldn't hurt the living directly, but indirectly? But even as he thought, he knew the answer. They had one rule for others and another for themselves.

He turned to Alma. 'Through the foyer, quick. Nobody will see us in the smoke.'

They pulled in their mists and rushed into the building, just another set of figures in the swirling ash. There were little fires everywhere. The Reverend hadn't left anything to chance. Above, the chandelier hissed and crackled, showering the marble floor with crystalline daggers. Luke ran ahead up the stairs – happy at least that the liftmen had gone – and burst into the Mayor's office.

Smoke wreathed the air. It smelt hot, metallic, like the furnace in Battersea. It nipped and stung his mists. He strained to see through the thick fumes.

The room looked off. The furniture had gone – had the Mayor moved it?

Then he looked down. Where the table had stood lay a pile of charred wood. The cabinets, too, were now mounds of ash.

Panic surged through him.

There was still a place they might have missed. He ran to the wall, to the panel hiding the safe . . . but as he opened it, acrid smoke burst forth. Even as a ghost, he coughed. All that remained was molten metal. The Reverend must have shut the panel after him. A little joke, perhaps.

'How did they know?' Luke asked. 'Wait – of course, they've been watching all this time.'

'They must hate half-ghosts more than I thought,' Alma said.

'Or maybe it's politics. They've wanted my job since I got it. This was a just a chance to provoke us, to ruin our plans.'

Luke pushed down his dread and tried to think of the map. Could he remember any of it? The shape of the shoreline, the pencil-drawn lines . . . a little, yes. But then he remembered the sea-mines. There had been so many. There was no way he'd remember those.

A thunder of footsteps sounded. Luke and Alma stepped back and hid in the smoke.

The Mayor appeared at the doorway with an assistant, smudged with smoke. They both wore gas masks.

'Here too,' he said darkly. 'That's every copy.'

A talkometer flashed. The lady glanced down. 'It's the same in the lab. The samples, the amber – all destroyed.'

The Mayor walked to the safe. 'They must have worked here. It's the only way they'd know.' He poked at the ashes. 'We'll need a press release and suspect – we can't look weak.'

'But who, sir?'

'Isn't it obvious?' He pulled at his gloves. 'I knew he was hiding something, I just didn't know what. He must have been working with her all along.' He turned away. 'Say it's Luke Smith-Sharma. Issue a warrant, tell the press, and send the guards to his boat.'

He paused. 'And take his friends – the plumber girl and that rice seller too. If he won't confess, one of them will.'

The Mayor turned and disappeared in the haze.

'They're pinning this on me?' Luke found it hard to breathe, and not just because of the smoke. 'Jess and Radhika too? But they've nothing to do with this!'

'I don't think he cares,' said Alma. 'So long as he's not blamed. And look around – the Reverend made it look like arson. It's what they wanted.'

The smoke grew thicker, opaque. His eyes stung with tears. His hopes of finding Ravi seemed like a distant dream. Now, he was a wanted criminal. And so were his friends.

He walked to the window. 'We need to warn the girls.'

'Wait. Not that way. If we fly through the centre, the Ghost Council will spot us.'

'Then how? We can't use the streets or the Mayor will get us.'

From the corridor, he heard the crackle of timber burning. The room grew stifling hot in the silence.

'I've an idea,' came a voice from the corner. Grating, wheezy. It was followed by a cough and rattle of chains.

Through the grey rose Terence, still trapped behind the thick iron bars.

'It's funny, Luke,' he rasped. 'But since you zapped me in that alley, I've seen all sorts of strange things. Shapes in the clouds. Faces in the storm.' He clutched the bars with bandaged fingers. 'Tonight, a shadow of a reverend walked in and burnt all my hard work.' He gave a crooked smile. 'But the funniest thing of all is seeing you two now. You and your friends have nowhere to go.'

'Neither do you,' said Luke, his loathing for the man almost calming his nerves. With everything else burnt, trust Terence to survive.

'Can I zap him?' Alma asked. 'Even with the smoke, he smells bad.'

'Wait!' Terence hissed. 'There's a copy of the map that ghost didn't get.'

'Rubbish!' said Luke. 'If there was, the Mayor or I would know.'

'It's a special one.' Terence smiled. 'It's the one in here.' He tapped his head with a bandaged finger. 'I know the way to Ravi. And I have a proposition. You set me free, and I'll take you to him.'

Luke looked at the man in the cage. Then at Alma.

'We can't trust him,' she said. 'Not an inch. Not a drop.'

'Of course you can't.' Terence chuckled. 'But for now, at least, our interests align. I want to be as far from the Mayor as you do. A little trip back to Europe will do the trick. Do you have a boat?'

'No,' Luke said. 'But I know someone who does.'

CHAPTER 19
THE MOTLEY CREW

While the east of the city sang with police sirens, on the north bank of the river, the water markets slept.

Jetties creaked like snores. Water lapped like a lullaby. The darkness lay thick like a raven-down blanket. It was a vigilant slumber. Owners peeked through the weave of their rocking hammocks. Mice squeaked as they scurried, on the lookout for cats. And the watchmen on the gates kept a careful eye. Nobody entered the markets without their permission. No thieves, no ruffians, and most certainly not the police.

That night, however, even the watchmen struggled. The mist on the river lay unusually thick. It drifted through the market like it knew its way. And amongst its hazy white, several watchmen heard footsteps – children's footsteps – but by the time they looked, the footsteps had gone, and all that was left was a whiff of chip-grease. The mist playing tricks, that's all, they said.

On the waterfront, however, the door to *Rajendra's Emporium* slid open, then shut. A light flickered on, revealing four tired faces and a brown-and-white cat.

'This boat isn't even seaworthy,' said Radhika, scowling. 'This is a total disaster.'

Luke shrugged. In some ways, it was a triumph. Alma and Luke had travelled miles through the sewers, evading the Ghost Council and the Mayor's best men, collecting Radhika, Jess and Stealth along the way. And Terence hadn't even tried to kill them once – though Alma's crackling blue fist might have had something to do with that.

'It's not perfect, sure, but we didn't have a choice. The Mayor was going to interrogate you.'

'Yeah, let's be positive,' said Jess. 'Compared to torture, this is lovely.'

'But this *is* torture,' Radhika said. 'Jess, you're too cheery. Terence, you smell. And Luke, you're the worst of them all. It's all your do-gooding that's got us into this mess. If I'd never met you, I'd be with my family right now.'

The mention of family took the wind from Luke's sails. They'd been so happy earlier that night. Playing chess. Talking about his mum. Tucked inside their boat safe and warm. Then Tabatha had come and changed everything. And they'd left in such a rush, he hadn't said goodbye. Not even to his sister – he'd just left her sleeping. It had seemed safest not to get their loved ones involved. Who knew how long it would be before they saw them again?

Jess sighed. 'I mean, a little hug from Mum might have been nice.'

'I don't know,' said Radhika. 'It might have been worse. I'm not sure I could have handled seeing the look on my parents' faces.'

Luke knew what she meant, but he didn't dare say it. It was like the New Thames Barrier: if he lifted it, the feelings would come flooding in. He had to keep them locked down, for at least a bit longer.

'Guys, I know it's hard, but we have to keep going. We just need to take it one day at a time.'

As he said the words, a siren wailed nearby, the darkness moved, and he thought back to what he'd seen on the boat. The hideous shadow – scuttling, sliding – and with it, he felt his hold on things slip. The dread swelled and threatened to burst its banks.

A grunt from behind pulled him out of his spin.

'Blah, blah, blah,' said Terence, his voice cutting the mood. He sat in the corner, hands and feet tied. 'This is all very touching, but

I'd like to get going. Because if we don't, I've a feeling we're going to get got.'

'For once, I'm with Terence,' said a wisp of mist seeping under the door. It curled upward and coalesced into Alma. 'You're all whining. It's boring. We've all made sacrifices. And really, guys, these are first-realm problems. My parents are both dead, so count yourself lucky.' She paused. 'Anyway, I've checked the market, and I can report that nobody saw us. But both the streets and sky are seething. The Mayor and the council are hunting us down. They need someone to blame. And what we need, Luke, is some kind of plan.'

He took a deep breath. 'It's simple enough. We leave London – it's not safe here – and make our way to the coast. Then we rescue Ravi, stop Tabatha and save the city.'

There was a moment's silence. Perhaps 'simple' hadn't been the right word.

Radhika's face did the spit-scowl again. 'You can't seriously believe that's possible.'

'We can fly. Fire lightning. And Terence knows the base. We've got a chance.'

'A chance in a million.'

'Do you have a better idea?' Luke wiped the dust from his hands.

'If Tabatha gets this weapon, or whatever she's after, we're not safe anywhere. She wants everything, she'll destroy it all. And I know your parents, my family, *everyone* will be in danger. Staying here, doing nothing, it's not an option.'

Radhika fell silent. She glanced to a picture on the wall. It was one of her and Ravi as kids. They were standing on top of the boat in the blazing sun, waving to the camera, not a scowl in sight. It couldn't have been taken long before Ravi was kidnapped.

'He almost escaped, you know,' Luke said quietly. 'By the Old Channel Tunnel. We'd got past Terence. Tabatha couldn't find us, but she said if he ran, she'd take you instead. He didn't even blink. He gave himself up.'

Radhika's face twisted and she turned away.

'Fine,' she whispered. 'I'll help you to the coast. But that's it – then I'm coming right back and getting my parents out of the city.'

'That'll do.' Luke sat down on the floor. He felt tired. Bone tired. 'Oh, one more thing. We've only got five days.'

The silence following that was worse than the arguing. Luke wanted to sink through the wood and hide in the hold. But instead of complaints, he felt a pat on his shoulder. It was slightly wet.

'Look, Wallbreaker,' said Alma with a wink. 'Why don't you take a break? Take a nap, you look awful. I'll play captain for tonight.' She turned to Radhika. 'Grumpface, stop scowling and start the engine. And Plumbergirl, you fix leaks, right?'

'Yeah, but in toilets. I'm not sure boats are the same.'

'Ah, it's just water. And I'm an expert at that. Come on, let's go below deck and start patching up.'

'And me?' said Terence. 'What about me?'

Alma turned and fired a spray of sparks to his neck. Terence fell to the floor with a *thunk*.

'Sorry, I know it's harsh, but his voice is so grating. He'll be fine in the morning. But tonight, I think we could all do with some peace and quiet.'

She opened the trapdoor and went into the hold, Jess following. Radhika frowned at Terence, then stomped over to the wheel and started the engine.

Luke looked out the window. Storm clouds were gathering to the east. They'd have to get past them to reach the sea.

The boat, however, turned the opposite way.

'Radhika, what are you doing? The ports are out east.'

'So we're going west. It's the last thing they'll expect.'

'But that's up-river. We need to reach the coast.'

'There are smugglers' canals,' she said, checking a map. 'If we move quick, there's a fairway we can reach by tomorrow.'

Smugglers' canals? He'd never heard of them. He supposed that was the point, though he didn't quite see how you could hide a canal. Not least one that led to sea.

'Can I do anything?' he asked. 'I steered our canal boat.'

'Let me see,' said Radhika. 'You've made me a fugitive. You've taken me away from my parents. And you want to sail my parents' boat to enemy waters.' She laughed mirthlessly. 'I think you've done plenty already.'

Luke nodded. He had done all of those things. And he wouldn't apologise. His only worry was whether he'd done enough. Enough for Ravi and his family, his friends and his conscience. They'd soon find out.

But right now, Alma was right, he did need a nap. So without another word, he walked to the cupboard in the corner, where there was a pile of blankets. He didn't even bother to lay them out. He shut the cupboard door behind him, curled up in the dark, and let the gentle rocking of the boat cradle him to sleep.

CHAPTER 20
THE RIVER

Luke woke to the smell of burnt toast. It was warm, and outside he could hear the river birds cawing. He didn't open his eyes – until he did, he could pretend he was still at home. That the events of yesterday had just been a bad dream.

But he could feel the boat sway in a way his home didn't. His houseboat was moored. This boat was moving at a clip. And then there was the smoke on his clothes – they stank of it. He thought back to the burning houseboat and Tabatha's sharp-nailed shadow . . .

He shook the image from his mind and opened his eyes. He was under a duvet in a cupboard of sorts. To his right, face pressed against the wall, lay Jess, snoring happily.

Quietly, he reached for the door. It squeaked open but Jess didn't stir. In the cabin, Stealth lay on the bed in the corner, Radhika's maps to his right, and beyond that, Terence, a chain round his ankle.

Though he'd seen Terence sleep in that cage at the Mayor's, this time he looked different – his face was almost smiling. Perhaps he was dreaming? He supposed it was possible. Terence was only human, after all.

He heard a faint clang from outside, followed by voices.

'Left a bit,' said Alma. 'There's a land thingy ahead.'

'You mean an island,' said Radhika.

'Whatever, Grumpface.'

'Look, if you call me that one more time . . .'

Luke sighed. He'd hoped some sleep might have eased the tensions. Evidently not. He stepped out on deck and into a blast of cool mist.

'Luke,' Radhika said, 'tell Alma to stop this ridiculous fog. She won't let me steer!'

'It's so we don't get seen!' Alma rolled her eyes. 'Luke, tell Radhika that I know what I'm doing. I'm the Council Deputy.'

'*Was* the deputy,' Radhika said. 'I've got a feeling you're fired now you're on the run.'

Alma's fist crackled blue. 'Careful, you might get yourself fired too.'

'Both of you, stop it,' he said. 'If you can't, take a timeout.'

Luke tried to give them Nana's 'look', then gave up. Best not to get too involved.

'I smelt toast — is there any left?'

Radhika sighed and passed him a slice. 'It's burnt. The toaster keeps sparking with you lot on board.' Then muttering, she went to the wheel, and turned left like Alma had asked.

He bit into his toast and scanned the water. In places, the mist thinned and he made out black trees and grass. A sandy path too, and the occasional dogwalker. No sign of this smugglers' canal, but they'd made good progress. It didn't get this green until at least after Richmond.

'Alma, you sure the council won't see this fog?'

'That's what I said,' said Radhika. 'But did she listen? No.'

Alma ignored her. 'Nah, I checked, they're all east.' She shrugged. 'But it seems that Grumpface here doesn't trust me.'

'Right, I warned you!' Radhika stepped away from the wheel. 'De-fog this river or I'll crash us.'

'Fine. It's your boat.'

There was a long pause while nobody did anything. Luke peered into the fog. Surely Alma would say if they were about to hit something? But from the look on her face, he wasn't so sure.

He put down his tea. It didn't taste the same any more.

Jess stepped out on deck, yawning. 'Who'd have thought cupboards would make such nice beds?' She looked at the three of them, then the unmanned wheel. 'Shouldn't someone be holding that?'

'Don't look at me. It's Radhika. She wants to crash.'

'I don't. All I want is to steer the boat – my boat – without fog.'

'Can we compromise?' Luke said. 'Could you thin the middle bit, Alma, but keep the banks thick?'

Another long silence. Alma sighed. 'Fine. For you, not her.'

The mist thinned suddenly and luckily too, for a hundred yards ahead, the river narrowed dramatically to a pair of gates.

Luke smiled. The land thingy hadn't been an island at all.

'It's a lock,' said Luke. Teddington Lock, if his memory served right – the first as the Thames rose uphill to the source. He'd always wanted to visit it, though not like this. Opening the gate would horribly expose them.

They didn't have a choice. They'd just have to be quick.

'Alma,' he said. 'Keep the mist double thick.'

The boat pulled in and Luke and Jess sprinted up the bank, shrouded in mist. They reached a lock-keeper's cottage with a trimmed privet hedge, then made their way to the winch post and began turning the handle.

Tink. Tink. Tink. Tink.

Luke had always thought locks were ingenious. With just two tiny gates and a winch, they allowed boats to do the impossible – defy gravity – and go uphill. It was sweaty work, though; the hinges were rusty and flaking in places.

'If they'd spent less time trimming hedges and more oiling hinges, this would be a whole lot easier.'

'At least it's fresh air,' said Jess. 'It's nicer than the sewer.'

Tink. Tink. Tink. Tink.

Jess had a point. He felt better already. The nerves of the last few days faded a little. With mist this thick, he felt almost safe.

'It's strange,' he said. 'We're on the run, but I slept better last night. It feels good to be finally doing something.'

'And with people I care about,' said Jess. 'Just like old times.'

Luke couldn't help but agree. Sometimes the 'who' mattered more than the 'what'.

The gates were almost open. The little boat approached, mercifully quiet.

'At least they've stopped arguing.'

'Yeah,' said Jess. 'I was starting to wonder if Alma might fry her.'

They had spoken too soon. A second later came an angry howl and the mist shot downriver, leaving them completely exposed.

A sheepish Radhika pulled into the lock.

'What happened?'

'She said I was useless.'

'And you said what?'

'That's there's nothing more useless than an unemployed ghost.' Radhika frowned. 'Sorry, perhaps I took it too far. She was about to zap me, so she took a timeout.'

Luke threw his hands in the air. 'You're like toddlers, you two. Now if anyone comes by, they'll—'

Stomp. Stomp. Stomp. Stomp.

Footsteps cut him off. Heavy footsteps. Coming from the cottage.

The door flew open and a puffy-faced man pinned eyes on them. He reminded Luke a little of the hag by St Paul's – he was the shapeless, unwashed, lurching type. But with eyes, thankfully, if not very good ones. They were squinting, red-rimmed, pouch-laden things, which a small marsupial might be happy to call home.

'What's all this shouting?' His pouched eyes narrowed on Luke and Jess. 'Funny,' he said. 'I just had a call from a man about a kid.' He shuffled up to them. 'You're a boy, I suppose, but you don't look half-Indian.'

Luke had often been told that. Normally it annoyed him, because, in fact, many half-Indians looked a lot like him: somewhere in between white and brown, with dark hair. But people wanted something clear-cut. Half a turban, perhaps, or an exotic accent.

For once, however, he was happy to disappoint. 'No, you're right, I'm not Indian at all.'

The man stared at Jess. 'And you don't look like a greasy-haired man.'

This seemed to throw Jess. Luke didn't blame her.

'No, I don't, that's true.'

'What about on board, is there a man there?'

'Nope,' Luke said.

'Not even one,' added Jess.

The man chewed his lip. Luke saw his cogs turning. 'Well, who's your adult, then? Your mum, I guess?'

Luke and Jess nodded.

The man smiled. 'OK, go fetch her.'

He'd got them and he knew it. There was a terrible silence. The man looked to Jess, Jess to Luke, and Luke looked up for some sign of Alma. They could do with a bit of her magic right now.

The man chuckled, then pulled out his talkometer.

'Now what was that man's name? Oberwink? Overthink? Something like that. I've his number somewhere . . .'

Luke's blood went cold. Oberdink? It had to be. But how could he have known?

Or maybe he didn't. If everyone else went east, Oberdink would go west. It was just his way. And either way, it was bad. They'd only been missing a few hours. They couldn't get caught now.

'Ah, here it is.' The man pulled out a card.

But before he could dial, there came a clatter from the boat. The man paused and looked down.

Luke looked too, with growing dread. Whatever was in there, it wasn't his mum.

The door burst open and Terence leapt out – but not as Luke knew him. He had a rug draped over his shoulders like a glamorous shawl. His ponytail was undone, his hair hanging lustrous and long past his collar. And his voice was different – warbly, feminine, with only a hint of grease.

'The name's Terencina, and the pleasure's all mine.' He curtsied daintily. 'Apologies for my outfit, but I didn't expect a man like you at a winch like this.'

The man frowned, trying to make sense of this eye-fluttering beanpole of a lady. If Luke read him rightly, he looked quite intimidated.

'Err. Sorry, ma'am,' he mumbled. 'It's just your children, ma'am, they don't look much like you . . .' He looked at Luke, then Jess. 'Or like each other, for that matter.'

'Different fathers.' Terencina winked. 'I was quite the looker in my youth. But raising a family, it does take its toll.' He sighed. 'Which is why I must return to my beauty sleep promptly. Unless, that is, you'd like to join me for a drink?'

The lock-keeper turned pink and leapt two feet back. 'No, ma'am, you sleep, I've work.'

A few hasty stomps later and he'd disappeared into his lodge.

Luke and Jess breathed, once, twice, and a third time for luck, then resumed. Luke's hands were trembling, but he couldn't be sure if it was the threat of Oberdink or Terence's dazzling turn that had shaken him so much.

When the gate finally opened, they climbed aboard the boat to find Radhika and Alma looking guilty.

'Sorry,' said Alma. 'I shouldn't have stormed off. Or called her Grumpface.'

'No,' said Radhika. 'I *was* a Grumpface. And I promise not to mention the job stuff again.'

'You'd better not,' said Luke, walking into the cabin.

Inside, Terence had transformed. The rug was on the floor. The ponytail re-tied. Any sign of Terencina had vanished. He looked at them darkly. 'If you mention that to anyone, I'll sink this boat with all of us on it. Got that?'

Luke nodded. At the rate things were going, he had a feeling they wouldn't need Terence's help – they were doing a sterling job of messing things up themselves.

'Well, the lock-keeper saw us and our mug shots are bound to be on the televisor tonight. It's a matter of hours before he raises the alarm.'

'Oh,' said Jess. 'That doesn't sound good.'

It wasn't. Once that happened, the Mayor would scour the area. Even if they made it to the smugglers' canal, surely they'd be spotted.

'Then it's probably time I shared the good news,' said Radhika as the boat rounded the bend. 'The fairway's moved nearer. In fact, it's right there.'

What? How could a canal move? He looked to where Radhika pointed. Pressed against the bank of the river was a funfair, with carousels, spinning tops and a giant Ferris wheel.

'But there's no canal. How do we get to the sea?'

'Oh, you'll see.' Radhika turned to the wheel and steered for the fair.

CHAPTER 21
THE SEVEN WIDOWS

The solution was obvious in hindsight, as they usually were. Within minutes of arrival, after a call from Radhika, some clowns appeared and began painting their boat. Minutes later, it was transformed into a 'Haunted Pirate Ship' ride, swinging back and forth on cables, set between the dodgems and the carousel.

Jess eyed it suspiciously. 'Are all these rides fake?'

'No. Just the ships,' said Radhika. 'That's why everyone pukes on them – they were never meant to be rides in the first place.'

With the boat painted, their faces were next. They had the full Hallowmas treatment. Luke, Jess and Radhika became red-fanged vampires, Terence a rat, and Alma, of course, a ghost. They fell in with the crowds, unrecognisable, and attacked the food stalls – buttered corn-fritters, smoky spiced beef, bowls of hot chocolate and candy-floss cones. But at the sight of the river, Luke lost his appetite. There, on the horizon, was a fuzz of red-and-blue lights.

His chest tightened. The lock-keeper must have reported them.

'Guys, the river police. Drop the snacks and hide!'

'No,' said Radhika. 'I've a better idea.'

She grabbed Luke's and Jess's hands and pulled them closer, following the surge of the crowd, until they came to a stop – along with Luke's heart – right on the riverbank, where a flotilla of police boats approached at speed.

'What are you doing?' shouted Luke.

'Trust me. I've got this.'

In any case, it was already too late. The police boats moved fast, carving paths through the water. A glittering black speedboat led the charge, manned by the Mayor himself. He cut a dashing figure – he always did – with his cloak flapping behind, curls flicking the wind, and steely eyes trained ahead down the river.

And though he waved at the crowd and their flashing cameras, he sailed right past Luke without a second glance.

'Smugglers' rule. If you run, people notice.' Radhika smiled for a change. She was enjoying herself. 'Sometimes, the best place to hide is in plain sight.'

The next two days proved Radhika right. The fair travelled south, entirely unnoticed, and with each passing hour, London felt more remote. City turned to suburbs, suburbs to towns, then to villages, hamlets and farmers' fields full of ridged black mud and mole-whisker shoots peeking up through the cracks.

And though Luke's name remained in the papers and Alma had banned him from flying in case the Ghost Council saw, he gradually found himself relaxing. He'd had word that his family were OK – a huge relief – and he was keeping himself busy. By day, Radhika taught him what she knew about seafaring: maps, currents, tides and the like. And at night, he practised his 'lightning' with Alma. She had figured out that, as a half-ghost, because he was still attached to the living, his lightning had to come from that realm too. He couldn't make it from scratch like a full ghost could, but he could channel it from electrical sources. The fairground was perfect, with its plentiful neon and terrible wiring. Though part of Luke wished he could do it like Alma.

'It must be a half-ghost thing,' she said. 'Our lightning goes down to the ground, but you lift yours up. It's cool. It's like you flow the other way.'

'I don't know,' said Luke. 'What about all the wall stuff – the creaking and rippling. Surely that's asking for trouble?'

Alma shrugged. 'What house doesn't creak? It doesn't mean it'll fall down. And when water moves, it ripples – that's healthy. Perhaps this pond has been too calm for too long.' She twirled a lock of dark hair round her finger in thought. 'And as for trouble, the council can hardly talk. Most of them should have gone to the End Place long ago. It's only them staying that draws the ghouls in the first place.' She took his hand in hers. 'You're different, sure, but you were made that way. You've a right to be here as much as anyone else.'

Luke looked at her. It was such a lovely to thing to say that he half-expected her to follow it with an insult. But since she'd left the council and her duties, Alma had been nicer to everyone. Well, except Terence.

Jess barrelled in with pancakes, Terence and Radhika behind. 'I got snacks!' She grinned. 'We're not late, are we?'

'Yes. But don't worry, the snacks make up for it.'

They sat round the table and Luke unrolled the map. 'We're here.' He pointed to a spot near the coast. 'We reach the sea tomorrow and sail at midnight.'

He traced his finger through the blue towards an ear-shaped cove. 'It'll take a day to cross over, according to Terence's map.'

Terence gave a superior grin, somewhat undermined by the dripping green zombie make-up covering his face. After they'd heard about 'Terencina', the circus had hired him to scare kids on the Haunted Ship. In the evenings, though, he'd stuck to the deal and worked hard on the map to Tabatha's base. Alma's glowing fist might have helped, but he'd been surprisingly diligent, even colouring in the sea-mines and patrol boats. It almost made Luke nervous.

'No offence,' started Jess, 'but if Terence drew this, can we trust it? What if he leads us to the mines?'

'Simple,' said Luke. 'He'll be on the boat. If we blow up, he will too.'

'Whatever.' Terence shrugged. 'I'm not helping, not really. I'll get you *to* the base, but I can't get you inside it. It's a fortress. It'll be fun, actually, watching you all get caught.'

'Quiet,' said Alma. 'It's fine, Jess. If it only takes a day, then we've a day left for a recce. Luke and I will fly over and find some chink in the armour. Then we'll rescue Ravi, zap Tabatha and destroy that lightning gun of hers.'

'Right. Easy-peasy.' Radhika crossed her arms. 'Your plan has more holes than this boat.'

'It's not watertight,' said Luke, 'but it is possible – Ma Boxhill said so – and it's the only way to save London and our families.' He looked at the moon, thought of his mum and felt a little braver. 'We've stopped her before, remember. Now, let's head to bed, we've got a long day tomorrow.'

Luke watched them pack away with pride. After the initial squabbles, he was proud of how they were working together. Radhika had showed Alma the maps. Alma had taught Jess to patch up the boat. Jess had used her first aid to tend to Terence's fingers – several were broken from the mayor's interrogation. And Terence, for all his grumbling, had softened a bit too: he even deigned to give Stealth a little stroke sometimes. Luke got the feeling he rather liked dressing up for the fair.

But as the others fell asleep, Luke found himself gazing out the window, searching for shadows. They'd lost the support of the Ghost Council, and what if *she* came back? The other night, he'd thought he'd heard something scuttling outside – just a rat, it had turned out, but still . . .

In fact, had something just moved by the window?

'Boo!' Alma's face popped up by the glass.

'Not funny. What are you doing there, anyway?'

'Flying, actually. I've declared the no-fly zone over. We're miles from London, the council won't see a thing. And the walking's driving me crazy. I feel like a groundghoul.'

'You're sure it's safe?'

Alma had a way of twisting Luke's arm, and he soon found himself gliding on his kite-cloud over darkened hills, through cool night air. The higgledy-spired town of Lewes cuddled up below, under an explosion of stars and a swollen moon.

It was nearly full. Three days left.

Luke turned to Alma. 'I keep worrying we'll get caught. Or that she'll find us, somehow. And I keep thinking back to what Tabatha said. It's not just about saving Ravi any more. She wants to take everything. She wants revenge.'

'She might,' said Alma. 'And who knows if your lightning will be able to stop her, but that's not a reason to mope — it's a reason to live. To savour every moment. Worrying, Luke, never did any good.' She glanced around. 'Look at this place. It's beautiful.'

Luke breathed it in. She was right. Beyond the town was a valley, where the river snaked across a meadow. Cows lay in the grass. Barn windows glowed. Church bells rang out midnight, and a few nightsparks shimmered up — butterflying green, blue and red through the air.

Alma sighed. 'I'd arranged a special soul-shepherding tonight. Ghosts from all four corners of the country were coming. I bet the council have cancelled it.'

'I'm sorry, Alma.' Luke watched a few float up. 'You could go back, you know. I'd understand if you did.'

'I know, but it wouldn't sit right. Who helps a hundred strangers, but then isn't there for their friend?' She shook her head. 'Anyway, come on, I've got something to show you.'

She rose higher and pointed south to a huge grassed ridge. Past it, the sky looked strangely black. Then his eyes adjusted. The black was moving. Lights twinkled on its surface, but not like stars.

He caught his breath. 'Is that what I think it is?'

'It depends what you're thinking.' Alma bowed with a flourish. 'May I present . . . the English Channel!'

Something flickered in his chest, bright like the lights of the ships on the water. 'It's so close. It can't be more than a day's sail.'

'There's more, come on!' Alma tilted her cloud, diving down to the ridge, where a powerful wind rocketed them east. Luke could barely look up for the strength of it, but when he did, he gasped. A set of magnificent cliffs curved into the distance, stained even blacker than the night sky itself.

'They're called the Seven Widows. They used to be white, they say.'

Luke could believe it. At the foot of the cliffs, in the shadows, floated hundreds of boats, each pumping plumes of soot up the cliffside. Ropes stretched up to the clifftop, along which juddered crates of goods.

'Smugglers?' Luke asked.

'Who else?' said Alma. 'The rich need to get their wine and cheese somehow.'

In the bay lay a sleepy, glowing town with a lighthouse, police station, pub and church, which was topped by a rusted weathervane in the shape of a cockerel. People chatted in the street, watching the action, exchanging coins, completely unfazed by the flagrant law-breaking. A cheery sign on the road read, *Smugglers' Cove*.

'Boats leave each night. We'll slink off with them tomorrow, once the fair gets here.' She looked at Luke. 'I'm telling you, it'll be fine. No one follows rules here.'

They drifted through the smoky air and settled on the church roof beside the weathervane. People spilt out from the pub to the street. A local policeman took some money from a woman; it chinked quietly in his hands. It was strange, Luke thought, but he found the crime reassuring. They'd never be stopped with all this going on.

Creak. Thud. Creak. Thud.

Luke's heart juddered like the weathervane beside them. That creak of leather. That confident step. He knew it, but no, it wasn't possible . . .

Yet unfortunately, it was: off the cobbled square strode the Mayor, broad, cloaked and quiet in the darkness. He stopped by an inn. The door opened and out stepped a familiar face in a thin grey suit.

'It's confirmed, Mr Mayor,' wheedled Oberdink. 'A fingerprint from the candy-floss matches Terence's. That'll teach him to drop litter.'

'But a funfair, really? It seems most odd.'

'You hired me because I am an expert on the boy,' Oberdink said. 'Well, let me tell you, he is odd through and through. And this town is the nearest smugglers' port. They're bound to be using it. My pineapple studies show—'

'Fine,' cut in the Mayor. 'So we surround the fair and the town, but what about the countryside? What's stopping them running?'

A bloodcurdling howl rose in the distance, followed by a chorus of wolf-like cries.

Oberdink smiled. 'Why, the dogs will, of course. They'll find his scent in no time.'

'Very well.' The Mayor opened the door to the inn. 'I need Luke alive. The rest . . . well, it doesn't really matter.'

Oberdink and the Mayor disappeared indoors. The wind picked up, sending the weathervane spinning, round and round like Luke's thoughts.

'What do we do? We can't stay with the fair! We have to make a run for it – we'll never reach Ravi if those dogs find us first!'

But Alma didn't reply. Her eyes were fixed on the rusted cockerel, which spun ever faster, jerking violently.

'Alma, come on! We have to warn the others. This changes everything.'

'No, *that* does.' She pointed at the weathervane, her eyes wide. 'A wind like this, it can only mean one thing.'

'What?'

'The Ghost Council are coming.'

CHAPTER 22
INTO THE WOODS

Crunch. Snap. Squelch. Drip.

They left that night through the woods, after a quick goodbye to the fairground owner. There was no time to lose. With the south wind so strong, the ghosts would reach them in hours.

'You sure we couldn't stay?' Terence grumbled, still dressed as a zombie. 'I got to terrify children, and I was paid for it too. I thought I'd finally found my calling.'

'That's because you're weird,' said Radhika. 'What I want to know is, why we can't take the road? This forest is creepy.'

'Let me think . . .' Alma glanced through the canopy at the dark night sky. 'Because the Reverend would zap you, the Crone would freeze you, and the Doctor would strangle you slowly with mist.'

Radhika muttered something and Luke and Jess exchanged a glance. It was like the first day on the boat. Jess didn't even try to lighten the mood, and wisely so, because what they really needed was sleep and shelter.

Crunch. Snap. Squelch. Drip.

They'd been walking for hours. Through the trees, they glimpsed fields and fences. The lights of Lewes glowed on the hill under the near-full moon. Luke's feet felt numb. Radhika was shivering. Jess's face had gone red from the cold. But in a few more hours, they'd reach Smugglers' Cove, where the fairground owner had said she'd leave the boat and Stealth – they couldn't risk losing him in the woods.

They just had to first survive the cold and being hunted by ghosts.

AWOOOO!

Oh, and the pack of hungry hounds sniffing the roads. If Tabatha turned up, they might as well throw a party, Luke thought.

'If the dogs find us,' Jess said, 'will they bite?'

Luke decided not to answer.

Crunch. Snap. Squelch. Drip.

Barely a drop of moonlight slipped through the branches overhead. Radhika was right: it was creepily dark – but at least they were hidden.

The wind picked up and the temperature dropped further. Luke wondered when they were going to reach shelter.

'At least with the dogs,' said Terence, 'the end would be quick. The Mayor's the worst. He stretches it out. Said he'd break all my fingers if I tried to escape.' He flexed his bandaged hands. 'Not sure these will ever be the same.'

The silence again. Luke didn't know what to say. In Battersea, Terence had done many cruel things, but he'd never once done anything like break someone's finger. It took a different kind of person to do that.

He still didn't trust Terence, or like him, but at least you knew where you stood with him. And he was tough too. The haunted house manager had even asked Luke if Terence might want a permanent job. Luke hadn't passed the message on. They needed him for now.

'Oh look, it's snowing!'

Jess was pointing to the edge of the forest. Fine white flakes drifted in through the trees.

'Snowball fight, anyone?' she said.

'No,' said Alma. 'Something's wrong. It never snows in November.'

'But I love snow!'

'Not this stuff. It's the Crone, I know it. The others will be with her. They're closer than I hoped.' She looked to Luke. 'A blizzardheart, a mist-wraith, and stormbreaker together – we don't stand a chance in a fight.'

'So what do we do?'

'A decoy,' she said. 'I'm faster. I'll draw them away, then lose them. I'll circle back here or to the town when I'm done. Just steer clear of the snow. There's a barn up ahead. Go there.'

And before Luke could protest, Alma darted away.

Crunch. Snap. Squelch. Drip.

They walked on. The dog howls faded. But the snow grew thicker. If Alma had meant to lose the Crone, it didn't seem to have worked. The snow now clumped in the trees, dancing closer in from the edges.

A creak overhead. A branch cracked, cascading white flakes through the air right where they'd just been.

Close. Too close. And was it him, or did the flakes look odd? Like circles, with hairs curling up at the edges.

Not circles, but ovals. Ovals like . . .

'Eyes!' said Radhika. 'I swear that snowflake just blinked!'

'Blinked?' But Luke knew she was right. Falling white eyes, blinking in the starlight. Was it for effect or could they actually see? If their rain glimpsed your thoughts, then it wasn't impossible . . .

Another branch creaked somewhere above.

'Change of plan,' said Luke. 'We run, now!'

They sprinted, stumbling over twisting roots and frost-crisped leaves. Branches scratched and thwacked left, right and centre, and the air danced with blinking white eyes – but so far, they'd not been hit.

Where was the barn? Where was Alma? Why hadn't her plan worked?

'Over there!' Jess cried.

Through the trees ahead slumped a tall wooden structure, drenched in moss and ivy – the barn, it had to be! They gave a final push, leaping over snow piles and ice, dodging shards from above, trees blurring by their sides. Then with a clatter of wood, they burst through the door, shivering.

Luke breathed. He checked the four of them. By some miracle, they'd made it. Not a flake in sight. He would have smiled if his face weren't frozen stiff.

He scanned the building, a large, steep-roofed, broad-planked thing. The place looked forgotten, but was entirely snow-free. Rotting wood crates piled up in the corners, wet leaves squelched brown at their feet and the air smelt musty and faintly of cheese. Or perhaps, Luke thought, that was Terence's feet.

Walking to the wall, he peeked through the planks. What if the snow didn't stop? If it blanketed the ground, would they have to wait inside until it melted? Or until they froze? He supposed death by freezing was marginally better than by lightning.

AWOOOOO!

Oh dear, Luke thought. He'd spoken too soon. It was a hound, definitely closer than before. And what was that? A rumbling engine?

'Quick,' he said. 'Behind those crates, before they see us.'

They squeezed in and, through the gappy walls, spied a truck approaching. Beside it, nose to the ground, loped a slobber-mouthed, black-furred, monstrous hound. It was heading straight for them.

It stopped, tail straightened, nose pointed to the barn.

'In there, eh, Bessie?' said the driver. 'Don't worry, we'll get 'em.'

A slow dread crept through Luke's body. Hiding was pointless. It would smell them out. They didn't even need a dog to do that with Terence's overripe feet.

Squelch. Squelch. Squelch. Squelch.

Two men reached the door, the hound beside them. Luke searched for a piece of wood, a nail, something.

'Can't you zap it?' hissed Radhika.

'If there were wires, but there's nothing.'

'Terence,' Jess said. 'You're strong. Could you bash it?'

'Nope. Dogs are loyal, they're a man's best friend.'

Luke thought this an odd time for Terence to develop some principles, but the men had entered the building, so they all fell quiet.

Creak. Squelch. Creak. Squelch.

Across the old boards, through the wet autumn leaves, the men approached. Luke shivered, but from fear, not cold. He covered his mouth to hide the steam from his breath.

Wasn't there anything they could do? Maybe Terence was right. He'd rather be struck by lightning than mauled by a dog.

The decision, in any case, was now out of his hands.

Hissssss.

What? Luke peeked through the boxes – the men stood in the centre of the barn, above a hole in the floor. Not a hole . . . a perfect square. A trapdoor – but why?

And why, come to think of it, had the smell of wet feet become so overpowering?

'Right,' said the driver. 'Load 'em quick, it's freezing. Then straight to Smugglers' Cove.'

'Five crates of cheese, and two of red wine, right?'

'Yeah, and no pilfering. He always knows.'

Luke's smile broke through the ice. Smugglers! They weren't hunting them at all.

The men disappeared into the trapdoor then emerged with a crate the size of a shed. The dog barked wildly until the man kicked its rump. 'Bloomin' dogs and French cheese. Go wild every time.'

Luke heard them stomp to the truck. They'd be back for the next one soon . . . which gave him an idea.

'Are you thinking what I'm thinking?' he asked the others.

Terence was already walking to the trapdoor. 'A ride in the cheesemobile? It doesn't get any better than that.'

CHAPTER 23
SMUGGLED

Three bone-jolting, lip-freezing, pungent hours later, the truck – and their cheese crate – came to a rattling stop. It was about time, Luke thought. It had snowed all the way and his fingers were ready to fall off.

Truck doors slammed, followed by snow-muffled boot squeaks, then a strange floating feeling: the men lifting the crate. Through the cracks, Luke saw the streets of Smugglers' Cove, the church, docks, warehouses and the blue-grey shadows of the past-midnight dark.

They were almost there – the sea at last!

The town vanished, replaced by stone walls and warm air. The crate was moving inside. A lantern's yellow glow filtered through and Luke felt them descend, stop-start, down steps.

THUNK! The crate dropped hard to the floor.

'Shall we unload it?'

Luke's heart skipped a beat. Even Terence looked scared, though the effect was offset by all the cheese smeared round his mouth.

'Nah,' said the other. 'The Mayor prefers his men to do that bit. They'll be here soon enough.'

Footsteps clumped off, followed by a door slamming and the clink of locks.

'The Mayor?' Jess squeaked. 'This cheese is the Mayor's?'

'Don't think, just help me with this lid.'

They emerged in a tumble of oozing French cheese, and after catching their breath, they stood, a little whiffy, surveying what looked like the cellar of a well-stocked inn. There were legs of ham hung from the ceiling, bags of salt and a wall-high rack stacked with beer kegs and wine. Oil lanterns burnt quietly in three of the corners and in the fourth stood a surprisingly deep pantry, like a walk-in wardrobe but for bags of flour. On the nearest wall, a window peeked out at pavement level, showing boots crunching on snow and a dark night sky.

It looked homely enough, almost cosy for a cellar, but they couldn't stick around. The boat could be waiting in the harbour already and, any minute now, the Mayor might get there. Not to mention the Ghost Council. Come to think of it, did the snow blink here too? Luke had better do something about the window.

He grabbed two bags of flour and blocked the view as best he could. The snow packed against the edges of the frame, as through trying to get in, but thankfully without luck. Through the pane, however, he saw something else: a grasping, thick, charcoal-grey mist. It crawled down the hill, its tendrils testing each door as it passed. It had to be the Plague Doctor's work. That couldn't be good.

Where was Alma? They needed her now more than ever. Or perhaps, he thought, she needed them. The first step, however, was to get out of this cellar.

'Could we knock on the door?' said Jess. 'Maybe someone will help us.'

'Maybe. Then again, they might hand us in to the Mayor.'

'Then we work together.' Terence picked up a rolling pin. 'You can zap 'em, I'll bash 'em, and by the time they wake, we'll all be long gone.'

Luke shook his head. 'Can you knock out a snowstorm, a mist-wraith, and a lightning bolt?' There was silence. 'I thought not.' He frowned. 'Our real advantage is that they don't know we're here. We need to keep it that way.'

He heard a tapping behind him. Radhika had her hands on the walls.

'Radhika, what on earth are you doing?'

'Smugglers' Cove is full of passageways, my parents said. They use them when there's a raid to reach the docks or hills.' She tapped a brick, listened, then moved to the next. 'They sound hollow, normally. There must be one somewhere.'

'OK,' said Luke. 'That's the best plan yet. Let's get tapping.'

But after a mere minute had passed came a new set of sounds. The clink of chainmail mane. A mechanical whinny and the clip of steel hooves. The crunch of boots against fresh-fallen snow.

Creak. Swish. Crunch. Creak.

Not just any boots, but the Mayor's. Nobody else in town could afford a robot-horse carriage. The confident crunch of his steps came closer, each beat of his boots like a stamp on his soul. Luke's heart raced. They were so close to the sea. If they could only have a little more time.

Squeeeeak.

It was the inn door's hinges. He'd entered the building. They had minutes – no, seconds – until he arrived.

Luke tried to think. Above, the booted footsteps grew louder, thudding heavily on the flagstone floor.

Static crackled from a walkie-talkie, followed by the Mayor's velvet voice. 'Oberdink, come down from your room, right now.'

Everyone held their breath. The Mayor had to be stood right outside the cellar door. He'd see them in seconds. Somewhere above, a second door creaked open, then came Oberdink's wheedling tones. 'Ah, Lord Mayor, you look rather . . . wet.'

'Wet. Cold. And rather angry.' His voice wasn't raised, but it cut through the walls. 'You told me that you were an expert on Luke Smith-Sharma. That you'd found his prints. That your methods would work.' A leather boot creaked. 'But there was nothing at the funfair and I have spent all night in the snow and choking mist. And do you know what your dogs found?'

'The culprits?'

'No. They found every warehouse of hidden cheese.'

'Ah. I see.' Oberdink cleared his throat. 'Well, that man Terence does smell quite cheesy. Awfully unhygienic. Basically an overgrown rat. So I suppose it is possible that the dogs got confused—'

'Then perhaps I can educate you as to the difference.'

Clink. Clink. Rattle. Clink.

Luke knew that sound – it was the key in the door. He glanced up the stairs and saw it glinting in the keyhole. Now the handle was turning. They'd be here in a second.

Creeeak.

With not a second to spare, they all dived for the walk-in-wardrobe of flour, just as the door to the cellar swung open. Luke tried not to breathe, blink or let his heart beat – anything that might give them away. The jolly sounds of the inn tumbled down into the cellar, followed by a heavier tumbling sound.

Thunk. Thunk. Squelch.

It was the sound of a thin grey detective, falling down thick grey steps, onto a hard stone floor and soft French cheese.

'Unload all that cheese,' the Mayor called. 'In alphabetical order. Memorise each scent. Or I'll peel off your fingerprints and feed them to the dogs.'

'But Mr Mayor, please!'

A door slammed above.

The hubbub of the inn faded. Through the door of the pantry, Luke watched Oberdink get to his feet. Cheese streaked his tie and moustache. Dirt from the floor dusted his face. But he didn't even try to wipe it off. Instead, he sat on the steps and cried.

For once, Oberdink had been on the right track. It was almost sad. But Oberdink's moods weren't Luke's problem any more.

The real problem was how on earth they were going to get out of this cupboard.

Luke felt a tap on his shoulder. It was Radhika, and she was smiling.

At the back of the pantry, between bags of flour, a panel had opened. Behind it lay a passageway leading into the dark. A secret passageway – she'd found one!

She gestured to him, then slipped through gap, with Jess right behind. Only Terence hesitated, his eyes on the pantry door.

It was then that Luke realised the crying had stopped.

He spun around. Oberdink stood in the doorway, his eyes like moons.

'Smithy,' he whispered. 'I found you at last.'

But before he could cry out, a giant leg of ham hit Oberdink hard on the head, and he fell the floor with satisfying thud.

'That's for calling me a rat,' said Terence. He whacked him one more time with the ham for good measure. 'And that was for you, Luke. We both know he deserved it.' He grinned, then loped through the secret doorway.

Luke followed him in. Though nobody could see it, for the first time that night, he was grinning too.

CHAPTER 24
THE WAREHOUSE

They inched down the tunnel between damp stone walls. In places, it narrowed to an uncomfortable squeeze, catching their clothes with salt and rock. In others, it widened, and the walls fell away into darkness. The only light came from Ravi's watch, which Luke held tight, while the sound and smell of the sea grew stronger. First a lap, then a wash, then a crash of waves; first a scent, then a tang, then a rotten-kelp stench.

But unpleasant as these things were, they weren't what worried Luke. What concerned him was that they seemed to be going deeper, and with each passing minute, the water was rising. It had started as a splash, then a soak up their shoes, but now it sloshed cold against their ankles.

'You sure this is for smugglers?' Terence grumbled. 'It feels more like a watery grave.'

'It must head somewhere,' said Jess. 'Nobody puts this

much effort into digging without reason.'

'To hell, perhaps?'

Luke frowned. The icy water was now up to his calves. 'It could be tidal. Maybe we have to wait until the tide goes out.'

'Or until the Mayor or the Ghost Council come down here to find us.'

'Fair point.' Luke sighed. He wished, not for the first time that night, that Alma was with them. Without her, they didn't stand a chance against the council or the Mayor. He hoped she was OK. 'Fine, we head on.'

They sloshed on in silence. Luke tried to remember what he'd seen of the town with Alma. What had been downhill from the inn? Where might they be heading? There had been a church, the police station, the boats at the end, but before that, it was vague.

'Wait!' said Radhika. 'Is that a light ahead?'

It was faint, but definitely there. They waded up to it with rekindled vigour, the water up to their knees and their teeth chattering. The beam of white light shone through a grate at least ten feet up. Through it, they heard the sea, voices and footsteps.

'Did anyone bring a rope?' Jess asked.

Luke shook his head. Even if they had, it would have been risky with someone up there. Luckily, he had a better idea.

'No rope. But you did bring a half-ghost.'

Moments later, he rose towards the grate, glancing down at his unconscious body, held tight in Jess and Radhika's arms. They'd better not drop him.

He reached the metal slats and let his mist rise through them, but as his mist reformed, he couldn't help but gasp. He'd expected another cellar, or a dingy basement, but instead he was met with a cavernous warehouse. Shelves stacked with crates towered above him, higher than houses, under sloped timber ceilings. Long windows ran the length of the roof, letting in shafts of moonlight, painting the room in stripes of shadow.

The warehouses, *of course*! He remembered them now, and if he remembered correctly, they were right by the harbour. They just had to find a way to get out unnoticed.

He scanned the room and smiled. It was too good to be true: in each of the towering avenues of shelves stood thin, extendable ladders and rope-pulley platforms for loading the items. It would be easy enough to get one down to the tunnel.

He began walking to the nearest when a bright yellow beam cut across his path.

'Hello? Anyone there?'

A guard stepped into the view at the end of the aisle, barely ten feet from Luke, and waved the torchlight back and forth – and right through him.

Of course, he saw only misty air, but Luke held his breath all the same. A long second passed, then the guard reached for his talkometer.

'Hello, Mr Mayor, I've checked the whole warehouse. All the confiscated goods – amber, poppies, the weapons too – they're all fully accounted for. Not a soul in here.'

Luke's mind raced. The Mayor's warehouse? Confiscated goods? He clearly hadn't just come for cheese and wine.

The guard walked on, his torch lighting up the crates – first boxes full of amber and dried red flowers. These must be the shipments for Tabatha that he'd intercepted, the ones she needed for the lightning gun. He turned to the boxes nearest the grate. They had thick wooden lids. Curious, he lifted one and gasped. Inside were stacked dozens of glittering red vials, light dancing inside them like liquid flames.

He'd seen them before. Tabatha had made them in her lab in Battersea. And when he'd dropped one, that time in the third chimney with Terence, it had made a fire that burnt a hundred foot high. That was one vial, but there must be a hundred vials in this box, and there were hundreds of boxes. What could they need them for?

The guard had already reached the loading bay door. He pressed some buttons and it rolled a few feet up, but before Luke could follow, it had come back down.

Luke pushed the contents of the boxes from his mind. He had to think. They needed to get out.

That door looked heavy, and without a passcode, they'd never get through . . . but with all those ladders and pulleys, they could possibly use the roof.

He glanced up. It was pretty high. He decided he'd better check it out first.

Without wind, a ghost couldn't technically fly, but a bit of momentum could go a long way, so he scrambled up the ladder, as light as air. At the top of the shelves, he took a running jump and easily caught hold of one of the roof's iron struts. A few leaps more and he was at a window.

The snow had now stopped, giving him a clear view of the harbour and the sea. Coated in snow, it was even prettier than he remembered. The jetties were strips of frosty fluffed ice. The tall, black cliffs stood like snow-capped mountains. The boats in the water bobbed like white whales.

But one boat stood out at the harbour's far end. The sign had gone, and the colour had changed, but he knew *Rajendra's Emporium* a mile away and it filled him with hope, just as it had for Ravi throughout all those years in Battersea.

Then he noticed the quiet. Not in the warehouse, but the streets. The inns had buzzed with people and laughter. Now it was deadly silent.

He glanced the other way and caught his breath. The snow had stopped, but the mist hadn't. The grave-grey mist was creeping down the hill. It had swallowed half the town. And was he imagining it, or had it stopped right by the inn they'd just left?

They had to move quickly.

He leapt down, landing by the grate. Focusing on his fingers, to keep them firm, he dragged a rope ladder across and slipped it down the drain.

He heard the *clunk clunk clunk* of his friends climbing up. Soon, they were there, dripping on the warehouse floor, and he was back in his body.

'We're so close, I can feel it,' Luke said. 'The boat's waiting, right there in the dock.'

'Then why are we standing here talking?' said Terence, heading to the roll-down door. 'Let's get out of here.'

'Not that way,' said Luke. 'That one has a code. We have to use the roof.'

Their faces fell. He looked up at the skylights. They seemed further up now he was back in his body.

Clunk. Clunk. Clunk.

What was that? Was someone coming? They looked back to the grate. A black leather gauntlet grasped at its rim.

'Don't use the roof,' said the Mayor. 'I'll escort you myself.'

The Mayor pulled himself up to standing with one heft of his hand, then smiled down on them from all six feet of his frame. His skin looked waxy, his eyes bloodshot. His long black coat and golden locks dripped with ice-cold water.

He drew a gun from his pocket and waved it at each of them in turn. 'You've given me a run for my money. Now it's time to come with me. And if anyone tries running, I'll shoot another of you dead.' He nodded to the roll-up door. 'Come on. Chop, chop.'

They stood there, silent. Beaten. Radhika's eyes were fixed on the gun. Jess shivered, pale and exhausted. Terence clutched at his bandaged fingers. They were too tired, too afraid to put up a fight. And Luke's stomach sank too. What could they do against a gun?

Unless . . .

Luke closed his eyes and listened – for that pulse of electricity, the beat of his heart – like he'd done when he practised with Alma. Surely there was a wire here somewhere . . .

'Luke, wake up!' the Mayor snapped.

Luke blinked. The gun was pointing straight at him.

It was no use. He felt nothing. Either that or he was too distracted – it was hard to let things flow with a gun in your face. He forced his feet to move after the Mayor.

Creak. Creak. Swish. Creak.

The Mayor stepped backwards, keeping the gun trained firmly on them, making his way towards the roll-up door. Luke hoped he'd trip on his cloak, but no such luck: big as he was, he moved like a cat. They had no choice but to follow, passing shelf after shelf of amber, poppies and the fiery red vials.

'Why the explosives?' Luke asked. 'You said you wanted to protect the city.'

'Tabatha made them, I just found them,' the Mayor said. 'But

I can't complain. You see, sometimes destruction is protection.' He opened a box and took out a vial. The red light danced in the dark of the warehouse. 'It's simple, really. Once you've told me the location of her base, we'll fill my zeppelin with these vials and drop them on it.'

'You can't just burn it!' Luke said. 'There are children in there!'

'I know, it's tragic, but in war, there are casualties. A few lives are fair game if it protects a whole city. And of course, people never need to know.' The Mayor pushed a curl from his bloodshot eyes. 'Really, Luke, this is all your doing. If you'd helped me build the lightning gun, it wouldn't have been necessary. I could have protected us with that. But with the documents gone, I've been left with little choice.'

Luke barely heard him. Burning rage drowned the words out. The children were innocent. Ravi was innocent. How could the Mayor do this? More than anyone, he should know better – he'd shovelled in Battersea like the rest of them.

Or, Luke thought, maybe he'd never cared in the first place. Maybe that's why the Margates had used him. At the core, he was as ruthless and rotten as they were.

Thump. Thump. Thump. Thump.

Suddenly he felt it. The pulse of wires from beneath the roll-up door; his heart beating in time. The anger flowing inside him had helped. If he could only draw a little down . . .

'Now, Terence,' continued the Mayor, gun in hand, 'what did I promise you if you tried to escape?'

'Errr . . .' Terence paled. 'But I didn't escape. They made me go with them!'

'Same difference, man. Your fingers. Now.'

Thump. Thump. Thump. Thump.

Luke's heart beat louder, and the pulse of electricity grew. Was the Mayor serious? Then he remembered all the men he'd sent to the Tower. Of course he was serious.

Terence lifted his hand, whimpering, and dragged himself towards the mayor.

Thump. Thump. Thump. Creak.

Luke felt the power grow in hands, felt the ripple in the air, and heard that same straining sound – the wall between realms. But he refused to be sorry. Like Alma had said, he was made this way.

'Come on, Terry,' said the Mayor. 'Your hand, or I'll shoot.'

Terence, shaking, took another step forward.

'No,' said Luke. 'Don't move an inch closer.'

The Mayor turned the gun on him. 'And why on earth should he listen to you?'

'Because I can do this.'

A bright yellow spark leapt out from Luke's hand straight to the Mayor's right glove. It singed through the leather and knocked the gun to the floor. Quick as a flash, Jess grabbed it and pointed it at their captor.

The Mayor stopped dead. He looked at Luke's glowing hand with disgust, or envy – Luke couldn't quite tell. Then Luke felt a hand on his shoulder. A bandaged hand.

Terence stood there, a strange look on his face. Tired, sad, maybe both. He squeezed Luke's shoulder a little too hard.

'Why did you do that?' His voice was a whisper.

'I don't know,' Luke said. 'I just did. It felt right.'

'Right?' Terence hissed. 'After what I did in Battersea? Why would you save me?'

'Because . . .' Luke trailed off. He wasn't sure. They needed Terence, but that wasn't why. It was something else. But before the words came, the Mayor spoke.

'It doesn't matter why, because it's over now.'

Luke looked up. The Mayor smiled. Unease trickled down

Luke's back. They had him cornered, with a gun and lightning to boot. Why was he smiling?

Then in the distance sounded a rhythmic stomp.

'Before I entered the warehouse, I called my men. All of them.' The military boots grew louder as he spoke. 'That's them right now.'

Luke knew he wasn't lying. He looked to Jess's gun, then his glowing hand. They didn't stand a chance against a troop of armed men. They had to hide, or run, or think of something. Anything.

The boots stopped. They'd run out of time.

'Come on in,' called the Mayor. 'Have your guns ready.'

The metal door rolled slowly upwards, but as it did, the sound changed. A howling wind followed by an odd gasping sound.

The air turned ice-cold. The mayor's smile faltered. Then the doors rolled up and the smile vanished altogether.

There, littered across the cobbles of the square lay the bodies of his unconscious soldiers. A grey mist writhed in the air, curling tight around their throats. And in the centre of the mist were three pairs of blue, glowing eyes.

CHAPTER 25
OUTNUMBERED

Luke didn't need to see their faces to know this was bad news. The Ghost Council had found them. Every bone in his body told him to run, but he stayed rooted to the spot, unable to look away. They didn't stand a chance.

The mist thinned and the Crone, the Reverend and the Plague Doctor stepped out, semi-transparent in the dim warehouse light. Jess inched back towards the shelves. Even the Mayor, for once, lost his swagger.

'No Alma?' said the Crone, tapping her cane. 'I'm disappointed.'

The Doctor rasped.

'Agreed,' said the Reverend. 'Must have seen sense and left.'

Luke felt a tiny thread of hope amongst the dread. If they expected Alma to be with him, they mustn't have caught her. But, then, where was she?

He forced himself to speak. 'What is it you want?'

'Isn't it obvious?' the Crone said. 'We want you gone, half-ghost. Always have. You're a threat to the balance, to the wall between realms, and to us. But now, finally, we have council approval. The vote was cast yesterday. You're to become a full ghost, whether you like it or not.'

Luke swallowed. 'What if I choose life? If I promise not to cross over?'

'Your word is worthless,' said the Reverend. 'It's action that's needed. But don't worry about death, you're halfway already. We'll make it look like an accident. An electrical failure.'

Luke's heart beat painfully in his chest. Had the council really approved this? Would they really kill him?

'Let me speak to Methuselah. I'll argue my case!'

The Plague Doctor croaked. A strand of his mist crept towards them.

'That's a no,' said the Crone. 'But we've come a long way; we may as well have a little bit of fun now we're here. You can have the first move, like in one of your precious chess games. How about a head start?'

'Run!' shouted Jess. 'Back the way we came!'

Luke glanced back. The others were already at the warehouse

shelves, disappearing within the rows. If they reached the grate they'd come through, might the ghosts miss them?

He ran, but a sharp cry drew his eyes back. The Mayor was tugging desperately at his black leather boot. What on earth was he doing?

Then Luke noticed the ice. Great claws of the stuff hooked round the black leather, trailing back to where the Crone stood.

'Help!' shouted the Mayor. 'I can't get them off!'

The grey mist reached him, snaked up his legs, waist, neck. His words became garbled. He grasped at his throat.

Luke slowed. He'd reached the shelves, could hear the others lifting the grate. He had to keep going. He couldn't help the Mayor now.

But the Mayor wasn't done. Though he gasped for air, with one last effort, he brought his huge fists down to the ground, shattering the ice round his boots. With an angry cry, he leapt forward. For a second he looked free – triumphant, even – but the cloak round his neck dragged him hard to the floor, where its velvet folds had frozen stiff.

The Reverend stepped towards him. 'My turn.' He raised his hand, as though giving a blessing. His palm glowed blue.

'For interfering. Heart or head? Any preference?'

Luke didn't stop to find out. He turned and ran as the air crackled blue behind him.

Thump. Thump. Thump. Thump.

That feeling again. His heart pounding, the static in the air, the lightning building somewhere inside his body.

'Whatever you're planning, half-ghost,' the Crone's voice echoed, 'It won't make a difference.'

'Except to his name.' The Reverend chuckled. 'We'll have to call him full ghost.'

Luke ignored them and ran deeper into the aisles of towering shelves, searching for his friends.

He spied Terence through a gap: he was at the grate. Jess and Radhika must have got down there already. If Luke could reach it before the ghosts saw, it might at least buy some time. Then maybe, just maybe, Alma might arrive . . .

Thump. Thump. Thump. Creeeak.

The charge kept building. He'd never felt it this strong. It flowed from the cables underground up through his feet. He let the energy gather inside him, with fear and hope.

Terence had disappeared. If he could just make it to the

opening before they saw . . .

Thirty feet . . . Twenty feet . . . Fifteen feet . . . Ten . . .

He skidded to a stop by the opening and reached for the cover.

'Ah,' said the Reverend, striding out from a shelf ahead. 'That's where they went. A drain. How embarrassing.'

Luke felt sick. Not only had they seen him, but they knew where everyone else had gone too. The Crone and the Doctor appeared behind the Reverend.

'So cowardly,' said the Crone. 'But what do you expect?'

They stepped forward. Ice and mist crept across the floor. But if it was meant to intimidate him, it did quite the opposite. Something stirred red and hot inside Luke.

'You're the cowards. It's three against one.'

Thump. Thump. Thump. Creeeak.

His hand glowed orange, the power throbbing fire-bright. For a moment, the ice and mist faltered.

'Intriguing,' said the Reverend. 'The half-ghost lightning. How delightful to see it first-hand. It's worse than I thought. The wall between realms is practically shaking.' His own fist glowed white-hot, dwarfing Luke's light like the sun to a candle. 'Forgive me, boy, if I'm not in the least bit worried.'

Luke hesitated. His own lightning had never been brighter, but the Reverend's was blinding. A stormbreaker, Alma had called him, and now he saw why. But he had to try.

'Not worried? Prove it. Leave those two out of it. Let's fight one-on-one.'

'One-on-*half*,' said the Reverend. 'Why not? A duel. Like in the old days.'

'Start from three. And at zero, we fire.'

The Reverend shrugged, unfazed. Luke felt the heat of his opponent's lightning even ten feet away. The scent of ozone zinged in the air.

But Luke didn't need that power. He had another idea.

Three . . .

Two . . .

Luke dived for the drain early, but not a moment too soon, just missing the bolt from the Reverend, who had also turned before time.

He returned fire. Not at the Reverend, but the shelves behind him, where Tabatha's red vials – a whole warehouse of them – ignited in an instant.

As he fell towards the icy water, shouting to his friends to dive, he heard an explosion like a thousand storms.

He sank beneath the water as a burst of fiery air blasted its surface. He held his breath, then emerged, and looked around at his friends – all fine – and up at the grate opening, where a roaring red blazed. Even twenty feet down, the heat was near unbearable. He didn't dare to think what it was like above.

He turned to Jess, Radhika and Terence, their heads dripping, and in the light of the flames, he noticed something else. The dank, water-filled tunnel was not so full as before.

The waterline had lowered. It indeed had been a tidal channel, but the tide had been going out, not in. And most important of all, at the furthest end, there was light – the shimmer of moonlight on waves. It was a smugglers' escape tunnel after all!

'Before this whole thing collapses, can I suggest that we go that way?' Jess said.

They surfaced minutes later under one of the jetties in the port. The streets were swarming with people running from the fire. Though 'fire' was an understatement – it was a veritable inferno. Crimson flames shot miles into the black night sky, while the warehouse was engulfed in a cloud of molten red. Heat blazed across the water in waves, melting a nearby postbox.

Nothing could have survived a heat of that magnitude. The three councillors had been surrounded on all sides. They didn't stand a chance.

And yet, what was that? A pale grey mist darted in the square, dancing around the front of the warehouse.

Had they brought reinforcements?

Then, in the depths of the mist, he caught a glimpse of black curls. And was that – yes, it was – a waistcoat and a dress!

'Over here!' he called.

The mist stopped, swirled, then shot over the waves right towards them. It coalesced under the jetty into a worried-looking Alma.

'Oh gosh,' she said, rushing up to each of them, with damp, heartfelt hugs. She even hugged Terence. 'Thank God you're alive. I thought . . .' She glanced back at the warehouse. 'Well, thankfully, I thought wrong.'

'You took your time,' said Radhika. 'Where have you been?'

Alma shook her head. 'Here! I've been here all bloomin' night! I drew away the ghosts, like I said, but when I went back, you'd gone. I checked the trees, the hills, but the trail had gone cold: not even footprints. So I hid in the docks and watched the streets and boats, and somehow, you appeared in the sea from nowhere. How on earth did you get here?'

'Cheesemobile,' said Jess.

Alma frowned. 'Anyway, once that horrible mist came, it was impossible to see. I didn't realise what was happening until I saw the explosion.' She glanced across to the fire. 'I assume the Crone and her cronies are in there?'

'They *were*,' said Luke. 'Though I doubt there's that much left of them now.'

There was a thunder of footsteps on the jetty above. People were fleeing the town, jumping on to boats and paddling out to sea.

'They've got the right idea,' said Terence. 'It's freezing. Can we get a move on?'

After a few shivery minutes of under-jetty wading, they climbed the ladder to their boat. Though they'd only been away a night, it felt much longer. Bedraggled and draped in seaweed, they stood shivering and grinning. They'd done it. They'd made it. They'd reached the sea.

The door creaked open and Stealth poked his head out. His whiskers twitched.

'I'm with Stealth,' said Alma. 'Let's head in and warm up before anything else happens.'

The others walked in but Luke waited, looking out across the waves. The sky was ink-blue. The near-full moon floated high above, but on the horizon sat an orangey haze – a warm, syrupy colour. Was it night or dawn? Or somewhere in between?

He shook his head. For a fleeting moment, in the amber glow, he thought he had seen a shadow on the water. The shadow had raised up its hand, as though in greeting, then it had disappeared with the waves.

Luke shivered. He watched the horizon a little longer, but nothing. Maybe he'd imagined it. Maybe he hadn't. But right now, all he cared about was getting some rest.

CHAPTER 26
AT SEA

It was early in the morning, the wind was calm, and puffs of white splattered the sky. A mile below them in the gusty salt air, the sea was painted with the shadows of the clouds – a swan-shadow, a kite-shadow, one that looked like an anchor, and a shoal of smaller minnow-like clouds. Where the light hit the sea, it reflected it back, bright like silver.

'For some reason,' said Luke. 'I thought it'd look more blue.' He kicked his feet over the edge. 'But from up here, with the sun, it's more like metal.'

'Yeah,' said Alma. 'Like all the mirrors melted and started swilling around.'

Luke couldn't help but smile. They were over the sea and talking nonsense because for the first time in days, they were out of danger. They'd left the ghosts and the Mayor far behind and, though plenty of peril waited over the horizon, for now, he wanted to relish the freedom of the sea.

He'd only seen it from the beach, never this high up – so the moment the sun had risen, he'd dragged Alma to the sky and they'd watched it sleepily. Even Alma, who liked the sound of her own voice more than most, seemed happy just to breathe it in and let the world drift below, with their little boat rumbling across the empty waves.

Jess was patching up the hull – 'boat plumbing', she called it – while Stealth watched with mild curiosity. Radhika, for her part, had her face in the maps, scowling but in a focused (not spitting) kind of way. Terence sat on deck rubbing his fingers. He'd barely said a word since the warehouse and Luke wasn't complaining.

'They're so quiet,' said Alma, removing her waistcoat and letting it slip into her cloud. 'The sea's quiet too. On the shore, it's so noisy. Waves breaking, dragging, all that frothing on the sand. Not to mention the seagulls and tourists. But out here, it feels still.' A briny breeze ruffled her hair and she breathed in deep. 'And it smells amazing.'

'I just can't believe that you've never come out here before.'

She squinted at the horizon. 'Seaside, yes. Out here, no. The council say it's not safe. That the ghosts that cross it don't always come back.' She frowned. 'But maybe that's because it's so nice out here.'

In many ways, the sea was a lot like the sky. Not just the colour, but how it moved. It was always changing, even its texture: sometimes bobbly like fabric, other times smooth like steel.

The anchor-shaped cloud passed high overhead, plunging them into shadow. It swallowed the boat in darkness and Luke's thoughts turned back to what lay ahead.

'Alma,' he said, 'How on earth are we going to get past her?'

'We'll think of something. We always do.'

She was right, Luke thought. They had managed so far. Who was to say they wouldn't now? Maybe soon, he and Ravi would be sailing home free. Not only free from her, but from guilt. They needed their luck to hold a little longer. Just two more days.

CLANG. CLANG. CLANG.

Luke looked down to see a little blonde dot jumping about on deck, bashing pots together. She managed to make a racket even out here.

'The breakfast meeting,' Luke said. 'We'd better head in.'

'Do we have to?' Alma sighed. 'I don't even eat food.'

'Well, I do. And we've a friend to save.'

Minutes later, they were sitting round the map, tucking into cheese they'd nabbed from the crate and a stack of burnt toast from their temperamental toaster. Radhika pointed to a spot between England and the European coast. 'We're here in neutral waters, and we're safe for now, but the Dover Strait won't be — it's as busy as anything and the coastguard might spot us. The best option is to hold tight and travel at night.'

Jess peered over. Luke caught a waft of pineapple. Somehow, she was still chewing Oberdink's putty. 'What are these? They look like hedgehogs.'

'Not up close,' said Luke. 'They're sea-mines. We need to navigate the gap between them and this windfarm to reach Tabatha's base.'

Alma looked to Terence. 'This is where you joke that we'll all be blown up.'

Terence just sighed and walked back inside.

'Do you think he's OK?' said Jess. 'He's been weird since the warehouse. Didn't touch his cheese.' She looked at Luke. 'It's almost as if he didn't want you to save him from the Mayor.'

'I heard him muttering in his sleep,' Luke said. 'I think he's nervous about Tabatha.'

They fell silent; Terence wasn't alone. For all their talk of stopping her, there was very little discussion about what happened if they didn't. Luke shivered. Something too horrible to imagine, no doubt.

'Anyway,' said Radhika. 'I'd suggest you all rest up. We'll be sailing through the night. I'll need you alert.'

And though Luke wanted to prepare, to make every second count, he had no choice but to wait. The day passed in a haze of sunshine and salty spray. He spent the afternoon making a rod from some driftwood and fishing on deck. He didn't catch anything – there were barely any fish in the Channel these days. It had been one of the many reasons for the war, his dad had said. Nobody could agree who the fish belonged to, so they all kept fishing until there were none left to fight over. That was one way of solving it, he supposed.

'No luck?' said Jess, who was hanging off some ropes to polish the hull, inches from the waves.

'No, but I don't mind. It's more to pass the time.'

'Yeah.' She peeled a barnacle off the boat. 'It's funny what's fun. Like this boat malarkey. I'm not sure I'm good at it, but I've really enjoyed it.'

'Not good at it *yet*,' Luke said. 'These things take time.'

A cold breeze picked up on the water. Dusk had fallen quickly. On the horizon, he spied the distant light of boats. Huge boats, if the height of them was anything to go by.

'We'd better go in. If we can see them, they can see us.'

Dinner was a sombre affair. They had turned their lights off, so as not to be seen, but the sheer level of darkness had caught them off guard. The black water swelled around them, the moon had disappeared beneath the clouds, and only the ship's radar kept them on track. Eating proved difficult – a fair bit of Luke's dinner spilt right down his shirt – though strangely in the dark, everything tasted better: the cheese tasted cheesier, the toast toastier, and the tea was malty and hot.

By the middle of the straits, the waves from much bigger vessels rocked their little boat so badly, they just sat there quietly, trying not think about sinking.

'Radhika,' said Jess, 'are you sure I can't go on deck?'

'Yep. It's not safe. A wave from a cargo-ship or a ferry could knock you overboard and we'd never find you in the dark like this.'

'Fine. So where's the best place to be sick?'

'Oh . . . Can you swallow it?'

'Erm. I can try.'

After what seemed like an eternity, they passed the last big ship and reached calmer waters.

'Guys, I think we're clear.'

The lights went on and Radhika smiled. Luke hadn't realised until then how stressed she'd been.

'We did it! Really?' Jess grabbed Radhika's hand and gave a little dance. 'So what do we do now?'

Radhika looked with dismay at the food on the floor. 'Clean up?'

Stealth's ears pricked up. On the waves, through the black, a voice carried. They rushed to the window. There was only darkness.

'Is it the coastguard?'

'Shh,' said Radhika. 'I don't know yet, do I?'

But as the seconds passed, the voices multiplied. First to a few, then a group, then an excited babble. Despite the noise, Luke couldn't make out a word. It made him uneasy.

'They're close now.' Radhika looked nervous. 'If we hit them, we might sink. Where on earth are their lights?'

As if in answer, a torch flickered on, about thirty feet off. It seemed to be drifting away. In the glow, Luke saw a flurry of movement.

'Phew,' said Radhika. 'We're fine. They've passed us already.'

'But look.' Jess was pointing. 'They're not fine at all.'

A lantern had now lit up the vessel. It wasn't a boat, but a raft made of barrels and wood and tied with rope. And it was crammed to the edges with people in tattered life jackets, moving in a blur of activity. It looked like they were shovelling. But shovelling with their hands.

'What are they doing?'

Luke swallowed. 'They're bailing out water. The raft is sinking.'

Nobody said anything. Over the roil of waves, a baby was crying.

'They wouldn't fit on this boat,' said Luke. 'We can't save them. We can't.'

Everyone nodded. All he heard was their silence.

CHAPTER 27
ONE GOOD TURN

They watched the makeshift boat a little longer. It could have only been seconds, but it felt like an age. There was a man fiddling with a rusty engine, tapping it. The woman holding the baby was crying now too, while a small boy tugged at her skirt.

They were so busy with their boat they hadn't noticed Luke and the others. Give it another minute and they'd be out of view altogether. Part of Luke actually wanted them out of sight. Part of him wished he'd never seen them at all.

But now he had, he couldn't get them out of his mind.

'Dying's normal,' said Alma. 'You can't save them all.'

'Or any of them, in this case,' added Terence, gloomily.

Something stirred in Luke's mind. 'But, Alma, that time we helped the baby at soulrise, didn't you say it was the journey that counted? Shouldn't we at least make theirs a little better?'

Before Alma could reply, the boat began turning. Luke looked around. Jess was at the wheel.

'Jess, what are you doing?'

'Something,' she snapped. 'We can't just talk. They've almost gone under.'

That was all it took for their collective resistance to crumble. Luke and Radhika gathered up materials for repairs. Terence, grumbling, checked for blankets and food. Alma helped with the tarp, though it kept slipping through her fingers, until Luke had an idea.

'Alma, couldn't you bail out the water?'

Luke practically saw the lightbulb turn on in her head. A great cloud of mist fell upon the dinghy – a freshwater mist that smelt of morning dew. Then as quick as it had appeared, it was gone. The boatpeople stood there, dry and clean – even their hair looked washed – in a raft bailed entirely of water. They looked around in shock, and when Alma appeared by Luke's side, one of the men almost jumped out of the boat.

'I read their thoughts too,' she said, smiling. 'They think I'm a miracle. A gift from God. Though a couple are worried I might be a demon.'

'Maybe they're all right,' said Luke, grinning.

Alma ignored this. 'There's a problem though: a dodgy radar.

It broke hours ago and they don't know the way.'

'What?' said Jess. 'They'll never make it. We have to take them!'

Terence choked. 'There's no space as it is!'

He was right. There wasn't. And even if there had been, they'd need food, water. And they could hardly take them *back* to Europe – to Tabatha.

Luke looked at the raft people, their eyes tired with hope. There were so many of them, and only one of Ravi.

Somewhere, in the darkness, the baby was wailing once more.

'I'll lead them back,' said Radhika, quietly. 'I'll use the compass. I know the way and all the coves on the coast.' She gazed out to sea. 'The water's calm. If we go now, we'll be fine.'

'But Radhika, we need you here.'

'So do they,' she said. 'And you don't, not really. I've shown you the maps and, Luke, you're a natural. Worst case, Alma can fly ahead. And Jess here's better at fixing boats than I ever will be.'

'But . . .' Luke said, struggling, 'we haven't finished. Your brother's still out there.'

She put her hand on Luke's. 'And if anyone can save him, I know it's you.' She unhooked the dinghy. 'It's what he'd want, I think – my parents too. They came here in a boat. They'll know what to do to help these people. Who knows, it might even give them something to live for.' She began inflating the dinghy. Stealth padded up to her side, as though to say goodbye.

Radhika looked at Jess and Luke. 'If I can, I'll tell your parents you're safe, and to leave the city. And I'll be rooting for you.'

Luke wanted to stop her, but it wasn't his choice. And deep down, he knew she was right. *When you know, you know*, as his mum had said.

But when Radhika and the raft disappeared into the dark, it still felt wrong.

'I'll miss her,' said Luke. 'I thought she might stay.'

Jess shook her head. 'I still can't quite get my head round it all . . . Those people would have died. Why would anyone take that risk?'

'Isn't it obvious?' said Terence. 'To start again. To get a second chance.' He shook his head. 'Some kinds of life are worse than death.'

The clouds moved and a shaft of moonlight fell on the boat. Luke looked up. It was almost full. Beside it, cirrus clouds stretched out like snow-covered headlands. Beyond, the constellations twinkled, watching.

He sighed. His breath misted in the cold night air. Then he

turned back into the boat and shut the door tight behind him.

Inside, the cabin was horribly quiet. Radhika hadn't talked much, but he heard her absence everywhere. The maps stared at him from the table. The wheel creaked unmanned. He wondered if its wood was still warm from her hands.

The others felt it too. Alma stood silently, gazing out the window. Jess made tea, but without the usual clatter. Stealth, always noiseless, was even stealthier than normal. Terence had disappeared below deck.

But when Luke thought of her out there on the water, along with the worry came courage. She was making a difference. She'd taken a risk. Now they had to make it count.

He checked his watch. The full moon was only one space away. One more night. 'Alma, we'd better go. We have to recce the base before it gets light.'

'You sure you're ready?'

'I never feel ready. It hasn't stopped me yet.'

He made his way to his bed and lay down. Closing his eyes, he readied his mind the way he always did. He thought of the sky, rain, clouds and wind. Then of death, the End Place, and his mum waiting beyond. He loosened his links to the world of the living; he embraced those that pulled him beyond. Slowly, the shapes beyond his lids blurred to shadow. Sounds became muted. A sense of weightlessness, drifting, up and out of his body . . .

'Wait!'

He opened his eyes. Below him lay his body on the bed where he'd left it, but beside it, someone sat trying to shake him awake. The figure looked like Terence and yet not like him at all. His hair was washed. His face de-greased. Soapy water glistened on his arms in the moonlight.

Luke drifted down behind him and tapped the man's shoulder with a finger that slipped right through. 'You showered, Terence?'

Terence spun round. 'Erm. Yes. It's no big deal.'

'Did you bash your head?' Jess asked. 'You sure you're well?'

'I-I'm fine. I've just been thinking.'

'Well, that makes a change,' Alma said.

Terence took a deep breath. 'I'm serious. I've been trying to figure something out.' He looked down at his bandaged fingers. 'When you stopped the Mayor hurting me in the warehouse, I didn't get it. I was so horrible to you in Battersea. You had every right to want some payback.' He sniffed. 'But you didn't. And then with that raft, today, you did it again.'

Luke frowned. 'Did what?'

'You were . . . *kind.*' Terence grimaced, as if it hurt his mouth to say it. 'You did the right thing. You helped another even though there was nothing in it for you.'

'Doesn't everyone?' said Jess.

'Not where I'm from,' said Terence. 'Where I'm from, there are other rules. But one of them is this: if someone saves your life, you owe them. And I figure I owe you.'

'Owe us what?'

'Some saving.' He walked up to the map and placed a grease-free finger on it. 'This channel between the mines that you're about to fly down . . . don't. Tabatha patrols it. She has boats with ghost-guns and she'll suck you right up. There's another way. A path through the wind farms to a secret cove.'

Jess put down her tea. 'A secret cove? Wow, thanks, Terence.'

'No,' Alma said. 'He told us to go down that channel in the first place! He was setting us up to be gobbled by a ghost-gun!' Her fist crackled blue. 'Give me one good reason I shouldn't zap you right now.'

Terence stepped back. 'Because I'm telling the truth. Because

I've changed my mind.'

The boat was silent, save for the slosh of waves. Luke looked at Terence. He didn't know why, but he believed him. Ever since the warehouse, he'd been different. There'd been no snide remarks. No smirks or scowls. He'd been quieter. Thoughtful. Burdened, somehow.

Alma was having none of it. 'He can't just take a shower and expect us to trust him. What if he's lying again?'

'He might be,' Luke said, 'but I don't think he is. And it isn't logical, either. If he wanted to trap us, why change his story? I can't think of a motive.' He looked at him. 'What changed? Why now?'

Terence sighed. Without the grease, his face looked flaky, tired. 'I don't know. I just *feel* different.' He squirmed, as though the words cost him. 'And because you saved my life, and nobody's ever done that. Because you're nice to me, and Tabatha never is. Because saving those people on the raft felt good, and I've never felt that before. I'm tired of being bad. I want to start again too.' He looked at Luke. 'And because, if I'm honest, I think you have a chance.'

Jess bit her lip. 'But you've always said it's impossible. That Tabatha's base is a ghost-proof fortress.'

'It is . . . but I nabbed these.' Terence reached into his pocket and pulled out three glass vials filled with red liquid flames. The light danced across the dark cabin. He must have pocketed them as they escaped the warehouse. 'Tabatha's weapon's in the zeppelin, and the zeppelin's ghost-proof. But these little bad boys, they'll do the trick.'

Terence stepped forward and put the vials in Luke's hand. 'Now do you trust me?'

'Well,' said Luke, 'it's certainly a start.'

CHAPTER 28
THE PLAN

An hour later, with their mist skimming low on the sea's dark skin, Luke and Alma stared uneasily at the horizon.

'I don't trust him,' said Alma.

'I'm not sure we've a choice.'

'At least by the end of the night, we'll know.'

Terence hadn't only told them a route, he'd given them a plan. His map of the base had every camera, watchtower and patrol route marked on it. He'd drawn an 'X' on every ghost-gun hidden in the vents. He'd explained how the cove was unguarded, on account of the sea-mines, which made approach by boat impossible unless you cut the cable that powered them, which was hidden in the gardens.

He'd not only saved them, but perhaps London too.

Though to be fair, he had also hedged his bets, so whatever side won, he'd be assured of safety. He'd made them promise that they'd never tell Tabatha, that if they failed – which, he reminded them, was still highly likely — they were to tell her he was horrible, cruel and a veritable monster. Terence had even made them put his chains back on, so he could claim to be their prisoner if Tabatha found them.

He was a funny old man.

'Wait, what's that?'

In the distance, a light flickered before being swallowed by waves. A boat, perhaps? It reappeared, fuzzy through the spray. No, the colour was different — a warm glow, not a boat's bright beam. It was too high on the water. And the way it moved too . . . a boat bobbed, drifted, but this light hadn't budged.

It could only mean one thing. Land!

A rush of excitement brightened Luke's mist. Another light appeared, and then two, three more, a string of sequins on the black horizon. To the right swayed the dark-feathered tops of trees. To the left, jagged rocks curled lazily in the water. The shape of the coastline matched Terence's map exactly — this had to be it.

But as the building emerged, it wasn't what Luke had expected. It was not at all like Battersea. Neat-rowed windows shone pretty and welcoming, its elegant roof sloped smooth and tiled, and a grey stone cross topped its central tower. It looked like a convent, and a nice one at that. It had flower-beds, lawns and soft-clipped trees, hanging baskets, gravel paths and statues in the garden. Not a chimney or a barbed wire fence in sight.

Then Luke thought to look down and saw a different welcome. Through the waves, the spikes of sea-mines poked up to greet him. Like hungry fish, they jostled for position.

'The whole bay is full of them. Terence wasn't lying.'

'There's still time for that.'

They veered right towards a moss-patched mooring post by the forest, then pulled in their mists and stepped on to damp earth. Pine needles pushed gently at Luke's feet and he felt the cool mud that lay beneath them.

This was Europe. They'd finally made it. They had faced off with the council, the Mayor and the treacherous seas. They'd left home, family, everything behind, and yet . . .

'Is it me? Or does it feel—'

'Just like home.' Alma finished his thought.

The grass, the trees, the moist evening air – they were all so familiar. He crouched and ran his fingers through a clump of clover. 'I expected it to feel different. Dangerous. European.'

'But there *is* something different. Really quite different.' Alma looked up through the trees. 'There are no clouds. Not one. I don't like it at all.'

Alma was right. Above the branches and the base hung a purple-black sky, the stars, the moon, but not a shred of a cloud. Luke hadn't noticed before; he'd been so fixed on the base. There was something very wrong about this place. He looked at the building across the bay. In an upper window, a shadow moved.

'Be extra careful,' he said. 'You heard Terence. Stick low, by the gardens and walls, and don't even try to enter the building, remember?'

'Roger that, amigo. See you here in fifteen.'

They split up and Luke followed the path through the woods. It was unguarded, unremarkable, just like Terence had promised, but as he neared its edge, he heard something new.

Swish. Thwack. Squelch. Swish.

The noises made him think of Battersea. But the swish was sharp, like the point of a spade. Luke walked towards it. Through thickets and trees emerged a swathe of red.

It was a field of poppies. One-eyed, black-staring, hairy-stalked things, that rippled on the surface like a pool of blood in the breeze. They poked finger-like from the black-oozing mud, spearing the air with their acrid scent. Luke had never smelt anything like it. Acid, sweet, sickly, cloying. No wonder the figures walking up and down the fields were sealed in white rubber suits.

Swish. Thwack. Squelch. Swish.

The blades sliced the flower-heads into baskets; the boots squelched through the inky mud. It was like the files had said: poppies on the battlefields, their roots drenched in graves of those long dead, harvesting soul-residue for who knew what.

He scanned the workers. For a field so big, there weren't many – maybe twenty or so. It was hard to see their faces through the visors. He moved closer, while staying part-hidden in the forest edge. He watched them slicing back and forth, the red petal juice sticking, staining, sizzling against suits.

Swish. Thwack. Squelch. Swish.

Then he saw it. Not a face, but a walk. A steady, strong, small-stepped walk – square of chin and straight of back.

It was Ravi.

And he was heading this way.

CHAPTER 29
THE FIELDS

Ravi approached, sickle in hand, swishing it back and forth across the red. Luke couldn't believe it. He felt like something might burst inside.

His friend was alive. Everything they'd been through was suddenly worth it.

Sixty feet . . . Fifty feet . . . Forty feet . . . Thirty . . .

He was closer now, near the edge of the field. He looked taller, his face a little darker. Luke wondered how else he might have changed and felt a twinge of nerves. It had been months since Battersea. What if he'd made new friends? Or if they had nothing to say to each other any more?

Twenty-five . . . Twenty . . . Fifteen feet . . .

After the nerves came a tight knot in Luke's chest. Guilt. All those months, that summer, Luke had done nothing to help him. He'd studied for his guild exams, flown with Alma and fished in the sun . . . while Ravi had suffered alone in this nightmare of a place. What kind of friend did that? The thought shivered through him, settling on his shoulders.

Then he shook it off. He hadn't done this: *she* had. And now he had a chance to fix it.

He stepped out from his shelter.

Ravi froze. The sickle slipped from his hand. He stared at Luke's faint outline without speaking, his features twisted in confusion and fear.

'Luke?' Ravi swallowed. 'Is that you?'

Luke nodded. A breeze caught him; his edges blurred.

Ravi's eyes widened. 'You're a ghost? No . . . They said you were safe. A detective. In London—' The words caught in his throat. 'What happened? Did she get you?'

'No, I'm fine!' He remembered that Ravi had only seen him as a ghost once. It took some getting used to. 'I'm alive. It's just a half-ghost thing.'

'Phew, I thought . . .' He rubbed his eyes through the visor. 'You know,' he said, his voice quiet. 'I never really thought I'd see you again.'

'I thought the same, if I'm honest.'

'I'm glad we were wrong.'

He reached out a white-gloved hand towards Luke's chest, where his heart would have been. Ravi held it there a second, then pulled it back. 'Sorry. I'm not sure why I did that. I still can't believe you're here.'

'It's OK. I don't mind.'

It was more than OK. It was good. Great. It seemed crazy that he'd ever worried what he'd say, when the truth was that he didn't need to say anything at all. Just seeing Ravi, just breathing the same air was enough.

Luke grinned and Ravi grinned back. It was still Ravi's smile: mischievous, dry, rarely shared.

A sharp cry sounded from across the field. Ravi glanced back, suddenly tense. A guard was shouting, his back towards them. They were safe, for now.

'It's weird,' said Ravi, 'but sometimes at night, when the bunk creaks, I pretend it's you. That if I can hold off checking till the morning, when I wake up, you'll be there.' He gave a small, hard laugh. 'I'm guess I'm going crazy.'

'That makes two of us. I keep dreaming we're hiding in cupboard full of blankets.'

Ravi laughed properly that time, and Luke felt the warmth surge inside him. It washed away any lingering doubts. This was why he'd come. He'd come to save his friend. Everything would be OK.

Thwack. Thwack. Thwack.

In the distance, the guard beat a worker with a stick.

Ravi winced. 'Look, you'd better go. It's not safe for you here.'

'Go?' Luke said. 'But we just got here. We're here to save you.'

'We? What?' Ravi's voice trembled. 'You mean like, the ghosts?'

'No – Jess, me and Alma. We've a boat, your boat. Just off the coast.'

And like that, Ravi's face changed. His eyes darkened. Concern became anger. His lips curled like Radhika's, but sharper, harder. 'You're here?' His features shook with fury and fear. 'Are you crazy, Luke? Sail back, right now! You great big idiot!'

'Idiot? But . . . I thought you'd be happy!'

Another sound started, a distant buzz. Ravi looked up. His left hand began tugging at his right. 'I *was* happy, knowing you were in London. Safe. With Jess. Doing your training.' He snatched his sickle from the ground. 'That's what's kept me going. But you've just thrown it away!'

'We haven't thrown it away. We're making it count.'

'Then count me out,' he hissed.

The buzzing grew louder. A dot appeared on the horizon and grew.

'You don't know this place, Luke. Every day, Tabatha adds new defences. The guards have knives. There are ghost-guns everywhere. And ghosts that are caught go to the lab – to be tested on.' He shook his head. 'Promise me you'll leave. Right now. Promise! Don't go near the house, or the gardens. Go back the way you came.'

The dot was now a zeppelin, and it neared the field's edge. A purple searchlight began swinging back and forth. There was something unnatural about the quality of the light.

'But, Ravi, we can't just leave you!'

'You have to – because if you try to save me, I swear I'll . . . I'll . . . I'll jump in that bay and let the sea-mines get me. I'm not letting you all throw your lives away.'

The searchlights swung ever nearer. Ravi turned back.

Swish. Thwack. Squelch. Swish.

And just like that, he was moving. Walking away.

'But I can't go back!' Luke shouted. 'She burnt my home. She's going to attack London.'

Ravi carried on as though he hadn't heard.

The warmth in Luke's chest slipped away like the tide; his doubts crashed inside him. This wasn't meant to happen. The full moon was tomorrow. He'd come all this way.

Luke had to persuade him. Where had he gone wrong? He played the conversation back, but as he did, something stuck in his mind.

'Wait, Ravi, what's wrong with the gardens?' Luke asked, as the engines rumbled closer. 'Terence said they were safe. Alma's there now.'

Ravi stopped, but didn't turn. 'They *were* safe, until Tabatha put in new traps.' He sighed, then his sickle swung back through the poppies. 'I'm sorry, Luke, but Alma isn't coming back.'

CHAPTER 30
THE VISITOR

'He said to go home. He said he wouldn't come back.'

The sea outside shook dark and restless, making the flames inside the boat's stove jump. Luke warmed his hands before it but stayed cold to his bones. Not even Stealth sitting on his lap could keep the chill away.

'Don't be silly,' said Jess. 'You must have misunderstood. Maybe he was joking?'

Luke shook his head. 'And Alma's still not back yet.'

He felt sick. They had to save Ravi tomorrow – that's what Ma Boxhill had said – but had losing Alma been part of the bargain? She'd mentioned sacrifice, but he never thought she'd meant this. They couldn't do it without Alma. And the thought of her trapped in some lab . . . It was suddenly difficult to breathe.

A jangle from the corner. Terence was fiddling with the chains he'd asked for, in case Tabatha found them. He'd sworn to Luke he hadn't known about the traps in the garden, but looking at him, Luke felt a rising anger. Had he tricked them? Or perhaps he never cared? He could always go running back to Tabatha.

Thump. Thump. Thump. Thump.

Luke's hand glowed, draining power from the boat's frail generator. Jess looked up in alarm.

'Terence,' Luke said, heat building inside him. 'You must know something. How do we get Alma back?'

Terence squirmed. 'I told you, I don't know. Tabatha never let me inside the lab.'

'You're lying.' Luke's fist crackled. 'I know you are!'

'Stop!' Jess stepped between them and the light left his hand. 'Terence is as afraid as we are. You know what Tabatha will do if she finds out he helped.' She picked up a pad from the table. 'Let's go through it again, one step at a time. First, the base. Did Alma deactivate the mines? Could we sail in and save her?'

'No,' Luke said. Despair crept up his throat, battling his anger. 'I checked as I left – they're still connected.'

'Then let's brainstorm. Any ideas?'

The boards creaked in the silence. The engine puttered over the slosh of waves.

'I've got one,' said Terence. 'Listen to Ravi. Turn back. It's the only option.'

'Shut up! You're lying! There must be a way . . .'

'I'm lying?' Terence laughed bitterly. 'Look in the mirror. You're lying to yourself. With Alma, you had options. But now you've none. Zero. Zilch.' He shook his head. 'You're just afraid of giving up, of failing like the rest of us. You'd rather bury your head in the sand and your friends in it too.' He leant in, his voice low. 'Have you forgotten what she's like? What she'll do when she finds you? She'll take it slow, Luke. She'll savour your suffering. She'll start with your friends and she'll make you watch, and then—'

'Be quiet!' Luke's fist began to spark hot orange. Terence scowled and slunk away to the corner. Jess was staring at him now and Luke couldn't bear it. He was acting like a child, losing his temper. Ashamed, he turned and walked to the window. The light drained from his hands as he watched the waves.

Maybe Terence was right. He'd lost Alma; he couldn't risk Jess too.

High above the waves, the moon watched, almost full. Before it had promised, counted the days. But it was silent now.

He wondered, had it ever really whispered? Had the 'glimpse' with Ma Boxhill meant anything at all? The moon was just a rock. A lifeless rock. Circling the Earth through space at dizzying speed which, despite all its effort, never got anywhere.

He wasn't much different. He'd made every second count. He'd never stopped to rest. And yet he was still trapped, with no end in sight.

He looked down at his mum's watch and felt a swell of anger. *Make a difference. Every second counts.* It was a stupid motto. What good had it ever done for her? She'd let him down and she'd left him alone in this world. And now he'd done just the same thing to his friend.

He tore it off his wrist, eyes wet, and raised his arm, ready to throw it into the waves.

'Wait,' said Jess. 'There's something you should see.'

He held the watch tight, ready to throw. 'What? Right now?'

'The toaster. It's odd . . .'

The toaster? He wiped his eyes and turned. He saw it at once – the toaster's little LED light fluttering red. Then the lamp and kettle did the same.

A cold shiver crept up his spine. It was like the street lights by St Paul's. Like his home just before it had plunged into darkness.

Was it her? Had she found them? Had Terence told her somehow?

Thump. Thump. Thump. Creeeak.

Despite himself, his heart beat harder, the charge building. She'd have brought her men, her guns, but at least he could try.

He clenched his fist and drew on the charge running through the ship's wires. Then he felt it. Another tugging too, from across the waves. Someone – or something – was coming.

Straining, he made out a shadow. He raised his hand, burning orange, ready to fire . . . and hesitated.

There was something different this time. The shape of it. The mood. He didn't feel scared. Then the moonlight caught it, and at once he knew why.

'Ravi?'

It was the strangest sight. His friend stood on the water, his edges blurring with the wind. Faint, barely there – Luke could see the waves right through him – but it was definitely him.

'You're a half-ghost too?'

Ravi nodded. A smile flickered across his face. 'More a quarter-ghost, I'd say. Tabatha has a serum. It's kind of a long story.'

With a clatter of steps, Jess joined them at the window. Words rushed out like the tears in her eyes.

'I knew it! We've been so worried! I've missed you so much. I – I—' She stopped herself and just smiled through her tears.

Ravi grinned. 'I've missed you too, Jess.' He pulled himself up on to the boat. His mist was dark, like Tabatha's had been. 'Knowing you guys were safe is what's kept me going. When I saw Luke in the field, it was like my worst nightmare. Sorry if I lost it.'

'I guess it was a lot to take on.'

'Understatement of the year.' Ravi raised an eyebrow, just like he had used to, albeit a semi-transparent one. 'When I'd cooled off, what you said got me thinking. About your boat, about Alma, but most of all, about the attack on London. It suddenly made sense. All week she's been talking about some special shipment. The guards too. The zeppelin's prepared and ready for a journey.' He ran a hand through his dark mist-hair. 'I guess you never were safe in the first place.'

Luke shook his head. 'None of us are. Not until someone stops her.'

Ravi's jaw tightened. 'Which is why I'm here. The shipment arrives tomorrow night – Bonfire Night. We'd better get planning.'

An hour later, the three of them sat on deck, hatching escape plans just like old times, though under the stars instead of underground. Despite the danger and his fear for Alma, Luke felt lighter. They were together again.

Ravi had filled in the gaps on Terence's map, including his dorm and the lab where Alma would be being kept, which guards to zap or distract, and which dorms would help and which wouldn't. They'd even pinned down the time – 9 p.m. the next day – which was when the shipment arrived and the guards and Tabatha would be most distracted. One issue remained: how to get the boat past the sea-mines.

'Could you zap them?' asked Jess.

'Probably,' said Ravi. 'But they'd hear the explosions and raise the alarm.'

'What if I fog up the watchtower and sneak in the front?'

Ravi shook his head. 'The patrol boat has ghost-guns, as does every vent in that building. I only escaped 'cos our dorm vent has broken.'

They'd been chatting so happily that Luke had forgotten that Ravi was a ghost at the moment. He hadn't even asked how that worked. 'What about this serum? Can't you all take some and zap her?'

'No, I wish, but we're not proper ghosts. It's artificial. She makes it from the ghosts she captures, and the poppies too. We can't zap, only spark – we can't fly, only float. She keeps trying to fix it, but she can't. It's been driving her crazy.'

Luke thought back. He'd assumed that Tabatha could do what he could, but it all made sense now: she didn't have the same power. That's why she'd used petrol to burn his houseboat. She'd had no choice. She'd needed something to spark.

It wasn't much consolation. She'd still managed to destroy so much that he loved.

Over the waves, the convent bells rang for midnight. Ravi stood. 'I'd better go. Someone might check.' He ran his hand along the boat – his boat. 'I always dreamt I'd get home, but I never expected my home to come and get me.' He looked at the boat, as if it might be the last time he'd see it. A wry smile crept to his lips. 'Oh and Luke, I know how you'll reach the land, but I don't think you'll like it.'

'This whole plan scares me. It can't get much worse.'

'I don't know about that,' said Ravi. 'Have you brought your trunks?'

CHAPTER 31
FULL MOON

'Swimming?' said Terence. 'Are you utterly insane?'

As Luke stared at the dark swelling sea, in only his trunks, he saw Terence's point. It was night-time, November and there was no land in sight. What there was, however, was a bay of vicious boat-bursting sea-mines.

'It's logical, actually,' said Jess, unfazed. 'Sea-mines detect metal, vibrations, the movement of boats. If they detected swimmers, too, every fish, shark or whale would set them off.'

'Sharks?' Luke said nervously. 'I didn't think there were sharks.'

'Not here. I don't think so, anyway. It was just an example.'

They'd spent the day practising their strokes, memorising the map and plan, and then packing their belongings into wax-sealed barrels. It'd been sunny, almost cloudless, and had started off fun. But then the cold had set in. Even after thirty minutes they'd started shivering, and when they had come in to change, they had struggled with their buttons because their hands were so numb.

And that, Luke thought, was in the heat of the day. As he peered out into the night, their boat hidden amidst the turbines of an offshore windfarm, he realised the dark was a whole new proposition. The water would certainly feel colder now.

'Here, drink this,' mumbled Terence, manacles jingling as he held out some tea. 'Then get going. All your worrying is getting on my nerves.'

Luke took it gratefully. He'd apologised for his words the night before, and Terence had been quite nice about it. Luke almost felt bad for the chains, but not too bad. Terence could reach the tea, the toaster, but not the steering wheel – just in case. He also had Stealth as company. The cat had taken a liking to him ever since his shower.

'We'll be back by midnight,' Luke said. 'But if we're caught, we'll tell Tabatha where you are, so you won't be in chains long.'

'Just don't drown, OK? Or nobody will find me.' He frowned. 'And remember, if she asks, I was horrible.'

'Absolutely horrid,' said Jess, grinning. 'I've turned the boat lights all off. Sorry, Terence, it's a bit creepy.'

'Actually I like it. It reminds me of Battersea.' He gestured to the bread in the corner. 'And at least I have toast. Now, you ready? I've got chains to jangle.'

They nodded and stepped out on to the deck.

'Three . . . Two . . . One . . . Jump!'

They plunged into the water.

Cold. Everywhere, and all at once. Dark and sharp and cold. Like an ice cream headache all over his body.

Luke burst to the surface, muscles screaming, but he kept his mouth sealed. They had to be quiet. So he did the only thing he could do: he swam.

Arm after arm. Kick after kick. He pushed through the water, waves soaking his hair and the cold searing his skull.

Even in the dark, he could see through the water. Murky shadows, fishes glittering and darting, the vague shape of Jess somewhere to his right.

He tried not to think of what might be beneath him: sharks, shipwrecks, sailors' bones. Or of how if he failed, his body would sink down to meet them.

Soon his teeth chattered. His fingers grew numb. A muscle in his leg cramped for attention.

Next he felt dizzy. Distant. Heavy-limbed. And as the swell of the waves lurched him high and low, he felt nauseous too. Who knew that you could get sea-sick while swimming?

He swallowed mouthfuls of saltwater, and the water swallowed him back, the dark waves gulping him in whole.

Still, he kept swimming along the current – he could sense it, like he sensed the rain – with Jess always beside him, as though they were being pulled on by a strange, compelling force. They had no choice. They had to reach the shore: everything depended on it.

And though he crashed into his friend, and forgot to breathe and spluttered, and though his fingers stuck together and he couldn't feel his toes, eventually, the black began to change. It gave way to muddy colours, which shifted beneath them.

Something slimy grabbed at his legs, then vanished.

Jess shrieked. 'C-c-cripes!' she stuttered, her lips blue. 'W-w-what was that?'

'I don't know,' said Luke, fighting back the fear. His mind jumped to the worst. A creation of Tabatha? A creature of the dark. Or could it be . . .

The slimy fingers grasped his leg again but this time, instead of kicking, he reached down and grabbed it.

It came off in his fingers. He pulled a handful to the surface.

'Seaweed!' He grinned. 'Which m-m-means . . . we're n-n-near land! The b-b-beach must be close!'

Suddenly the energy came back to him. He found himself sprinting alongside Jess. Past the rusting spikes of entangled sea-mines. Through a forest of slimy leg-grabbing kelp. They pushed through more icy water and aching breaths. They were getting closer.

The black gave way to yellowy-grey as the sand rushed up towards them, only a few feet away. Luke wanted to stop, to check it was real, but he was so tired he feared he might not make it if he did.

Then before he knew it, they were standing. Hugging. Jumping, too. The sand wet and springy under his numb white feet. He was shivering, violently, but warm inside. They'd done it! They'd been lucky, perhaps, but the plan had worked.

He looked across the cove to the base. A solitary searchlight swept across the bay. Now they had to hope their luck held up.

After a lightning-lit fire, three pairs of socks, five biscuits and at least two mugs of hot water, Jess and Luke had stopped shivering enough to study the map. They set off, following Ravi's markings, staying low behind the rocks – stumbling and cursing their frozen feet – then cut in through tall, dark woodland, where a sweet-sap smell mixed with the salty-breeze.

The compound's outer wall rose ahead, a dry-stone thing flecked with pale-green lichen, and they spotted the crooked oak Ravi had mentioned at once. Jess pulled out the rope-gun, fumbling a little with her frozen hands.

'I practised at home. It's quite straightforward.'

'Don't you want to wait for your hands to warm up?'

'I *want* to,' she said, glancing at the moon. 'But we don't have time.'

She squinted, paused, then pulled the trigger. A thin black cord flew up into the green, hooking on a sturdy branch near the top: a perfect shot. Jess couldn't help but grin. Moments later, they were rising through the leaves, Luke clinging awkwardly to Jess like some inept koala. He decided he preferred his own way of flying.

Through the treetops, they saw the whole complex – the distant fields of swaying red poppies, the neat green gardens that circled the building, and the convent itself, all sloping roofs, speckled tiles and hidden ghost-sucking vents. In the central courtyard, instead of a fountain or flowers bobbed a monstrous black zeppelin. A tethered silk whale, like the Mayor's, except larger still.

Crunch. Crunch. Crunch. Crunch.

Footsteps on gravel. Luke glanced down. Two guards were patrolling the outer gardens. Ravi said they passed every few minutes. It was just a question of timing – of crossing from the trees to the roofs in the guardsmen's gaps. Then from there to the dorm.

'Ready, Jess?'

'This branch is kind of bendy. But I can definitely try . . .'

They watched the guards turn the corner.

Three . . . Two . . . One . . . Go!

The rope shot across, hooking quietly around a strut on the roof. She was good, Luke thought. That couldn't have been easy. But Jess continued without fuss, fixing the rope to the branch where they stood. Then, with a nod and a jump, they zip-lined down, whizzing through the air.

She turned and laughed. 'Now this is fun, right?'

Luke was about to agree, when . . .

SNAP!

The branch gave way. They lurched down and hurtled towards the gravel below.

Air rushing. Rope hissing. A silent scream.

Then a change in direction – not just down, but forward too

— as the rope, which was still attached to the compound roof, became taut and swung them up in a great looping arc towards the building. Its neat, creamy bricks sped towards them. At such speed, Luke felt sure they'd be knocked out in an instant.

But at the last minute, Jess threw her weight to the side. They veered into an open window and tumbled on to the floor, their fall muffled by a thick white carpet. The rope zipped back into the gun with a whirr and a stutter.

Crunch. Crunch. Crunch. Crunch.

The footsteps reached the window. They held their breath. The steps faded away. Luke lay still a moment longer, then finally breathed. The guards hadn't noticed them. Nobody had heard. And by some miracle, he was alive. He pulled himself to his feet, sore but grateful, and took in his surroundings.

Rich wood panels. Persian rugs. A mahogany desk the size of a bed. And behind it, on the wall, a hundred little screens showing every nook of the compound. The red rippling fields. The jetty in the east. Dormitories. Toilets. Offices. Kitchens.

But no sign of the lab.

Luke stepped closer, while Jess fiddled with the rope-gun, which was badly dented. Then fleetingly, on a corridor on the lower levels, he saw something move. A tall, slim shadow, just out of shot. Not a guard, but *her*. Tabatha. Walking fast . . . but where?

He scanned the other cameras but he couldn't see her.

Jess dropped the rope-gun and tried to use her foot to bend it back. She pulled a face. 'What is this place? A control room? Do you think they've a spanner?'

Luke shook his head. He wished it were, but his growing anxiety told him otherwise. From the silk chaise-longue to the silver-dished trolley in the corner, it was far too nice for the guards. And then there was the smell.

He touched the ashtray on the desk – still warm.

'It's Tabatha's office. And she hasn't been gone long.'

CHAPTER 32
THE OFFICE

Jess's face went pale. 'Tabatha's office?' She looked to the broken ghost-gun, then to the door. It didn't even have a handle, just a sensor of sorts. 'How do we get out?'

The anxiety in Luke's stomach gave way to a gnawing feeling, like he'd swallowed some creature that was trying to get out. 'Check the drawers for a key card. I'll check the panels.'

Frantically – quietly – they searched the room, hoping nothing was alarmed. Luke found immaculately stacked cupboards with neat rows of files. Then refrigerated ones, with tubes of blood and glowing liquids. The last cupboard had an enormous model of London, in bewildering detail, from the patchwork-slummed south to the boulevard-lined north, scattered with tiny lifelike figurines.

No – not scattered – but carefully placed. Individually painted. And strangely familiar.

A hot unease rolled over him. In the eastern canal, by a burnt yellow boat, stood an old lady and a girl – Nana and Lizzy. Just across, in the arches, stood Jess's mum and uncle. Then another boy, from the Bakers Guild, who'd been at Battersea too.

'Jess . . .' He scanned the model. 'You've got to see this.'

Everywhere he looked was a child from Battersea, their families too. All accounted for and up to date – if his dad's figure by Great Ormond's Street Hospital was anything to go by.

'Jess, come on!'

But when he turned, Jess hadn't moved. She was staring at the screen, paler than before.

'I think I just saw her. On that screen, there.'

'Floor two? Isn't that this one?'

Then from beyond the door came the sound he'd dreaded.

Click. Swish. Tap. Click.

Tabatha's heels. Her coat, her nails. It reverberated through the chambers of Luke's heart. He had no key card. No ticket. No way out. He felt like he was back in Battersea again. Room furnace-hot. Heels approaching. The certainty in his bones that there was no escape.

Click. Swish. Tap. Click.

No. That was then. Things were different now. If they couldn't get out, they'd just have to hide. He scanned the room. None of the cupboards were big enough – there was no clutter to hide in them. It was neat, minimalist, all in place.

Click. Swish. Tap. Click.

It was louder now.

'The curtains?' said Jess.

Luke shook his head. They were flimsy white things; the light from the window would show them up easily. Then he saw it.

'Quick, the trolley!'

The top laden was with silver platters – cakes, a cold steak, some kind of fruit salad – but the bottom half was covered by a thick white linen. Luke lifted it, and to his delight, it was empty.

Click. Swish. Tap. Creeeeak.

They dived under it just as the door swung open. Through the white sheet, the dark shadow moved.

'I've told you, if they don't harvest enough, you just have to shoot one.' Tabatha's voice sounded bored. 'That'll wake them up.' A faint tinny sound; she must have been speaking on the talkometer. 'No. I don't want them in the lab. We'll be leaving tonight.'

Tonight. Ma Boxhill had been right. He had a horrible feeling he knew where they'd be going.

'Delays, yes,' she went on. 'But the shipment will arrive. He is nothing if not reliable. And once it does, I will use it.' Luke heard a smile in her voice. 'The Europeans are counting on me. It'll be a Bonfire Night to remember.'

The talkometer snapped shut. The steps clicked closer.

Click. Swish. Tap. Click.

The shadow stopped by the trolley. He made out the silhouette of her boots. He could smell the leather and her musky perfume. Her nails clacked and chimed against the silver-domed lids. An aroma of fresh fruit wafted down.

She picked something up, stopped, sniffed.

'This fruit ... It smells odd ...' The talkometer snapped open. 'Cook, why does my pineapple smell damp? Like some child's wet hair.'

Luke looked at Jess. Beneath her still-sodden hair, her face was pinched with terror, no doubt the mirror of his own. Sweat pooled on his lip. He felt sure it would start dripping any minute.

Another tinny response.

'Then why on earth does my room smell like the sea?'

The talkometer clicked shut. Her nails drummed against it, then stopped. The shadow stepped back. The head tilted. Luke felt her look right through the linen and into his soul.

He was shrinking again, helpless. He couldn't breathe, think or move. Where was his lightning? Why wouldn't it come?

The leather boots creaked into a crouch.

The arms reached forward. Through the white, Luke made out the curl of her hands.

A single black nail ran across the cloth.

The talkometer beeped.

The figure pulled back.

'What? Really? Forget about the fruit. I'll be right down. Tell all the guards to head to the jetty at once. I need everybody there when the shipment arrives.'

With a swish she was gone, the door shutting behind her.

Luke and Jess stepped out and breathed. That had been close. Too close.

The door had sealed shut again. But Tabatha hadn't had a key card. How had she opened it?

'Jess, can you come and check out this sensor?'

Jess had other concerns. She was staring at the platters of quiche, pastries and tropical fruit. 'She didn't even eat anything. She's inhuman, she must be.' She touched a bronzed, flaking croissant and sighed. 'I mean we're clearly going to die here. Maybe we could just eat and call it a last supper.'

Luke watched her; his jaw dropped. It wasn't the food he'd noticed, but Jess's ear. Or what lay behind it, to be precise: a splodge of blue putty that certainly wasn't gum.

'We're not dying yet. Now pass me that pineapple.'

CHAPTER 33
THE ESCAPE

For once, Luke was grateful for Oberdink's training. After he'd removed the putty from behind Jess's ear, he swiped Tabatha's fingerprints from the pineapple in seconds and used it on the sensors – the fingerprint sensors – that operated the lock. With a quiet click, the door inched open and, after a check of Tabatha's screens, they tiptoed down the guard-free corridors up to Ravi's dorm.

Another swipe of the putty and the door swung open, revealing lines of bunks in a dimly lit room. White linen was tucked over sleeping figures in each bed. From a few barred windows, some light seeped in. All was still as stone. Only the drifting dust motes looked vaguely alive.

A single sheet moved, and a figure sat up. A figure that grinned with a dimpled smile.

'You made it!' said Ravi. 'I can't ruddy believe it!'

'I'm not sure I can either,' said Luke.

'Wait, weren't you meant to come in through the window?'

Jess pulled a face. 'Change of plan. Had a ropey rope-gun. Anyway, you ready?'

Ravi whistled twice. All at once, across the dorm, children sat up. A couple yawned, but within seconds they were lined up by the door in their off-grey pyjamas. Their feet were bare. Some looked nervous; others plain terrified.

'Don't worry,' Jess said. 'He's done this before.'

'I haven't, actually.'

'But you can make lightning,' said Ravi. 'So stop moaning.'

The kids looked less than convinced. The knot of nerves in Luke's stomach tightened.

Outside, beyond the bars, a ship's horn blared. The shipment, it had to be. They didn't have long. Soon the guards – and Tabatha – would be heading back. Soon she'd have what she needed for the weapon.

Luke pulled out the vial of red liquid. 'Now, let's get to the zeppelin.'

They walked down the corridor, soft of step, past tall arched windows and whitewashed walls, cold stone floor and thick oak doors. Through the shutters and darkness, he glimpsed the poppy fields.

'The end of this corridor, then down the stairs,' said Ravi. 'He's probably sleeping.'

Luke was about to ask 'Who?', when he heard a hideous snore, like plug-hole water and the gasp of balloons. There was only one person he knew who snored like that.

'Elvis is here?' he asked incredulously. Fat Elvis had guarded his dorm in Battersea, and he'd spent most of his shift snoring. 'I thought Tabatha would have fired him by now.'

'I'm sure she would have, but she's short of staff. Only so many made it through the Channel Tunnel in time. That's why the doors have sensors instead of guards. She can't get Europeans because officially it's still a convent.'

'Then how does she explain the children?'

'We're an orphanage too, apparently. Building character and all that.'

'I hate that phrase. It has a lot to answer for.'

They reached the bottom of the stairs and saw Elvis bulging, one eye half-open, like a giant squid stuffed into a chair. Luke felt sorry for the chair.

He closed his eyes and breathed. His mind reached into the darkness.

Thump. Thump. Thump. Creeeak.

It came easily this time, unlike in Tabatha's office. The cables pulsed in the walls to the beat of his heart. Quiet, at first, but then louder. He breathed slowly and let them flow in.

The hall lights flickered. His hand crackled. He opened his eyes and saw a hot orange glow. He watched it a moment, like Alma had taught him, then stepped forward and touched Elvis's head.

A spark jumped from his hand and the snoring stopped. Elvis slid from his seat, unconscious, then bounced along the floor. He came to a stop by a door with an iron-ring handle.

Ravi pulled it open. 'It's just a cupboard with blankets. He'll fit fine in there.'

They began wedging Elvis in, but Luke shivered. It was just like in his dream. The cupboard, its iron-ring handle, the blankets – it was all the same. And he knew how that went: with the click of heels, a nail through the keyhole, he and Ravi cornered and caught by her amber eyes.

Fear rose in his chest. Ma Boxhill's dream had been right – who was to say his wasn't too? He glanced behind, but there was only silence. In the distance, the boat horn blared again.

He pushed the fear down. This was no time for doubts.

'That should do it,' said Ravi. He turned to the stairs, where the other kids stared at Luke's glowing hands. 'Stop dawdling, you lot. That was the warm-up. Now get to your stations.'

The kids nodded and dispersed, Jess running with them, while Luke waited with Ravi by the door – a big one – watching the seconds tick by on his watch.

Thump. Thump. Thump. Thump.

Luke closed his eyes and drew all the power he could. His hands grew hot and crackled. Through his lids, he saw orange light fill the room.

'You ready for this?'

He opened his eyes. 'Ready as I'll ever be.'

Ravi pushed and the door swung open into the monstrous courtyard, the glittering black zeppelin in its centre. Arched walkways ran around the sides and intricate balconies leant overhead, while below, heavy black chains tethered the airship to the ground.

And beside each chain sat a guard with a gun.

Thump. Thump. Thump. Crack!

With a burst of orange light, the nearest guard fell before he'd even stood up. The second reached for his gun but – *CRACK!* – he fell next. The last two ran and dived for cover in the arches, where they were leapt upon by nine kids apiece: two for each limb and one for the face.

The courtyard fell quiet, save for the sound of ropes and gags being tied. Luke felt a little shaky – he wasn't used to using this much lightning – but he forced himself towards the airship. Jess reached up into black silk skin, felt around a bit, then tugged hard. With a click, then a hiss, the gondola door hissed open.

'How d'you learn that?' Ravi said.

'What can I say? The Mayor's driver took a shine to me.' She gestured Luke in to where a glass-and-steel pyramid sat stacked with amber. 'And I've a pretty good idea where to put these explosives.'

Minutes later, the vials were in the weapon. Some of the kids set off to the swim-point, while the bravest stayed by the zeppelin. They were to set it off at the last moment, to give them time to save Alma.

Alma, Luke thought, *we're coming. Hold tight.*

He turned to Ravi and Jess. 'You know, you don't have to do this. You could head to the swim-point.'

'And leave her down there?' said Ravi. 'When she came to save me?'

'And to be honest,' said Jess, 'I'd like to see her zap Tabatha.'

So without any more discussion, they descended the stairs to the lab. The three of them. Underground again. Just like old times. But this time, Luke had a feeling they would all see the sun.

After a spate of guard-zapping, which left Luke's hands zinging, they stood before an enormous steel door. Luke pulled out the putty and the door hissed open to reveal an enormous oval space, like a stadium with lower ceilings. Its curving white walls teemed with shelves and cables, and overhead ran criss-crossed steel-girdered walkways. The air was different: colder, damper. It buzzed and clinked and had a faint metallic smell.

And like in the lab in Battersea, Luke could feel the rain. There were ghostclouds here, somewhere ahead. That was where the ghost chambers – and Alma – had to be.

'Come on,' he said. 'I think she's at the far end.'

They set off past tables, microscopes and dissection tables, past tanks with UV lamps and trailing green creepers, past shelves of bottles and tubes and powders. Luke wanted to stop and study them, but they didn't have time. But when they passed a wall of monitors, flickering with CCTV, he couldn't help but notice that a cargo-ship was pulling up by the jetty. Was that the shipment? Amber perhaps, or something else?

Guards lined the path as the boat pulled in.

'Wait,' said Ravi. 'Is that *my* boat?'

It didn't make sense, but it was there in plain sight. *Rajendra's Emporium* bobbed on the monitor, attached by a rope to the cargo-ship. He peered closer. It was definitely their vessel. He could make out his fishing rod hung up on one side.

The hope dried up inside him. How had she got it? And more importantly, if she had, how were they going to get home? And what about the kids at the swim-point – what if they had set off early? He didn't dare think about it.

Luke tried to breathe. He felt like he was drowning.

They'd hidden it among the wind turbines. Had the shipment boat spotted it?

He didn't have to wait long for the answer.

On the screen, the little boat's cabin door swung open and Terence stepped out, cut chains dangling from his hands. He grinned, waved, and the guards rushed to greet him.

Luke felt ice in his chest. 'He betrayed us. After everything.'

Then the lights went out and they disappeared into darkness.

CHAPTER 34
LIGHTS OUT

The dark was as thick as a blindfold and twice as tight. From somewhere above came a muffled explosion.

'What's going on? You guys OK?'

'I'm fine,' whispered Ravi, from somewhere to his left. 'Aside from a we're-totally-dead kind of feeling.'

'But those explosions,' Jess said, 'that's good. They must have blown up the zeppelin. The weapon's gone. London's safe.'

But there was doubt in her voice and Luke felt it too. How could they be sure? And then there was this darkness. It had come *before* the noise.

He reached out with his mind for electricity, hoping he could summon a glow to his hand. But no, nothing. The power-outage was total. And with it, his lightning.

Something told him that this wasn't an accident.

Hissss.

The door to the lab opened.

He turned his head. Everything was pitch black. He strained his ears. No step, no voice. Had he imagined it?

No – wait – there was a sound, barely audible . . .

Breathing. Someone was breathing back there. And he knew, he just knew, who it was.

The creak of leather.

The tap of nails.

The swish of fabric against a cold hard floor.

'I know you're in there,' said Tabatha. 'I suggest you start running.'

Click. Swish. Tap. Click.

They ran in the dark, staggering, clattering past tables and shelves, while behind them, Tabatha made steady pursuit. She knew this place; they didn't.

'Doesn't this feel familiar?' Her words danced through the black. 'Me, hunting you, in my lab, with a gun.' Her voice was quiet, but it carried through the room. 'And just like last time, you're meddling with my plans. So selfish. Putting your friends above the needs of a city.' She laughed. 'But I can't complain. I do enjoy a rematch.'

The needs of the city? Luke ignored her and stumbled on. If the dark had been a blindfold, it was now a noose. A bookshelf, a pillar leapt out suddenly, only inches from his face. He wanted to slow down, but he could hear her gaining on him.

Click. Swish. Tap. CLANG.

The clang of metal — she was climbing up to the walkways. Why? She must have known they were on the laboratory floor. Then he remembered — she'd mentioned a gun. Up there, she'd have a better view. She could pick them off one by one.

'It's been a hard year,' she continued. 'Banished. Badmouthed. Trapped out here . . . watching while my network and good name crumbled, while my achievements and contributions were wiped from the record. I have looked forward to repaying the favour, Luke. But then I wondered, would a bullet be sufficient? It's too swift. Merciful. Why not draw it out?'

Luke heard the smile in her voice and felt a surge of hate, which he knew was exactly what she wanted. She thrived on hate, fear, all those things. It was another way to dominate, a way to control.

He winced as his hip jarred against something hard. He wasn't paying attention. Her voice was throwing him.

'It's funny,' she said, nearer still. 'But do you know where the name Luke comes from? It means "light-giving". Which is ironic, given you're always stumbling about in the dark, chasing shadows. You've never really lit a path of your own.' The footsteps stopped. 'And who needs light anyway, when you've night-vision goggles?'

Night-vision goggles?

CH-CHIK.

The sound of gun cocking.

Luke didn't think; he dived.

Phht. Tzing!

A bullet whizzed past. Glass shattered. Sparks burst through the air as Luke crashed to the floor. His elbow hurt from the landing, but the bullet had also been useful – for a fleeting moment, the sparks had chased off the darkness. He'd seen Jess and Ravi to his right, and a sheltered path ahead between bookshelves.

They darted towards it.

CH-CHIK.

She had cocked too late. They had made it. They were safe for now.

Clang. Swish. Clang. Swish.

Her steps became muted. He stole a moment to think.

The shelves were safer, but not safe. If she walked right

overhead, she'd have no trouble hitting them. But beyond the shelves, he made out a faint light. Was there still some power down there?

He reached out with his mind – if he could only draw down a little – but he heard nothing. No pulse of electricity, no crackle of static . . .

But there *was* something. Not a sound, but a feeling. And as the light grew stronger, it took on a colour: a calm, grey light, like an overcast sky.

The light of a ghostcloud.

Clang. Swish. Clang. Swish.

He turned and whispered to the others. 'We're near the ghost chambers and Alma, they must be past the shelves. And she's made a mistake. With the power off, the ghost vents are too. If we can break Alma's chamber, she can zap Tabatha. The walkways are metal – they'll conduct, so one bolt should do it. And if it does, this will all be over.'

Hope leapt in his chest. It shone in Jess's eyes. Ravi, however, jerked his head at the walkway. Suddenly, seriously, he put his finger to his lips.

Jess hadn't noticed. She was reaching into her bag.

'I nabbed a gun from a guard. That should shatter the glass, but—'

CH-CHIK.

Luke looked up. A red dot of light wavered overhead.

Phht.

Jess cried out and fell, her bag clattering to the floor. Her body shook, then stilled, a tiny black dart embedded in her neck.

Luke found himself flying backwards, dragged by Ravi to the next shelf along.

'What are you doing? We can't leave her there!'

'We have to.' Somehow, Ravi had Jess's bag in his hand. 'Tabatha had us in her sights. We can't save Jess if we're shot. We have to keep moving.'

CH-CHIK.

The noise was nearby, the steps growing louder. Ravi turned and Luke stumbled after, willing his legs forward. They felt heavy, as though they weren't his own. As though he'd left a part of himself with Jess.

How could he have left her? She'd never left him. In Battersea, when he'd found the tracker and wanted to quit, she had pulled him up, got him back on his feet. Why hadn't he done the same?

'Poor Jess, what a waste,' Tabatha said from the darkness. 'But then again, she was wasted in London. Overlooked by the guild just because she's girl, even though she had double the talent and worked twice as hard. I know how that feels. Perhaps you do too?' She sighed. 'My father, the ghosts, those in power – they only took me seriously when I gave them no choice. It shouldn't be like that. It's time things changed.'

Clang. Swish. Clang. Swish.

Her voice was everywhere, worming its way into his thoughts. Images assailed him. Jess smiling each morning even though the guild put her down. Her bravery with the groundghoul after Alma's disdain. Her patching up the boat and hijacking the zeppelin.

Her lying the floor with a dart in her neck.

What was in it? Poison? No. Surely not. If Tabatha had wanted to kill them, she could have just used a bullet . . .

Clang. Swish.

The footsteps stopped. The silence was worse. What was she waiting for?

Ravi tugged his arm and at once he knew.

They'd reached the edge of the shelves. Rows of ghost chambers waited ahead, just like in Battersea – squat blue-black metal contraptions, halfway between an oven and a diving bell. But it wasn't the chambers that scared him, it was what came before them – an exposed stretch of floor at least thirty feet long.

'We'll never make it,' Luke said. 'She'll have a clear line of sight.'

'If we both run at the same time, then one of us might.'

Ravi was right. It took time to reload. One of them might make it, but never both. The thought of it made his throat dry with fear.

'Look,' said Ravi. 'The guards will come soon. We've got to try. It's like you said, if Alma zaps Tabatha, this will all be over.' He squeezed Luke's shoulder. 'If something happens, don't be a hero. Just grab the bag and run.'

It was Russian Roulette. And Luke didn't want to play.

Still, they readied themselves at the end of the shelves.

'Go!'

And they were running towards the glowing ghost chambers. The polished grey concrete rushed under their feet.

They made it four steps. Then eight. Then, somehow, halfway, and Luke thought maybe he'd been wrong. Maybe she'd misjudged. Maybe they'd make it.

CH-CHIK.

Phht.

Then he was alone. His feet skidding forward, trying desperately to turn, but slipping and sliding towards the chambers.

He came to stop, in the shelter of the ghost chambers . . . but not with Ravi. He lay a few meters behind, face down, a dart in his back.

Despair lurched in Luke's throat. This wasn't the sacrifice he'd been promised. What was the point if it ended like this?

Then he saw the bag on the floor, a few feet from the chambers. Ravi must have thrown it as he fell. Luke darted out and grabbed it.

CH-CHIK.

Phht.

A thud in his leg. He'd been hit.

And yet he was moving, diving back into the shelter.

He looked down. The dart had pierced his pocket. Why hadn't he felt it?

He reached down and realised. Broken glass and dented metal. He pulled out what was left of his mum's watch. Its face was shattered, the engraved words unreadable.

Bitterness and anger twisted inside him.

'Shame about Ravi,' said Tabatha, above. 'A very clever boy. Could have been anything – a shopkeeper, an industrialist. But of course, he never would have, because he he's from the water markets. Came over on a boat. The guilds never would have let him. Such a waste. And I do hate waste.'

'Shut up!' Luke shouted. 'Don't pretend you care. You just shot him!'

Her laugh tinkled like broken glass. Her footsteps quickened.

Luke cursed – he'd given himself away. He ran deeper through the ghost chambers, scanning as he passed. A sea of hazy figures swam by. A man wringing his hands, staring down at his feet. A featureless lady, moaning quietly. In others, propellers whizzed, tearing shapes in the steam.

What if that was Alma? What if he'd come too late?

'Luke, is that you?'

He turned towards the voice, and he saw her. She was smiling sadly, hands pressed against the glass. Her dark curls were faint. She looked pale, weak.

'You came,' Alma whispered. 'I knew you would.'

Relief surged through him. He wanted to tell her everything – about Ravi and Jess, about all that had happened, about how happy he felt just to see her face. But he couldn't, not now. There was no time to lose.

It was just like last time: a single bullet stood between failure and freedom.

He reached into the bag, drew the gun, pointed it at the glass and fired three times.

A crunching, tinkling, hopeful sound. Smoke clouded the air, then finally cleared.

What on earth?

The three bullets had crumpled, mid-shot, within the glass. Cracks webbed out from them, but the glass held strong. Alma hammered her fists desperately behind it.

Laughter in the darkness. 'Bullet-proof glass,' said Tabatha. 'You see, Luke, I never make the same mistake twice.'

Click. Swish. Click. Swish.

Luke spun round. The steps had clicked, not clanged . . . She was down on his level.

'Do you know, Luke, why light can never beat shadow?' Her voice echoed around him. 'Because wherever you turn, the shadow's always behind.'

CH-CHIK.

Phht.

Luke felt himself fall.

CHAPTER 35
THE RETURN

Metallic thrumming. Hydraulic hissing. The curl and thrust of muted wind. Something cold pressing against his head, with the smell of engine oil and dry, high air.

'Look, he's moving,' said a voice, but Luke ignored it. He was far too tired and his head throbbed with a pain that started near the bridge of his nose and splayed out through his forehead.

'Luke, wake up!'

The urgency of the voice stirred something in him. Memories flashed in his mind. Ravi . . . They'd found him, broken into the base . . . but things had gone wrong.

He forced his eyes open.

He blinked once. Twice. The world came into focus. He was standing in a capsule-shaped room about the length of a bus, dimly lit and with walls of dark glass. Ahead, in the corner, lay a table and grey teardrop lights. At the slanted windows hung plush velvet drapes. Beyond that, only cloud and sky.

Tabatha's zeppelin. It had to be. The gondola looked just like the Mayor's.

He glanced down. They were a thousand feet high, and through the tinted-glass floor moonlight trailed across the rippling night sea. In the distance stood the black cliffs of the English coast.

'Over here,' hissed Ravi. 'Quiet, or she'll hear you.'

He turned, still dizzy, to see Ravi in the corner, handcuffed to a pipe with Jess. Beside them sat Terence, looking sorry for himself. Finally there was Alma, pale, faint and angry, sealed tight inside one of Tabatha's glass chambers.

Luke felt a rush of relief. They were alive! He stepped towards them, but his head met with a *THUNK*.

Hard, angled glass. Triangular glass. With growing unease, he realised what it was: the pyramid. The weapon. But instead of looking in, he was looking out . . .

'Can someone tell me why I'm *inside* the pyramid?'

'It gets stranger,' said Alma. 'Check out your hands.'

Luke did, and if there'd been room, he knew he would have jumped – for his hands had been soldered into metal gloves on chains, through which black cables ran down to an opening. In the

Mayor's zeppelin, the same cables had run through the amber in an attempt to power the weapon.

'This doesn't look good.'

'That's because it isn't,' said Terence.

'Shut up,' snapped Alma. 'This is your fault. If you hadn't betrayed us, we'd have—'

'You'd have what?' cut in a voice.

Tabatha leant against the control room door, pipe glowing in hand. 'Let me guess. If it weren't for Terence, you'd have defeated my guards? Blown up my weapon and sailed into the sunset?' She put the pipe to her lips and walked to the window.

Click. Swish. Tap. Click.

She breathed out and stared at the cliffs below. The zeppelin was fast; it had almost reached the coastline. Luke made out the twinkle of Smugglers' Cove.

Tabatha turned. 'If you had escaped, I'd have stopped you at sea.'

'We'd have found a way,' said Luke. 'Just like last time.'

'Last time, it was the ghosts that saved you.'

'There's still time for that,' said Alma.

Tabatha blinked and turned back to the window. They passed

over the town of Lewes and the rolling South Downs. The haze of London hung on the horizon.

Click. Tap. Swish. Click.

She approached Luke's chamber. Her amber eyes peered through the glass. The pupils were small. Bored. The teardrop scar beneath them gave her a mocking look.

'If the ghosts come, I'm ready. You see, Luke, *you* were the shipment.'

'What? No . . .' He wouldn't believe it. She had to be lying. 'It was an amber shipment. The Mayor told us.'

'Then the Mayor knew nothing.' She ran a nail gently against the pane. 'It was never the amber, it was the insects inside it. Trapped in this realm, yet half-gone to the next – they were hole, a chink in the wall between realms.' She shrugged. 'But the fossils were so rare that I had to buy whole mines of the stuff, and in end, the hole was always too small. The best I ever managed was a ghoul here or there.'

'So you did make the leaks!' said Jess. 'I knew it. And the groundghoul.'

Tabatha paused, as if deciding whether this merited a response. It didn't, it seemed. She turned back to Luke.

'With the amber not working, I knew I needed something

stronger. More in-between. I sent Terence back for my research and samples to see what I'd missed. I even crossed over myself, to keep a close eye . . . but it was only when I visited your houseboat that I solved it. When I saw – no, felt – your lightning in action.'

She took another draw on her pipe. 'It seems a genuine half-ghost is rare thing indeed. None of my experiments, my serums, ever came close to what you could do. It was marvellous to watch. The colour, the way it drained me dry – it defied all my expectations. With my serums, I can cross over, I can make a spark or two, but you are different. A strand runs from you right through the wall to the other side. Your charge lifts *up*. It flows the *other way*. You're not a chink in the wall, but a valve, a floodgate. A lock in the canal that needs breaking open.'

A floodgate? What? 'But why break it open? The wall is there for a reason!'

'Is it?' Tabatha said. 'In my experience, boundaries rarely are. North and south. Rich and poor. Master and apprentice. Women and men. Boundaries are upheld and protected because they serve certain interests. Progress is always about tearing them down.'

'But between the living and the dead? Surely that's a boundary that matters?'

'You tell me. You cross it all the time.' She walked to the window. 'But less talk, I think. It's time for a demonstration.'

Luke didn't like where this was going. He pulled at the chains and manacles, but they only dug deeper.

'If you struggle, Luke, I'll drop a friend overboard.'

He stopped.

She smiled. 'Good, that's better.'

The zeppelin juddered. Tabatha steadied herself against the glass. Outside, the wind grew. 'Well, it's finally time. I hope you're all ready.'

'Ready for what?'

Luke followed her eyes to the window, just as the zeppelin turned, and there on the horizon was a storm – a storm like none he'd seen before. A monstrous black thing the size of a mountain, with a thousand heads and grasping arms. It looked solid as rock, but it moved like the sea, a black-oil sea gobbling all in its path. Eyes, feelers, tentacles and horns, all were tangled within it as it trailed down in a haze to the fields below.

'The Ghost Council,' said Ravi. 'They've come for us, haven't they?'

'I think you'll find that *we've* come for them,' said Tabatha.

'After Battersea, I knew that I wasn't safe until they were gone, but the question was how. With some help from Luke, I think I've cracked it.'

They could hear the storm now. A discordant shriek, like a murder of crows. A massacre, more like. It was impossible to think of anything else. Terence began to whimper. Tabatha walked back to the control room.

Until that moment, Luke had hoped that the ghosts might save them, but now he wasn't so sure. The storm looked merciless. It crackled with blue-white fire. It bulged hungrily at strange angles. It didn't look like it was saving anyone anytime soon.

The zeppelin pushed on, sailing nearer, and a buzz of electricity built in the air, along with the spike and scratch of static. Jess's blonde hair fuzzed up at the edges.

'Tabatha,' Alma shouted, above the din, 'there's still time. They don't interfere unless they have to. If you abandon the ship, they might spare you.'

'Why would I do that?' said Tabatha, now at the wheel. 'So I can cling on to life like you desperate ghosts? I don't want that. Nor fame like the Mayor. I want to live on through my actions. Or, as Luke puts it, to *make a difference*.' She smiled. 'That's true immortality. To change this world before we go to the next.'

'But it won't work,' shouted Luke. The buzzing hurt his ears as the storm filled the sky. 'My lightning's no match for something like that.'

'I disagree. The limit of your powers has always been the source. If you take the scraps from fairgrounds, your bolts will scrappy. Here, however, is something quite different. A zeppelin packed full of soul-fuel – a floating power station wired right through you. There is no limit. They won't know what hit them. The ghosts and their wall don't stand a chance.' She put her hand on a lever.

'Wait!' shouted Luke.

She pulled. The lights flickered and the gondola fell into darkness.

Thump. Thump. Thump. Thump.

Luke felt his heart beat, but not like his own. It was slower, beating to the rhythm of some other drum.

The engine thrum faded. The propeller stopped ticking. Time itself seemed to shrink and slow. And in the quiet dark, he felt something else – the zeppelin. It was like it was part of him: it was his skin being buffeted by the storm-winds outside, its criss-crossing wires were his arteries and vessels, its enormous engine pulsing in sync with his heart.

He was part of its circuit.

Thump. Thump. Thump. Thump.

The beat was louder now. It hurt his chest. It pressed in his skull. He was caught in its rush, like a raft on the waves.

He reached out with his mind and tried to stop it, calm it, to draw it down, like before. He thought maybe he could divert it somehow.

But nothing. It was useless. He was a cog in its gears, and she had the wheel. And in the engine, he could feel the power building, buzzing, like a raging torrent. Like a flood at the gates.

Thump. Thump. Thump. Creeeak.

The floodgates opened, the power from the zeppelin rushed inside him, bright white and burning hot through his arms. It screamed in his ears, jabbed metallic on his tongue. His muscles, his skin felt ready to burst into flames.

Then it stopped.

He felt a sudden lightness.

The black faded and the gondola flickered into light. His friends were still there. The storm still raged. Nothing had changed.

Perhaps it had failed?

Then a deafening shriek from the beyond the window. The zeppelin's steel nose glowed, crackling and spitting out sparks of orange light. *His* light.

The light bulged like the sun, blindingly bright. With a crack, a blade of sunset shot across the sky. Not fork-like lightning, but straight like a knife. It hit the storm with an almighty scream and blotted out the sky.

A dusty smell settled in the air. The wind breathed and the grey cleared.

A black, jagged crack ran through the mountain of clouds – it sparkled darkly, like a star-speckled sky. Mesmerising. Frightening. Strangely quiet. A breach in the wall, a rip between realms. It hurt to look, and yet Luke couldn't look away.

In the jagged darkness, something moved. Ever so slightly, but Luke knew he'd seen it.

A lung-rattling gasp echoed through the sky.

Out from the rip poured shadows of every shape, shade and size: a ravenous-jawed dragon with a strange twisting neck, a slavering hound with curling claws, a gaping-mouth squid, a long-fingered lady, and hundreds more eyeless figures.

Ghouls. Everywhere. The whole sky was full of them.

She'd torn through the wall. Luke couldn't move or think. The ghouls, however, got straight to work.

The long-fingered lady was first – she grabbed an elderly man-ghost and dragged him back through the crack into the darkness. Next a dark-slime leech suckered a dove-cloud and did the same. One by one, ghosts fell, pulled through the tear in the realm by the ghastly figures.

The council's cloud-mountain collapsed in a landslide of black.

'Don't begrudge them,' said Tabatha. 'They're only doing their job. Those ghosts should have passed over a long time ago.'

Luke's knees buckled. The Ghost Council had been right all along. He had been a danger to everyone.

'Don't be down, Luke,' Tabatha said. 'You're still making a difference – just not how you planned.'

She turned back to the wheel. 'Now, for London.'

CHAPTER 36
LONDON BURNING

A horrible silence fell on the cabin. There was nothing left to say. They'd come to stop Tabatha, not help her. It had gone wrong so fast.

Outside, black ghouls swirled like an oil slick of shadows. Ghosts tried to outrun them, diving down or flying north towards London, but wherever they went, the ghouls followed. Swarming, searching, sniffing the air, their eyeless faces pressed against the gondola glass. Some peered in, testing the panes, but they were thankfully sealed shut.

There was no way in and no way out.

'Stop it,' said Ravi.

'Stop what?'

'Blaming yourself. It's not your fault, it's hers.'

Ravi looked angrily to the control room. Through the glass, Luke saw Tabatha and Terence at the wheel and beyond them, the city he'd always called home. The zeppelin had reached London's outskirts. He could see its shadow slipping over fields towards the edge of the slums, where bonfires still smouldered and people lay sleeping in hammocks and tents made of tarp.

Luke wanted to scream, *She's here, look out!*

But nobody looked up. Even if they had, they would have ignored it. It was just another zeppelin in a cloudy night sky. They wouldn't notice its strange spear-like nose, its black-whale shape, nor the ghoulish clouds that flocked around it. People didn't look closely. They didn't pay attention, even when their life depended on it. Even when the answer to their problems was right in front of their—

Wait. There, by his nose, was a mark. A chink in the glass. It had to be where his head had thunked it. *Which could only mean . . .*

'Guys! This glass isn't bullet-proof – it's breakable! Do you think if we smashed it, we'd break the circuit?'

Jess sat bolt upright. 'It'd be a start.' She frowned. 'But we'd need some pliers to cut those gloves or the wires.'

'Pliers?' said Ravi. 'Where on earth will we get pliers?

'How about there?' Alma pointed to wall panel. The word '*Maintenance*' ran across the bottom, printed and centred. Organised as ever, Tabatha had labelled it. 'I bet there's a hammer there too. Serves her right for being neat!'

Her voice burnt with excitement. It fizzed up in Luke too.

'But, guys,' Ravi hissed, 'we can't reach that cupboard. Not in a million years.'

They all slumped. Ravi was right. Luke and Alma were trapped behind glass. Jess and Ravi were chained. And yet, half an idea was still better than none. They just had to find a way.

Hisss.

The doors slid open and Terence loped in: stooping, muttering and greasier than ever. Disgust and anger swilled in Luke's stomach. They needed ideas, but they couldn't talk with him there. He was ruining it again.

Terence the traitor. Terence, who he'd trusted. Terence, who he'd saved from the Mayor's gloved hands.

Then he saw Terence's hands. They were worse than ever: bruised, bandaged and with burn-marks too – Tabatha's, no doubt. Come to think of it, he even had a black eye and a limp in his step. He looked altogether wretched, like some wounded street dog. A dog loyal to his master, however cruel she was. A dog they'd helped, who couldn't help but bite them.

Despite himself, Luke felt a pang of pity. Some wounds, he supposed, were too deep to heal.

Alma had no such dilemma. 'You disgusting, treacherous weasel of a man!' Her eyes glowed blue. 'You betrayed us! We trusted you! This is all your fault! The sky's black with ghouls – it's like the end of the world!'

Terence didn't react. Didn't smirk or sneer. His eyes stayed on the floor.

'Stop that, you coward. At least have the decency to look us in the eyes!'

Terence didn't. Luke followed his gaze down. Through the glass, Luke could see the Thames – the tiny riverboats, Tower Bridge opening, the dots of slum-dwellers wading in the shallows.

The zeppelin turned and Terence's head turned too, slowly, like a ship weighing anchor. He looked at Luke. His eyes were wet. A tear slipped down his cheek, followed by a trickle of words.

'I didn't betray you.'

He was lying, he had to be . . . and yet, Luke felt doubt.

'But we saw you on the screen! You met the guards. They were cheering . . .'

Another tear hit the dark glass floor. 'I didn't, I promise. I waited in the boat, in the dark, with Stealth. I was rooting for you, hoping, checking the horizon. I thought about our journey – the freedom, the fairground, what I'd do when I was free. And then I thought about the cheesemobile, and I guess I got hungry. So I made some toast.'

He stifled a sob. 'That was my mistake: the toaster. It finally broke. Burst into flames. Smoke everywhere. Tabatha's cargo-ship saw and thought it was a signal. When they saw me chained up, they said I was a hero.'

A stunned silence. Luke's mind ran with the possibilities. Surely the fate of London hadn't been decided by a toaster?

'Even after they caught me, I tried,' Terence said. 'I hid Stealth – he's safe – and I didn't tell them you were onshore. I pretended to pass out from the fumes when they asked. It was only at the jetty that Tabatha smelt a rat.' He whimpered. 'I wanted to help, I promise. I told myself that if you beat her, then I'd take it as a sign. That I'd start again like those raft people.' He looked at their chains. 'I guess the sign's pretty clear.'

'I don't buy it,' said Ravi. 'Why didn't you tell us that Luke was the shipment?'

'I didn't know!' Terence said. 'She told me she wanted you, but she didn't say why. And I guess I was scared. She'd said she'd kill me if I let anything on.' He bit his lip. 'I did try to put you off – with the mines, the fields, the traps and so on. But nothing made you turn back.' He shook his head. 'I'm sorry. I really am. But that's life, I guess. Things never work out the way I want.'

'Wait,' Luke said. 'Terence, there's still a chance—'

Hissss.

Tabatha entered. Terence hid his tears but she didn't even look his way.

'It's time, children. I think we'll start here. Symbolic, no?' She gestured behind her, to where, wreathed in ghoulish black clouds, Big Ben's green-glowing clock face stared back. They'd reached the heart of the city: Parliament's bomb-proof domes, the frilly bureaus of Whitehall, grand Westminster bridge and the bubbling Thames. Even at this hour, people walked the streets, though the office windows were mercifully dark.

Tabatha tapped her pipe and watched the embers fall. 'We'll stop the clock. Start again. Burn off the old and make way for the new.'

'Burn?' Luke said. 'You said you'd fix it.'

'Yes, but first we need to set an example. The guilds. Mansion

House. The New Thames Barrier. And Parliament, of course.'

'They'll never support you if you burn half the city!'

'They won't have a choice once the European army gets here.' She smiled. 'Once the city's in chaos, they'll invade and instate me as mayor. I'll rebuild Battersea. Imprison those who resist.'

'Tabatha, wait—'

She was already walking back. Her hand was on the lever. She pulled it down.

Thump. Thump. Thump. Thump.

It happened quicker this time.

The engine thrum faded. His heart slowed. The zeppelin wires pulsed, quickened, throbbed with power. Then the power rushed through him – crashing like the waves of a river bursting its banks – and thundered out into the ship.

A hundred bolts of orange-black lightning snaked towards the clock of Big Ben, which exploded into sparkling black flames. Veins of electricity ran down the building sides, charring bricks, shrivelling the tower like a lightning-struck tree. The streets plunged into darkness, the life sucked out of them.

With a juddering creak, the clock face fell to the ground and shattered on the pavement. An enormous minute hand shot outwards, ploughing through traffic, before disappearing, sizzling, into the Thames.

People screamed. Fire rained from the tower, carrying on the breeze and sparking nearby rooftops. It leapt hungrily, unnaturally, in all directions.

The control room door hissed shut, leaving only an outline of Tabatha's figure.

'Oh god,' said Ravi. 'This is her plan?'

'She's just getting started,' said Terence.

Luke felt weak. Dizzy. Terribly responsible. But he forced himself to catch Terence's gaze. 'No, she isn't. Not if you stop her.'

Terence spluttered. 'I can't. I already tried. It didn't work.'

'Then try again.' Luke nodded towards the panel. 'There's a toolbox up there with a hammer, maybe pliers. Use it to smash this glass, then cut these wires. Then all this will stop.'

Terence shook his head desperately. 'I can't! It won't work! It never does.' He was begging now. 'And even if it does, what then? I've nowhere to go. They'll send me to jail.'

Luke felt his grip loosening. Terence turned back towards the control room.

Jess grabbed Terence's hand. 'What about the fair? You loved the fair. They don't care about the law – they'll take you in.'

Terence stopped. He could have pulled away, but he didn't. He looked at Jess's hand on his. 'The fair,' he said, something stirring in his eyes. 'But they'd never want someone like me.'

'They did!' Luke said. 'I didn't tell you at the time because we needed you, but the lady offered you a job.'

'Me? Really?'

Jess nodded. 'I heard it too. She said, and I quote, that you "scared the pants off those kids".'

Behind him, in the control room, Tabatha pulled the lever again.

Thump. Thump. Thump. Thump.

The surge came hard and fast, burning down Luke's arms, screaming in his chest. Blades of orange-black lightning shot over rooftops, towards the ship-like pretty-timbered buildings of Temple, the seat of the guilds. The rolling green lawns blackened. The ground convulsed, then caved in. The lightning spidered outwards, sending the trees and brickwork up in flames.

But it wasn't just there. All around them, now, the fire was spreading. Sirens blended with the wails of civilians below. Rising black smoke mingled with ghouls in the sky, till the whole city was bathed in a choking smog.

'Well, she got her bonfire,' said Alma.

'And we can still put it out,' Luke said. 'Terence, please?'

Terence hadn't moved, but his eyes had a faraway look. 'She really said that?' He whispered. 'That I scared the pants off those kids?'

Luke nodded. 'And that you worked hard. And were strong.'

Slowly Terence smiled. Not a smirk, or a grimace, or a gurn, or a sneer. But a genuine smile. And though his teeth were still greasy and his face bruised, it lit up his face. He looked so much younger – and nicer.

Faster than lightning, he leapt to the cupboard, pulled out the toolbox, unlatched it, and whipped out the hammer. With an almighty swing, he brought it down on Luke's chamber, shattering it into a thousand glass pieces.

'The gloves!' Luke said. 'It'll break the circuit.'

Terence jammed the clawed end of the hammer under the lip of a glove, then levered hard, tearing at the metal and the skin of Luke's wrist. It loosened down the side – Luke could feel it at once – but he still couldn't get his hand out.

'Try the pliers!' said Jess.

'There aren't any, you idiots!' shouted Terence.

Then he did something strange. He bent down through the glass, though great shards dug into his skin, and sank his teeth in – to the rip in the metal – and pulled.

The metal screeched, tearing.

'That's it, it's working, Terence, keep going—'

A shot cracked through the gondola. The acrid scent of gunpowder. Terence fell to the floor.

Tabatha stood in the doorway, pistol smoking, her eyes like the fire in the city beneath. 'What a waste,' she hissed. 'All that for a finger?'

Luke looked down: only the tiniest strip of metal was loose on his little finger – he could barely move it. And on the floor, he saw the cost of it all. Terence, face down. Not moving.

Click. Tap. Swish. Click.

'You did that, Luke. He was mine and you killed him. And all for nothing.'

She was right. It had been for nothing. His hand was still trapped. He could barely angle it away from himself. He looked again to Terence, so lifeless on the floor.

'And now I'm angry.' She looked at his friends. 'But before I drop this lot overboard, I've a better idea.' She pointed out the window. 'Recognise that?'

In the distance, beside a broken minaret, stood the modest red-bricked building he'd seen at soulrise. Of course he knew it. It was Great Ormond Street Hospital.

'Your father's still in there recovering after his little boat fire. It's time you showed him what you can do.'

'No!' Luke cried. 'Leave him alone!'

'Maybe you should have left Terence alone.'

Tabatha walked back to the wheel. The zeppelin turned. Luke's whole body shook like the winds outside. It wasn't just his dad in there; there were thousands. Children mostly. The government offices they'd hit would have been empty this late, but a hospital never slept.

He pulled desperately at his hand, but it still wouldn't give. He could hardly move the finger Terence had freed.

'Guys, please.' He turned to his friends. 'We have to do something. Anything.'

They only stared back in horror as it came into view.

It looked just like it had at soulrise. Tucked away quietly amongst showier buildings. He remembered the glowing bright souls, the nightsparks, butterflying up. He'd been worried at the time about his apprenticeship, the council, and so many silly things. What he'd give to go back to that moment now.

Thump. Thump. Thump. Thump.

His heart slowed. The sounds dimmed. The lights in the city clouded beneath him. The power built and buzzed inside the zeppelin, and another memory came – that of the baby's soul he'd cradled in his arms. *We all have a time*, Alma had said. *It's the journey that counts.*

And suddenly, he knew how to break the circuit.

They'd made so many sacrifices. What was one more?

So Luke bent his finger, the fraction that he could, then shot his brightest spark right at his heart.

Thump.

Thump.

Thump.

Silence.

CHAPTER 37
SACRIFICE

Luke's soul slipped from his body. It had many times before, but this time felt different. Final. Freeing.

He looked over the cabin with a strange dispassion. His body slumped in the chamber, glass shards at his feet. His friends shouting, desperate, unable to reach him. Tabatha furious, trying to slap him awake. All the while, the zeppelin's buzzing grew louder as it powered up, reaching its limit.

But without him, it was broken — the power had nowhere to go.

The scene felt slow and faded, like a memory. As if the outcome didn't matter because it had already happened. *Any second now*, he thought, *it will be over*.

The buzzing stopped. There came ominous creaking, a deep wrenching sound, like river ice breaking. But louder. Nearer. Right above his friends' heads. From the belly of the ship.

They all looked up, even Tabatha, and for a fleeting moment, Luke thought he saw a flicker of fear in her eyes. An instant later, with a deafening screech, sparks exploded from the central chamber, sending her flying with a crunch into the glass.

Smoke streamed through the cabin, followed by the stench of burnt rubber. The creaking grew deafening. More bursts of sparks, each brighter than the last. The whole airship juddered and shrieked. The energy trapped inside had nowhere to go.

But Luke did: he could feel it pulling him. High above, the stars called out to him. He belonged there now. It was finally time.

He took a step through the glass and glanced back at his friends. The carriage was in chaos, lurching this way and that. Tabatha was dragging herself across the floor, nails-first, towards the control room, her legs trailing limp behind her. Jess and Ravi snatched the hammer from Terence's hands and turned to use it on their chains.

Luke wanted to stay, to help, but the pull was too strong. It wasn't up to him any more. His time had passed. He felt himself slip into the cold air beyond.

Then he was rising, shimmering, like a light at soulrise. He was a nightspark, butterflying ever higher into the sky. Ghouls swirled all around in the smoke, but they didn't pay him any mind; he was already on his way. In any case, they looked different now – like shadows, only as scary as you gave them credit for. They were just doing their job. They were part of the plan.

The air grew thin. Snapping, icy, tugging at his sides. He was over the clouds now, then higher still. The only thing between him and the stars was the moon. It hung full and white and round above him, showering him with light.

He thought of his mum. Would he meet her up there? He hoped so. He had so much to tell her.

He turned to glance down on his home one last time. Little fires jumped from roof to roof, engulfing the city centre, carrying east and west on the wind. Great Ormond Street Hospital was safe, for now, but he wondered whether it would last the night. How would he know? Perhaps his friends would tell him, one day, when they reached the other side.

He turned back to the stars. A single gossamer strand stretched up into the black. The next step was his. He just had to take it.

A breath. A sigh. He reached out towards it . . .

Thump.

A noise. A tiny, faint thing. A single thread, trailing back.

Thump. Thump.

Again, that sound, stronger this time. Not a thread, but a string. Not a trail, but a tug. Small, insistent, holding him back.

Thump. Thump. Thump.

Louder. Stronger. Not a string but a rope. A fierce embrace. Too strong, too warm, for the End Place to hold him, and suddenly, silently, he was hurtling back down.

Thump. Thump. Thump. Thump.

Blinding light. Shrieking metal. Smoke, choking and thick. He opened his eyes. He was back in the zeppelin. Alma crouched beside him, her hand on his chest.

A spark to his heart. She'd brought him back.

'Not on my watch,' she said. 'You're not going anywhere.'

'Actually,' said Jess, thrusting a parachute into his hand, 'he is. Right now. Because this ship's going to blow.'

It didn't take an expert to know she was right. Dark cracks scuttled across the tinted glass. Shuddering gasps convulsed the carriage. The hot metal stench of burning wires stung their nostrils.

Ravi rushed over. 'I've opened the hatch, come on!'

Jess helped Luke stagger to the opening. The air howled through, carrying the reek of the burning city.

Luke looked round the gondola. Terence lay still, Tabatha was slumped face down by the control room. Unconscious, but breathing.

'What about them?'

'Terence is gone,' Jess said, pain darting across her face. 'And Tabatha, well, there aren't enough parachutes. They only had three.'

Luke wavered.

'You can't save everyone,' said Alma.

A hideous new sound came from above. The snarl of fabric. The silk whale's belly ripping open. They didn't have time.

'I guess you can't.' He grabbed Jess's and Ravi's hands. 'The wind isn't right but we'll have to chance it. Ready . . . Jump!'

They leapt together out over the clouds. Air rushing. Faces stinging. Clothes flapping at their sides.

It wasn't anything like flying. The sky screamed in their ears, but couldn't shift them an inch forward or back. They moved eye-wateringly fast, but stayed above the exact same spot. Everything looked so small. Time seemed to slow. It was hard to say if they getting any nearer.

But then suddenly they were. Buildings expanded, little by little. Luke made out shapes in the trees. The dots became people. The picture came alive.

And the flames multiplied in hundreds of shades of red. They were everywhere now, tongues, fingers grasping up towards them. Just one spark and their parachutes would probably catch fire. They couldn't land here. They wouldn't stand a chance. Where on earth was the wind they needed?

Then the clouds moved, letting white moonlight wash across the city. A whispering breeze reached Luke's ear like a gentle voice. A mother's voice.

Then it was drowned out by a far louder sound.

'Wind!' he shouted.

Not just a wind, but a powerful swell, which lifted them up and away from the fire and towards the parks in the north. A wind like a guide. Like a helping hand. The hand of someone long gone who was still looking out for him.

He squeezed his own friends' hands. 'Count of three, remember. We need to be clear of one another.'

They nodded and let go.

'Three . . . Two . . . One . . .'

He pulled the cord.

CHAPTER 38
HOME

They sat round Luke's kitchen table, having one of Nana Chatterjee's epic breakfasts, the table piled to the rafters with fruit, dosa, waffles and eggs. But today, Luke took the time to enjoy it. After weeks on the run eating nothing but toast and cheese, he appreciated it now. No more seizing the day; he was soaking it up.

'More mango?' said his sister.

'Yes, please,' said Luke.

'Actually, I was offering it to Ravi, but there's enough to go round.'

He'd decided to take some time off. Most of London had, really. After Tabatha's rampage, they didn't have much choice – normal business had ground to a halt. The zeppelin had crash-landed into the New Thames Barrier, and though the ensuing floods had helped quell the fires, the centre of London now looked like the east: waterways instead of roads, boats beside houses, and all in all, a slightly slower pace of life. The south had benefited too – the slum-dwellers' flood defences had fared surprisingly well, and a rush of central Londoners had moved south, renovating houses, opening shops, embracing a dryer, more urban kind of life.

The change of mood was also helped by the glorious sunshine. On Alma's orders, of course. Luke looked out the window. The black-streaked ruins of buildings stood before him. Somehow, in the sunshine, they still looked nice. Everything looked nice on a sunny day.

'How long do you think she can keep up this weather?'

'As long as she likes, she's the head of the council,' said Luke. 'When they moan, she just tells them to soak it up.'

'Your grandma's not complaining.'

They could hear her whistling above. It was unseasonably warm for November and her roses were blooming. Stealth looked blissful beside them, curled up in the sun. Luke's dad was happy too: he was leading an investigation into mayoral corruption and equality in the guilds. Even Radhika had stopped scowling – she'd found a new role managing a shelter for refugees. She'd called in on the way this morning to say hello.

'Are you sure she's coming?' said Ravi.

'As sure as I ever am.' Luke checked his watch and looked up at the sky. 'She'll be here any minute now.'

His sister looked up. 'Who, Alma?'

Luke grinned. Alma visited his family most days now. She'd changed the rules. Though ghosts still were discreet, the family of a half-ghost was an exception. And though at first his family trod carefully around Luke and lightbulbs – and his grandma kept getting him to light fires with his hands – they were getting used to it. And Luke slept a lot better without having to carry so many secrets.

But today, the person in the sky wasn't Alma.

'You ready, guys?' Jess called down, hanging from the side of a small, bright yellow zeppelin. 'My boss said we've got it for an hour. Anywhere we like.'

She was beaming almost brighter than the sun, and had been ever since she'd switched apprenticeships. It'd been easy enough, she said – apparently zeppelin hydraulics were just 'plumbing with air'. Though Luke had a feeling she was being modest.

The zeppelin tooted and the ladder thunked down.

'Mind my roses, Jessy,' his grandma shouted.

Luke and Ravi climbed on to the boat deck, then ascended the ladder. As Luke looked down on the city, parts charred and flooded in the dazzling sun, he felt strangely lucky. Despite all of Tabatha's efforts, and though thousands had been hurt, there'd been almost no deaths. Some said it was a miracle. Divine intervention. And when Luke thought back to the pull, and the wind that had glided them to safety, he wondered if, for once, they weren't far off.

There had of course been a couple of casualties. They'd found the two bodies in the gondola cabin. And though Tabatha wouldn't be missed, Luke still wished that they could have done something for Terence. If it weren't for him, it could have all been quite different. Luke looked up above the clouds. Hopefully he knew that too.

Then, gliding down from the sky, not late any more (it helped, he supposed, that she ran the meetings), was a magnificent white swan-cloud with Alma on its back. She waved, the breeze flicking her hair.

'Sorry,' she called. 'The council were moaning about the weather again. I said if we're really a democracy, we should ask the lifers too. They're the ones who actually get wet. That shut 'em up.' She winked. 'You know, I've been wondering if we couldn't do with a little less cloud-cover generally. More downtime for us clouds. More sunshine for you guys. We'll blame global warming. Everyone wins.'

'Sounds good to me,' said Luke.

'Anyway,' said Alma. 'You ready for the flying lesson?'

They clambered into the gondola, and Luke and Ravi sat on the floor. Ravi pulled out a vial of Tabatha's serum from his bag. Most of the bottles and Tabatha's lab had been destroyed, but they'd kept just a few. For special occasions.

Ravi opened the top and looked at it wistfully.

'You know, Luke, if we ever open that shop, we could sell this stuff for millions.'

'We could, but we won't,' said Luke. 'Anyway, who wants to be rich? It's not about what you've got, but who you're with.'

'Hear, hear,' said Jess, walking up to the control room. 'Now come on, let's do this.'

And if anyone had thought to look up that day, they would have seen a wonderful sight: a sun-yellow zeppelin accompanied by three bright white clouds in shifting shapes, which seemed to dart, dive and soar, to and fro, with apparent disregard for the direction of the wind.

But nobody looked up, because they never do.

ACKNOWLEDGEMENTS

I'd like to thank the readers. It still feels such a privilege to have these things I wrote, on my computer in the attic, being read in homes and schools across the country. And for anyone who took the time to review *Ghostcloud* or let me know they liked it – an extra thanks. It's so important for new authors and such a joy – hearing your feedback is absolutely one of the best things about this job.

Then there are my amazing beta readers (who I forgot to thank last time!). Particularly Julia Kelly, Adam Connors, Davina Tijani, Sharon Boyle, Steve Catling, Collette Riggs and Dan Jolin – I don't think you'll quite realise how instrumental you were, with words of encouragement and advice when I was very, very stuck. Thank you and then some.

To all the wonderful booksellers, bloggers, journalists and organisations who spread the word. Having your little book out in the world is terrifying at times and your support and kind words make a real difference. Special mentions to Steph Little, Erin Hamilton, Jacqui Sidney, EmpathyLab, Scott Evans, Emma Kuyateh, Imogen Russell Williams, Mrs Nicholas, Vincent at Enchanted Books, A New Chapter, as well as everyone at the BookTrust, Toppsta and Waterstones for including me on various 'best of' lists.

To my superfans: Jen Dunne and Katherine Miles (for the Surbiton stock shortages), Lucy Scheinkonig (for the Sheffield ones), Liz Burke, Janet Pollak, Ally Mintz, Nikhil Richardson and Philly Cod. I'd also love to do a shout-out to everyone who voted in the epic 'cover war' – from India to Ireland, from Canada to Mexico and beyond. I still can't quite believe that we won!

To the many tireless librarians and teachers who set up visits so I could speak to their students and hear their wonderful questions. It's such a joy connecting with readers like that – thank you. And to all the students I've ever taught, you taught me more than you know.

To all the brilliant other authors who have given invaluable advice or help promoting the book. Especially Piers Torday, Lindsay Littleson, Ross MacKenzie, Candy Gourlay, Liz Hyder, Ross Montgomery, Vashti Hardy, Matthew Fox, Annaliese Avery, Sara

Grant, Simon James Green and Maisie Chan. And to my writing buddies: Mike Bedo, Kate van der Borgh, all The Good Ship 2021 gang, UV2020 gang, the LWA, CityLit, Curtis Brown and City Uni gangs. I'm so grateful.

To my dream-team at Hachette. Lena McCauley for the spot on structural edits; my calm voice of wisdom – from pace, to plot, peril and title – you were always right. To Jenna for the encouragement, patience and wordcount-cutting wizardry, as well as inspired line edits and dairy-free similes. To Anne McNeil, for your passion and belief in me – it wouldn't have happened without you. To Lucy Clayton for tirelessly sorting school visits and placing articles, and to Flic and Krissi for the brilliant marketing and Twitter tips. To Nic Goode and her Sales team and Tracy Philips and her Rights team for getting my book out there and across the seas. And of course to Sam Perrett and Chaaya Prabhat for another STUNNING cover. I love it so much. Can you win the cover war twice?!

To my wunder-agents Steph and Izzy – I feel so supported, championed, and very lucky to have you both in my corner. Whether it's about the story, the cover, Amazon logistics or deal-making . . . I still don't quite understand how you do everything, and do it all so well! Thank you.

To Kate Oliver, Schnitzel, to Alex (for the mole whiskers). To Diane because I should have thanked you the first time! To Jonathan Stroud, Neil Gaiman, Roald Dahl and Kate Bush for sparks of inspiration. To my Channel swimming buddies and the Lesvos refugee volunteers.

To my mum, dad, Shani, Gill and Kris – I couldn't have finished it without your help with the kids and unfailing support. To Rosie, Duncan, Jack and your families – I love you all to bits. To the Shanks for putting up with me writing secretly on holidays.

To Sarah, Chris, Meg and Leia. I am a writer, but I don't think I'll ever find the words to thank you properly for what you've done for us.

To Joe and little E and S – because you're everything to me. You keep me going. And I can't think of better company for the adventures ahead.